Keep A'Livin'

a novel in verse
by Kathya Alexander

aunt lute

San Francisco

Aunt Lute Books, P.O. Box 410687, San Francisco, CA 94141
www.auntlute.com
Cover design: Sarah Lopez
Text design: Stevie Sokolouski
Senior Editor: Joan Pinkvoss
Production Team: Shay Brawn, Bianca Hernandez-Knight,
María Mínguez Arias, Emma Rosenbaum, Sheree Bishop, and
Evelyn Kuo

This book was funded in part by the Zellerbach Foundation and the San Francisco Arts Commission.

Print ISBN: 978-1-951874-06-3
eBook ISBN: 978-1-939904-42-3

This copyright page is continued on page 305.

Library of Congress Cataloging-in-Publication Data

Names: Alexander, Kathya, author.
Title: Keep a'livin' : a novel in verse / by Kathya Alexander.
Other titles: Keep living
Description: San Francisco : Aunt Lute Books, 2024. I Summary: In 1963 Arkansas, twelve-year-old Mandy and her mother Belle experience the extraordinary events of the Civil Rights Movement, finding strength through tragedy along the way.

Identifiers: LCCN 2023056633 (print) I LCCN 2023056634 (ebook) I ISBN 9781951874063 (trade paperback) I ISBN 9781939904423 (ebook)
Subjects: CYAC: Novels in verse. I Mothers and daughters--Fiction. I Grief--Fiction. I Racism--Fiction. I Family life--Fiction. I African Americans--Fiction. I Arkansas--History--20th century--Fiction. I LCGFT: Novels in verse.
Classification: LCC PZ7.5.A437 Ke 2024 (print) I LCC PZ7.5.A437 (ebook) I DDC [Fic]--dc23
LC record available at https://lccn.loc.gov/2023056633
LC ebook record available at https://lccn.loc.gov/2023056634

10 9 8 7 6 5 4 3 2 1

Dedicated to
Lacy Alexander
Berdine Alexander Ready
and
Willie and Valerian Alexander Summerville
and to all those colored teachers
who demanded excellence no matter what

Prologue:
THE LAND OF UZ

Now there come a day when the sons of God
came to present theyselves before the Lord.
Satan come late. (He God son too.)
And the Lord say, "Satan, now where was you?"
Then Satan answer the Lord and say,
"From going to and fro upon the earth,
and from walking all up and down in it."
The Lord say, "Is you done found any of my servants
who is as diligent as thou art?"
And Satan answered and said, "No, Lord. Not one."
And the Lord said to Satan, "Hast thou considered
my servant, Belle? That perfect woman
who fear Me and hold Me in her heart?
She escheweth evil and love the Lord."
Then Satan answered the Lord and said,
"Doth she fear you for naught? Hast thou not made a hedge
about her and about all her house?
And about all she hath on every side?
Thou hast blessed her with the work of her hands.
And her substance increaseth in the land.
But put forth thine hand and touch all she hath
and she will curse you to your face."

And the Lord said unto Satan, "Didn't we go thru this before
when you convinced me to torture my servant, Job?
And did you not learn in that time
that there are some souls as diligent as thine?"
And Satan answered the Lord and said,
"Yea, but thy servant Job, was he not a man?
One that, in his day, wielded authority and power.
Belle ain't nothing but a po' colored woman
living in a land that don't care nothing about her.
Take away the hedge thou hast placed about her.
Verily I say, touch all she hath
and she will curse you to your face."
And the Almighty God said unto Satan,
"Behold, all she hath is in thy power.
Only upon herself put not forth thine hand."
So Satan went forth from the presence of God.

I
BELLE AND A.D.

1
ANGELS IN UZ

The heat float down the hall and dance off the walls of my bedroom.
Mama in the kitchen. She got the oven on
for the biscuits she making. The sound she make when she fluff
the dough with her hands is what wake me up.
Whup whup whup, the dough say like it is talking to Mama,
telling her if she got the consistency right.
I done wake up to the sound of my mama making biscuits
every morning, every day, for all of my life.
Every day. Not just in the middle of winter.
But every day. No matter how hot
the weather already is. This is summer in Arkansas!
My head hurting so bad, I can't even sit up.

Today the 4th of July. So even tho it's scorching hot
my mama done already started cooking a pot
of turnip greens. I can tell by the smell.
It ain't even seven o'clock yet, but it's already hot as hell
in our house. Mama also is cooking our breakfast.

She make biscuits and gravy, pork chops and bacon,
smothered potatoes with onions, and she is boiling some more
potatoes for the potato salad that she making for later on.
Today is also Mama's birthday. I have got her a present.
I paid for it with the money that I make from Cud'n Thetta
running to the store getting her Kent cigarettes and short Cokes.
It ain't much cause Cud'n Thetta don't really pay all that much.

I had planned to get Mama something really nice for her birthday.
I ask Daddy if he would come and take me to town
so I could go shopping at Sterling Dept. Store.
He said that he would, but then he didn't come home.
He was at the church having a deacon meeting or something.
Mama get mad at him because he didn't show up.
I know she get mad sometime for him doing his preacher business,
so I had planned to jump out of bed to show her how much I love her.
But it is too hot! My head feel like it's splitting.
Mama cook like this every day, but I don't usually get sick.
When I ask her one time why she cook such a big breakfast,
she say it come from growing up on a farm when she little
and the men would go out to the fields after breakfast.
Well, not just the men. Women work the fields too.
I told her it would be all right if we eat a tuna fish sandwich
and she start yelling at me at the top of her lungs.
I do not understand it. She act like I told her
that I didn't want to eat none of her food.
And, of course, wouldn't nobody never say nothing like that
cause everything she cook be screaming go-oo-od!

My head is pounding and I feel sick to my stomach.
Every breath that I take fill my lungs up with hot air.
I try to lift my head so I can get out of the bed
but arrows of pain shoot all thru my scalp and my neck.
I can hear Mama take the top off the pot that the greens in.
I hear the sound of the spoon scraping against the side of the cooker.

I can see in my mind the dish towel on her apron
she use to wipe the sweat off her face. I hear her take the sugar
bowl off of the table to sprinkle into the pot.
She say you have to use a little sugar so the greens won't be bitter.
She mash the leaves down into the pot liquor that she make from the fat
that she season the greens with. She call it streak o'lean bacon.
The air coming from my fan feel real damp and real warm.
I hear Sissy in the living room. She is mopping the floor.
She like to do her work in the morning, in the cool of the day.
But ain't no sucha thang, really, with Mama cooking the way
that she do every morning. I do not understand
how she can be in that kitchen. I hear her pull the pan
from out of the oven. The biscuit dough finally ready.
I can hear the radio in her bedroom. It sound scratchy with static.

Sweet Willie Wine, the DJ, talking about the Children's Crusade.
That's a bunch of colored children down to Birmingham, Alabama
and the things that they did that's done changed everything.
My brother, Quinton, was a DJ on the same radio station
before he leave Little Rock and move to Jackson, Mississippi.
Now he a DJ in Jackson for WOKJ,
although he move around a lot following all the Civil Rights demonstrations
and reporting on the radio all the things that go on.
Today Birmingham taking the 'whites only' signs down.
If I did not see it for myself, I wouldn't have never believed it.
Daddy say, "Belle, this go to show you God can use any thang."
Mama say, "God ain't told nobody to use n'an one of them chir'en."
See back in April, Rev. Martin Luther King
had planned a big march to force integration
in Birmingham. He had planned for Negroes
to turn out in large numbers and to get arrested.
But didn't hardly nobody show up so he went to jail hisself
and he wrote a letter to all of the white preachers
talking about them real bad cause they wouldn't get involved and help.
Mama say, "A.D., one day that man is gon' get hisself killed."

Rev. King wanted Negroes to come out and get arrested
because he wanted them to overwhelm the whole jail system.
They can't lock up everybody, Rev. King had said.
But when the grownups didn't show up, all the DJs in Birmingham
had asked the kids to walk out of all of they schools.
And 2000 colored children did. They met at the park at noon
that was across from the 16th Street Baptist Church.
The DJs talked in code. Told them to bring they toothbrush
so they could brush they teeth after they eat they lunch.
But what they was really saying to the kids was that
they need to be prepared cause they might not get to come home.
And most of them children had not even told
they parents they was doing it. 931 children
got arrested during the walk out. That was back in May.
The whole country was glued to they television that evening
when they let loose dogs on them children. They call it D-Day.
Then the next day a new wave of children walk out of they schools.
They had to put the kids in the stockyards cause the jails was so full.
They lock the children up in cages that was meant for the animals.
They call that Double D-Day. More than 20,000 students
skipped school to go to jail. See, that's what I want to do.
I want to take part in some protests. Mama say, "Mandy, I will kill you
if I catch you being caught up in this Civvie Rights mess.
I will beat you 'til the skin fall from off of your back."

It don't sound like nobody else is up beside Sissy.
My brother, Lucky, ain't at home cause he got football practice.
My brother Jake and his wife, Dara, is still in they bedroom.
I can hear Jake Jr. in there talking and playing by hisself.
Uncle Jesse sound like he is still on the back porch.
Daddy turn it into the boys room when Jake and Dara get married.
They bedroom use to be the boys room but since they have a baby
Mama say that they need a room all to they self
so they can keep Jake Jr. in the room with them.
They been living with us for almost a year now,

but they getting they own apartment and moving out next week.
I want to tell Mama about my headache but it hurt to open my eyes up.
My head feel like bombs is going off inside my skull.
I get headaches a lot, mostly when it is time to start school.
Mama say that is because I get way too excited.
But sometimes I get them when I'm not excited about nothing too.

Mama cook like we have got air conditioning or something,
but don't nobody have air conditioning in Uz where we live.
Folks thank being cool is just a total waste of money.
It is mostly just white folks that have air conditioning.
Like the white woman house that my mama work at.
I like going over there when my mama go to clean.
They have two twin girls that's about my same age
and they mama let us play in the sprinklers and everything.
Don't nobody in Uz have no sprinklers neither.
Mama say the Lord make the grass and He also make the rain
so why she want to run her water bill up
when, if the Good Lord made it, He will always provide
a way to make it grow. Then she start to complaining.
"I have a hard enuf time getting anybody to even cut the grass.
All y'all lazy chir'en laying round the house all summer
and not n'an one of y'all cut the yard 'less I ask."
And then she start talking again about how children is ungrateful.
Every story she tell seem to come back to that.
I throw the covers off myself but I still can't open my eyes yet.
I wait to see if the bombs in my head settle down a little bit.
I hear Mama turn the water on again in the sink.
Sound like she is washing more greens for our dinner.
But then I hear her take the mixing bowl out.
That mean she making a cake. Her cakes is my favorite.
And that's when I smell the custard for the homemade ice cream.
She just put in the vanilla. The smell swim down the hall.
Well, she might have put it in the cream before that.
Sometime you can't smell stuff from the kitchen for a long

time. It's like when Lucky be cooking at night.
By the time the smell come and wake you up,
he already be thru eating whatever he cook.
He always smile when he tell me all the pork chops is gone.
Lucky make me sick. He love being in the kitchen with Mama
whenever he be at home so he know how to cook.
And she love to teach him all of her recipes.
I might could do that, but it is just too hot.

When I get too hot, seem like the world start to spinning.
Seem like I start to wheezing and I can't hardly catch my breath.
One time when I was six I fall on the floor screaming.
Mama just look at me and say, "Mandy, if you don't get up
off of that floor acting like you ain't got no sense
I'm gon' give you something for you to fall on the floor about."
She act like I fall on the floor cause I like it.
I can't help how I act when I get hot like that.
It make me feel like some arms is holding me too tight
trying to cut off all of my circulation.
And I have this thing about being closed in.
It make me go crazy – stark, stiff and raving.

I think that come from living in Uz.
Uz is a small Negro settlement
across the Arkansas River in North Little Rock.
Didn't nobody found it. Didn't nobody settle it.
It is a land of daffodils and willows that weep.
Sunflowers and all of the little colored girls hair
grow wild from the rain they mamas catch in tin tubs.
Look at the corner of any house and you'll find one there.
The old ladies in Uz pat my head with they hands
and then gnarled fingers reach out and caress me around my throat.
Mama say God created the heavens and the earth
and then He made Uz with the stuff He have left.
The very air in Uz is stale and sweet.

The creeks is as clear as they is deceiving.
The stars shine brighter. The night is more black.
And the people stand rooted and grounded in believing
things that don't make no sense to me no more.
Like all this 'thou shalt not, thou wilt not saith the Lord.'
And if I say anything to Mama about it,
she say, "That's what it say in His Holy Word."

I hear Mama take the biscuits from out of the oven.
She start to humming as she take them into the dining room
and sit them on the hot pad that she put on the table.
Then mama start to moaning a Dr. Watts hymn.
She is gon' start to singing in a minute.
That is what she always do.
I can tell what kind of mood she gon' be in
by the song that she sing. This morning she choose

> *Father, I stretch my hand to thee*
> *No other help I know*
> *I-I-I-f thou withdraw thyself from me*
> *O whither shall I go*

This is one of my mama's favorite songs.
She usually sing this one when she feeling sad or lonely
like she ain't got nobody down here on earth to lean on.
She sing this song a lot when she is mad at my daddy.
I think she sing it this morning because
of the argument her and Daddy had last night.
Mama always fussing at Daddy about something.
He always making her mad doing what she think ain't right
even tho my Daddy the one who is the pastor
so you would think that he is the one who know
what God expect from out of His servants.
One time I hear Daddy call Mama holier than thou.

My daddy got a voice that sound like the angels in heaven
is ready for him to put on his long white robe
and take his place beside them in the heavenly choir stand.
But he don't never hardly sing when he is at home
like Mama do. He got a laugh that's like music
and that's what you hear mostly coming out of his mouth.
Daddy just sing on Sundays when he is in the pulpit.
Usually Amazing Grace. That's the song he like most.
When I ask him one time why he don't sing more at home,
he look over at Mama and say she sing enuf for both.
But it's something about the way that he say it
that make me think that ain't all of the truth.

Mama already dressed to go to work this morning.
Her white lady love parties. She planning a big one today.
Mama probably won't be home until late in the evening,
but she will get a nice present since today her birthday.
Her white lady always give all of us some good presents.
She don't shop at Sterling. She get her presents from Blass.
But she don't never think about letting Mama off for her birthday.
Sometime I think that it is just too bad
that my Mama's birthday fall on the 4th of July.
If it wasn't, maybe sometimes she would be off.
She get paid two extra dollars when she work on her birthday,
but still seem like her white lady would give it some thought
and realize my Mama would like to rest on her birthday.
But her white lady don't seem to think nothing like that.
Mama she to go to work like it is any other day
and her white lady don't see nothing wrong about that.

Sometimes I do not understand about white folks.
Especially white women. White women cold blooded.
On TV they always show mean white men like George Wallace
or in Birmingham, they usually show Sheriff Bull Connor.
But white women seem like they would understand

since they almost bad off as us. The stuff they put up with from men.
But it don't make them act no more nicer to us.
They should be, but they ain't. I seen that for myself
one time when a white woman in a black car was driving by.
She had a lace handkerchief wiping the sweat from off her brow.
I could see clear as day the red on her husband's neck.
Somehow I knowed she'd been by here a hundred times and had missed
even seeing colored folk living here. Hadn't seen children in the yard.
Course, back then most white folk only come thru Uz
on they way to Jacksonville or taking the short-cut to Stuttgart.
I see her like in slow motion. She holding a fancy cardboard
store-bought fan clasped tight in her white little hand.
And the black vinyl seats, I knowed was sticking to her legs.
I knowed the legs of her panty girdle had started to rise
and a tight, sour muss was rising from in between her thighs.
I don't know how I knowed this. All I know is I did.
Her hands was pale and manicured. She dropped the store-bought fan
and closed all ten of her fingers around her own self's throat.
And then, all of a sudden, she start to choke herself.

She have on a Peter Pan collar with a single pearl button
at the small of her neck. Her hands reach out and rip it
right off. Her husband he reach over and slap her,
never taking his eyes off the road. It was a swing he had practiced.
Real straight and real smooth. The white man hit her so hard that
the woman fall over and she grab onto the door handle
and out the car the woman fell. Right there in our ditch.
The white man stop the car so fast that it make his brakes screech.
Her legs was wide open. Somehow she had land on her butt.
And the white man come stand over her, but he didn't pull her out.
He say, "Bitch, get in the car!" I can't believe what I'm seeing.
He didn't hit her again, but you could tell that he wanted
to. But it was like something come and grab the white man by the sleeve.
His hand was held up straight toward the sky and he was leaning
over the woman. He start to look around

like he trying to figure out who holding him by his arm.
They car was still running, stopped on the side of the road.
I was standing shock still out in our front yard.
That's when Mama come out. She run straight thru the screen
to go see bout that woman. To help her up off her knees.
She jump in the ditch to grab her. The white woman trying to stand
so Mama go over in front of her and she reach out her hand.
And the white woman spit at her. Yes, Lord. Yes, she did!
You talk about biting the hand of the one who is trying to feed
you! And, just like that, God let loose the man hand
and he start to beat on the woman right in the ditch where he stand.
He throw her into the car and they go on they way.
I hear him yell something about niggers as he drive away.

When I start to ask my mama about all of this,
she grab me by the arm and pull me onto the porch.
She tell me don't go back out in the yard. I ain't got no choice but to obey.
Lucky for me, Jewel come over so I don't have to stay
on the porch by myself. I tell Jewel what happen.
She say she bet my Mama shame. So I don't keep asking her about it.
But I often think about that white woman a lot.
I can hear Mama stirring the turnip greens in the pot
and I wonder if she ever think any more about that white woman too.
About what make white women hate colored people the way that they do.
Why that white woman was madder at my mama than she
was mad at her white husband. He the one who beat
on her. But she rather get back in his car
than to take a colored woman's hand that was trying to help her.

The sun done rose like a hot biscuit and is shining into my window.
Feel like it is already over 90 degrees outside
and it's probably twice that hot inside of our house
with all the pots on the stove. I feel like I'm dying
between the heat and the headache. My eyelids feel like
they is both stuck together from the scorching heat.

When I am finally able to open up my eyes,
I see a angel by my bed stretching out both her hands.
The angel don't seem real. More like a hallucination.
I get them sometime when my headaches real bad.
But this time the angel make my headache feel better.
Not like the other headache hallucinations I done had in the past.
The rays of sun in the room turn the light in the air
into a fiery heat that is a shimmery red.
The angel wings is flapping to the throb of my headache
and every time she move, seem like my head hurt a little less.

Mama teach me about spirits and angels all the time,
but I don't never expect to see one standing in my bedroom.
So what I'm seeing is scary and I am totally shocked.
Seem like she is standing just beyond the reach of my arms.
To me this feel like a dream or something.
Mama tell me this world is all most people see,
but there is a world beyond what you can see and touch.
And when I see beyond this world God is trying to tell me
something. I don't know what it is that God want me to know,
but I wish He would find another way to show
me than having these explosions going off in my head
with a angel with fire wings standing at the foot of my bed.

I can't see the angel face cause it is blurred by the pain.
All I can see real clear is her dress and her wings.
They both look like they done gone up in flames
and look like fire is coming out from her outstretched fingers.
I lay back still as a corpse on my bed this morning,
in this halfway place between wake and sleep,
with the bombs going off inside of my head
and the angel flapping her wings and reaching her hands out to me.
I can see her there like she is on the television.
Feel like the fire is wrapped around me like hot sweaty sheets.
Mama say, "Most people don't believe the things that they seeing.

But, Mandy," she say, "always believe what you see."
Mama tell me that day when that white woman come,
"Everybody got a guardian angel assign especially to you."
She say, "The angel is there to guide and protect you."
I ask her, "Mama, do Gov. Wallace have a angel assign to him too?"
She tell me, "Mandy, God ain't no respecter of persons.
That mean He give everybody a chance at His grace.
But just like the angel is there to aid and assist you,
God can always come and take the angel's hand away
and leave you to deal with this life all by yourself.
It's a terrible thing to fall into the Living God's hand
without a Comforter that is there to balance the scales."
I am not sure I understand exactly what she was saying,
but I know that white woman had a angel to protect her.
Even tho I couldn't see it, I know it held back the man's hand.
The angel in my room disappearing in front of my eyes
and I can feel the pain starting to disappear inside of my head.
I am still not sure whether the angel real or not
or if she some kind of vision set off by my headache,
but I feel like God showing me I got a angel to watch over me.
So I whisper a prayer of thanksgiving and I finally get out the bed.

2
THE BREAKFAST TABLE

When I go in the bathroom I can hear Daddy in the back yard
where he is talking to our next door neighbor, Uncle Virgil.
I brush my teeth and I wash my face.
The cool water make my head feel a little mo' better.
Mama don't allow nobody to sit down at her table
with the stink of a night's sleep still clinging to them.
She say, "The least y'all can do after I done cooked all this food
is to sit down at the table like somebody been raised."

Daddy and Uncle Virgil voice float in thru the window
riding on a breeze so heavy that it don't even move the curtains.
They been out in our back field looking for water.
Uncle Virgil can find water. They call him a diviner.
My daddy want to dig a new well in the field out back
so he don't have to walk so far to water the corn and the peas.
We got three acres of land on this side of the track.
Uncle Virgil say, "A.D., we can always try it again
and look for water on another parcel of land later on."

Our house sit smack dab in the middle of our three acres.
Daddy grow soybeans on another seven acres cross the track
and he grow peas and corn mostly everywhere else.
Mama got a truck patch where she grow tomatoes and greens
and the other stuff that she grow for our kitchen table.
So we got a deep freezer that is always full
because they pretty much grow everything that we eat mostly.
That's how everybody is that live in Uz.
And when one person got, everybody else have got too.
You can walk in a person's house and get you some bread or sugar
even if that person ain't home. Everybody help each other out too.
When the time come for us to pick all of our vegetables,
Daddy give Uncle Virgil great big bushel baskets
cause him and Big Mama too old to plant they own garden
and they just got the one daughter. That is Cud'n Thetta.

Daddy and Uncle Virgil is also talking about the news
and them school children who take part in the Children's Crusade.
Daddy say, "The Supreme Court been done ruled against segregation
in the schools in the south when that Thurgood Marshall,
argued the case when he was a lawyer for the NAACP.
The judges said it was illegal way back in 1953
for colored and white children to be going to separate schools.
But Governor George Wallace, that old red-neck fool,
don't care what that Court say. He would rather die than
have coloreds and whites be together." Him and Uncle Virgil slap they hands
together in agreement. "He don't care what the Court say.
And taking them signs down ain't gon' mean nothing neither," Daddy say.

When all them children marched, Bull Connor got so mad
that he sicced the police dogs on them and blasted them with fire hoses.
They even turned the water pressure up to try to take the children skin off.
It was on the CBS Evening News with Walter Cronkite on television.
Daddy say, "Belle, it say in the Bible, and a little child shall lead them."
Mama say, "I don't believe that the Lord ain't never told nobody

to put no chir'en in front of no dogs and water hoses.
Don't put that foolishness on God. This just a bunch of grown folks
who too scared to put they own necks out there on the line.
So they let the chir'en get bit and knocked down on the ground.
God don't like ugly, mark my words, A.D." my Mama say.
"And He ain't too particular about pretty," my daddy answer that day.
He say, "Everybody need to take some kind of a stand.
If it ain't something you would die for, then you ain't a real man."
My Mama say, "Being a man is putting food on the table.
Not sitting in jail, losing your job, looking like you is crazy."
My mama and daddy is always fussing about this.
I don't know why cause in Uz ain't nobody doing nothing.
Folks act like ain't nothing wrong with colored people being treated
like they is less than whites folks. That's just the way that it is.
And all us children in Uz is way too scared
to go against our mamas. Them children in Birmingham
must have mamas that don't whip them like our mamas do.
If my mama even thought that I was about to do
something that put me in a cage where some animals be kept
she would whip me 'til my whole body was covered with whelps.

When Mama hear me stirring round she start to sing even louder
like she want Daddy and Uncle Virgil to hear the song that she singing.
I think she is trying to drown out they conversation
cause she don't never want me to hear nothing about no demonstrations.
So she don't want me to hear them talking about the Civil Rights protests.
But it is on television every night so it ain't nothing she can do.
Everybody in the whole country is talking about it.
Even President Kennedy talking about it after what them children go thru.
And then I hear my daddy come on into the house.
He go into the kitchen and kiss my mama on the mouth.
She say something I can't hear. Her voice sounding gruff.
But my Daddy just laugh and then he pull his chair out
at the head of the table and take him a seat.
Then my mama yell out, "Come on, y'all, and let's eat!"

Everybody go wash they hands and come sit round the table
while she set the pork chops she make on the dining room table too.
Then she go back in the kitchen and she start to scramble some eggs.
She ask each one of us if we want one egg or two.
She start to singing again while she is beating the eggs
like the song in her throat have just got to come out.
You can't sing at the table because that bring you bad luck
so she singing in the kitchen before she come to sit down.

> *I came to Jesus as I was*
> *I was weary worn and sad*
> *I found in him a resting place*
> *and He has made me glad*

When she come back with the eggs, my daddy he say the blessing
before everybody start to reaching for the food on the table.
"Belle, pass me them biscuits," my daddy say when he thru.
I wipe the sweat off my face with a paper napkin.
It's even hotter in here than it is in my bedroom
cause now I am even closer to all the fire on the stove.
The fan in the dining room is pointed directly at Daddy
but it is a circulating fan that move the air back and forth.
I lean over and follow the fan whatever direction it move,
trying to get what little air it is blowing around.
But the heat feel like it is chewing up all the breeze,
so the sweat on my face is running all down
into the crease of my neck. Daddy always sit at the head of the table.
Mama always sit on his right hand side.
That is the chair that is the closest to the kitchen
and since she be hopping back and forth all the time,
that is the place that she always sit at.
I always sit in the chair that is right beside her.
When I was younger she used to cut up all of my food.
I use to have a hard time with that because of me being left-handed.

"Mandy, how you doing?" Mama put her hand on my forehead.
"You look like you is feeling kinda peak-ed.
You got another one of your headaches again?"
I nod my head. She say, "You will feel better
after you put some food into your stomach."
That is my mama cure for everything.
That's cause Mama food taste like manna from heaven
that God send down to our table on angel wings.
That make me think about the angel in my bedroom.
I wish that I could tell Mama all about it,
but now ain't the time with everybody at the table.
Uncle Jesse would probably just laugh at me about it.

I watch Uncle Jesse root round in the hog brains
that Mama fix for him and Daddy special.
I wouldn't be caught dead eating none of that mess.
I use to 'til Uncle Jesse he tell me
that you got to be careful when you eat hog brains
or else one day you gon' start to squeal like a pig.
Ever since that day, I ain't ate no hog brains,
but off into that platter he dig.
He laugh and say that just make more for him.
He grunt around in his plate like it's a trough and he a hog.
I'm glad I learn about hog brains in time.
The heat making my head feel like it is in a fog.
Uncle Jesse is sucking on the bone of a pork chop
like he drinking Jordan River and looking back for the cross.
Whenever ain't nobody home except me and Uncle Jesse,
my mama always tell me to go stay at Jewel 'nem house.

For long as I knowed him, my Uncle Jesse
done worked as a janitor at the Arkansas State Capital
Building over in Little Rock.
Uncle Jesse is my mama's youngest brother.
And he the one get Daddy the job as a janitor

after him and Mama sell off they cow
and move to Uz from the old place Down Home.
That's what my Mama tell me anyhow.
Even tho my daddy is the pastor of our church,
they don't pay him enuf so he still have to work
at another job. Sometime he even give his money
that they pay him back to help out the church.
My mama don't like it when he do that.
I hear them arguing about it in they bedroom
when we all is in the bed at nite.
"A servant worthy of his hire," my mama always tell him.

Uncle Jesse just move back in with us.
He a short little bitty blue-black wall-eyed man.
His skin it look like a black walnut.
He talk real loud and got real bow legs.
Mama say one time he got offered a job
with some follies come round West Memphis way.
That's close to Down Home where Mama and Daddy 'nem from.
She say Uncle Jesse dance good as any white man in that day.
Back then, she say, he was young and fine.
(I cannot even begin to imagine.)
But she say he can't take the job because
he cannot sign the contract that them white folks give him.

"Where y'all sanging at again there, gal?"
Uncle Jesse he turn and say to Sissy
with his ugly ole wall-eyed self.
One of his eyes is looking across the table
and the other one looking over where Sissy is sitting.
Sissy sitting at her regular place at the table –
as far away from Uncle Jesse as she can get.
She start pulling on her bangs. She don't even answer.
Sissy don't never answer Uncle Jesse when he talk to her.
I don't know why. But she never do.

I think something musta happen when Uncle Jesse live with us before.
That was back when I was round one or two.
So I can't say that I remember what happen.
I just remember how my mama say
that Sissy start seeing little pretty booger-bears
whenever she go outside to play.

Sissy seven years older than I am
so that would have made her around eight or nine.
That's why I can't remember back then too good.
But I remember Uncle Jesse living with us at that time.
And as far as it go with Uncle Jesse dancing,
one time I seen him do the jerk.
And one other time I seen him dancing with Sissy
in the living room when Mama stay late at work.
Sissy must have been around 12, and she do not want to do it.
I remember she had tears running down her face.
Uncle Jesse was drunk and doing more rubbing than dancing.
When I come in the room, Sissy she run away.

Lucky usually sit where Uncle Jesse is sitting.
He five years older than me. And he play a lot of sports.
He play basketball and football and he run track.
He real good at that, but he make Ds and Fs.
Not like me. I always make straight As.
But I don't like sports so I don't play none.
My teachers always want me to because I am so tall,
but I don't like to lose so I just don't play at all.
Lucky real quiet whenever he is at home.
I done noticed he not like that when he is at school.
He always talking smack. All the girls want to date him.
He got good hair he always brushing and he act real cool.

Jake and his wife, Dara, sit across from me
on the side of table where Uncle Jesse is sitting.

Jake Jr. sit in his high chair next to his mama.
He always reaching for me so he is always wiggling.
Jake and Dara they just got married
a little bit over a year ago.
They been staying with us ever since they wedding day.
When Dara got pregnant, Jake had to drop out of school
and get a job at Goodyear Tire and Rubber.
But he still go to college. Now he go to nite school.
Dara graduated from high school with Jake Jr. in her stomach.
Her mama cried all thru they wedding ceremony
which they had on the porch out in our front yard.
It was pretty and all, except her mama was so sad.
I hadn't never seen a mama cry like that before.
Especially not on the day of somebody's wedding.

Sissy she sit on the other side of me.
I'm gon' be real sad when Sissy go away to college.
We done slept together in the same room for all of my life.
I do not know what I am gon' do without her.
Sissy she is the middle sister
and she is always – always – on her job
as the peacemaker of the family.
She name after a holy city of God.
Siseria. That is her real name.
And she is the good girl of the family.
She is going to college when this summer is over.
My sister, Sissy, she real dear to me.

Sissy take elocution cause she sing in the choir.
That's why she always talk so proper.
She even been on T.V. and everything.
So far, she my Mama most famous daughter
because Sissy sing just like a angel.
For real! If you ever hear her, you will see.
She teach me Doris Day songs she hear at the movies.

One call, Que Sera Sera. In French, that mean 'what will be will be.'

The future's not ours to see
Que sera, sera

Sissy take French four years at Pulaski County.
That's the colored high school over to McAlmont.
She was the salutatorian of they senior class.
The valedictorian a cripple girl name Velma.
And Sissy she think that is only right.
That's just the kind of person that Sissy is.
Plus she was editor-in-chief of the school yearbook,
she direct the senior class play, and march on the Mighty Panther Drill
Team as the leading pompom girl.
And she comb my hair and have supper waiting on the table
every nite when Mama drag herself in from work.
Cause when Mama come home she ain't hardly able
to eat her dinner before her head start to bobbing
up and down against her weary breast.
Sissy wash up all the dishes and help me with my homework
then she lay my head upon her chest.
That's when she sing to me the love songs
that she always seem to hold so dear.
I love the way that Sissy voice
sound falling gentle on my ear.

I ain't told nobody but I am scared to sleep
in me and Sissy's bedroom all by myself.
What if the fire angel come in again
if Sissy is not with me in there?
She leaving next month to go to Haiti, Missouri.
She gon' babysit for our sister-in-law
who used to be married to our brother, Azra Lee.
He die from cancer about seven years ago
and his wife done got married to somebody else.

And she done had that other man's children.
Sissy is gon' keep them for the summer
while our sister-in-law is finishing up with college.

I wish we could get Quinton's radio station
but it don't come in clear during the day
except on Sunday. We can hear it the best
late at night. Jackson is too far away.
The heat is hovering in the corners of the dining room
so my head real foggy while I'm sitting at the table.
I feel like I do when I'm gon' get in a fight.
Last fight I had was with a girl name Mabel.
Mabel the onliest person I done fought my whole life.
One day she come into the lunchroom and knock my books on the floor.
Seem like Mabel Ann done always been jealous of me
from all the way back since we was four.
"What you gon' do now, huh? Huh? Little pretty girl,"
Mabel Ann she say all in my face.
I walk away to the door that lead to the lunchroom.
Rain done start falling from a sky that is dark and gray.
She follow behind me selling some wolf tickets.
Then she push me in a corner where the janitor leave a broom.
The onliest thing that I can remember
is that I could not breathe in that room.
When I come back to myself,
the broom in one hand and Mabel Ann earring in the other
where I done ripped a slit thru the hole in her ear.
And I'm trying real hard to rip her another one.
All I could hear was Mabel Ann screeching
and hollering and screaming all up in my face.
It's people like stupid old Mabel Ann
that make it hard for the entire colored race.

Miz Fourth-Grade Phillips (to tell her apart
from Miz Fifth-Grade Phillips – one is married to the other's brother)

is pulling me by the tail of my coat.
She yelling at the kids, "Somebody hold her!"
I take inspection of myself
and see that I'm all covered with sandy hair and blood.
Somebody pry my fingers from off the broomstick.
Mabel Ann's hair sticking up and I'm covered with mud
where we done fought back out in the school ground.
I don't even know how we got out there.
I look over in the direction of Mabel Ann.
She crying like a baby. And I don't care.

Since then, I ain't been in no more fights
with Mabel Ann nor with no other mother's daughter.
Mabel Ann tiptoe around me now most times.
And when she in my face, she act like she oughta.
But I still can remember back in time
when I was closed in behind a table.
That is the feeling that I am getting this morning.
Don't watch out, somebody be pulling my coattail before I'm able
to stop myself from hurting somebody.
And this is not how I want to be.
I want to be like them kids in the Children's Crusade
and make this a better world for colored children like me.

We sing happy birthday and get the presents for Mama
when breakfast is over before she go to work.
My head ain't hurting at all no more
and I am feeling better now that I done ate.
"Happy Birthday, Mama." I give her my present.
Everybody else give her they present too.
Mine is some Avon talcum powder.
It have a soft furry top that I love to
rub up against my face and skin.
Sissy she give her some pearl earrings.
Daddy he tell her he will have her present

when she come home from work later on this evening.
Jake and Dara give her a big box from Jack Fine.
My mama she cannot wait to open it.
Jack Fine is the most expensive store in Little Rock.
It's a pearly white dress with a cape that go over it.
"This some kind of birthday," my Mama laugh.
"Come on, A.D., before we be late.
Mandy, don't you forget to hang out them clothes."
Then she kiss me on the forehead and head out for work.

3
KEEP-A-LIVIN'

We eat barbecue ribs for the 4th of July
that my daddy cook in a hole in the ground.
That's because we do not have a grill or nothing.
He take a rack out the oven and he lay it down
on top of the hole after he done fill it with charcoal.
I like bbq best when he cook it like that.
Sissy she season the ribs and the chicken
and Jake and Dara watch it while it cook.

Daddy go to town to buy Mama a present.
He buy her some panties and he buy her a hat.
He spend a lot of money on both of them things.
The panties is in a big box that he get from Blass.
The hat come in a round yellow hat box.
When Mama come home, he give her her presents.
She grunt when she open the panties box up.
And then she frown and sneer at my Daddy like thunder.
Deep down in her throat. It make me feel funny.

I can feel the storm clouds roll around in her neck.
This go back to the argument that they had yesterday.
Mama bit Daddy on the finger. She was just that mad!

"You ain't never even bought me a pair of panties!"
Mama scream at my Daddy last nite in the hall.
The cedar chest in the hallway had the door wide open.
Mama reach inside and she pull out her shawl.
I did not know they was even arguing 'til then.
I was watching Gunsmoke so I wasn't paying no attention.
"But, Belle," Daddy say, as he come out the bedroom,
"if you want to go somewhere, then come on, I will drive you."
"If I get in that car with you, A.D., I'm gon' kill you."
Her voice full of storm clouds. Fat ones. Black with rain.
Daddy come into the living room following my mama.
His voice sound like fog. All whispery and thin.

"But, you don't drive," my daddy say to my mama.
"Quit acting silly and go get in the car.
You act like I done done something so wrong you can't forgive me."
After he say that, Daddy stick his finger out
and put it right up in my Mama's mad face.
He shake his pointer finger at her like he do in the pulpit
when he is making a point to the congregation.
Mama look at him like he crazy. Then she turn around and she bite him!
Daddy look at his finger like it don't belong to him.
Like he don't know what happen to make it feel like it do.
Mama walk across the linoleum floor in the living room.
She never look back when she leave. Then Daddy go out the door too.
I don't know why my mama get so mad at my daddy.
He brought her flowers and everything when he come home from work.
And he always bring her a special kind of flowers.
Don't nobody else in Uz never get no flowers like that.

He bring them flowers again. Chrysanthemums. Just like always.

Belle think he like the name more than he like the bloom.
Saying it make him feel like he is some kind of different.
Something special. Something smarter. It wasn't special to
say roses or daisies or lily of the valley.
Nobody said chrysanthemum. That make him feel better than them.
More educated. More knowing. Somehow more romantic.
So she never liked the big yellow pillows atop the thick green stems
cause the flowers tied up in the strings of deceit.
Far as I know, it's always that way. And it always had been.
So she sink down on the mattress and think about why they got married.
Waiting to absolve her husband of yet another sin.

When Belle and A.D. meet, she was out in her garden.
She was stooped over the squash and had her wide, ample bottom
stuck straight in the air. She was feeling the ground
to test it for planting when A.D. come around
to the back of the house. He ask her for some water
from the well out back. He say, "You Mr. Fredrick's daughter?"
Belle say, "That's what my mama tell me. Here. Here is yo' drink."
Then she turn her nose up at him like she think that he stink.

She know exactly who he is. His daddy Levi Anderson.
And A.D. is his daddy only begotten son.
His name Aaron David. But everybody call him A.D.
And that man bout as pretty as a colored man can be
and still be called a man instead of a god.
Belle look down and see that his manhood is hard.
It's pushing at his zipper like he ready for sex.
And the look in his eye say he think Belle gon' be the next
woman he sleep with. But if he think that, he wrong.
Izzie Belle Carr ain't bout to give her possibility away for a song
like them other women Down Home who think they gon' be the one who he marry.
And, in that instant, she know she will be.
Know it sho' as po' is hard to carry.
When her heart tell her mind that, she can't believe what it say.

But she know she gon' marry this pretty man that same day
that she meet him. It's something that she see in his look.
And even more important to her, A.D. carrying a book.
Plus the fact that the Andersons own more than five hundred acres.
A.D. look at Belle and he say, "How you doing, Miz Lady?"
"I'm fine. How you?" Belle ask him right back.
"You sho' is fine. Now, you sho' right about that."
"You can't thank of nothing to say that's mo' original than that?"
"Well, I think I'm at a disadvantage standing in your truck patch.
Why don't you go with me to the club come this Sat'day nite?
Then I'll see if I can find the words to express myself right."
Belle say, "I don't go to no clubs. They ain't nothing but the devil's work.
But you sho' is welcome to accompany me next Sunday to church.
You can come calling if you want to go with me to Mt. Zion."
Her hair standing all over her head like a lion.

'It's something wild about this woman,' A.D. think to hisself.
He bend over and stick his whole head down her well.
He holler her name.

> *Baaaaabyyyy Bellllle*
> *Baaaaabyyyy Bellllle*

The sound echo right back.
Belle look at him and say, "You got to do better than that."
He say, "You sho' is a hard woman to please."
Belle say, "But worth pleasing."
A.D. say, "And you a tease.
You better be careful, Belle Carr," he wink his eye and he say.
"You might just look up in 30 years and rue the very day
you ever trifled with me."
"I might," Belle agreed.
"But it might be you who the one that fall down on they knees
and beg me for mercy. You ever think about it that way?"
A.D. eyes they twinkle. Belle stare at his pants and she say,
"Well, I guess you gon' just have to go to church with me to see
what it look like to have me looking up from my knees."

Then she stroke the shaft of a squash and she give it a squeeze.
Then she bend over and lick it! Just as big as you please!
A.D. he almost swallow all the spit in his mouth.
He take a deep breath and, real slow, blow it out.
'That gal don't know, Lord, what in the world she is doing.'
Down in A.D. pants he feel a sho' nuff storm brewing.

A.D. say, "Er-er. Uhmm… I think I know one of your brothers.
And I'm sorry to hear that y'all done just lost your mother."
Belle say, "We managing. Yeah, we managing just fine."
A.D. look in her eyes and see that she is crying.
He reach out his hand and wipe her tears with his finger.
He push back her hair and he let his hand linger
at the crown of her head. Belle breathe in a deep breath.
She say, "A.D. Anderson, you best behave yo'self."
"I'm just comforting the sorrowful in a time of great need."
"Well, if you want to help somebody, here. You can chop down them weeds."
She hand him a hoe and he go right to work.
She look at his muscles bulging out from under his shirt.

"Why you think it is that you and me ain't never met?"
"Well, it might be because you so full of yo'self."
A.D. walk over to Dolly. He throw his head back and laugh.
He scare the po' cow, who ain't much more than a calf.
He stroke the cow's head. He look down at her udder.
He say, "This cow sho' need milking. Maybe instead of me hoeing,
I oughta milk her for you. I can still help with the weeds."
"Is you trying to say you can be all that I need?"
"Well, I don't know what you need. But, if you tell me, we'll see."
Belle say, "Man, I ain't got no time for you to be playing with me.
I'm the oldest of 14 chir'en. Ain't a minute my own.
Specially now that my mama dead and gone, rest her soul."
"I can't imagine how I'd feel if my Mama left me."
"Ain't no need for you to 'magine. You keep a' livin', you gon' see."
A.D. hit Dolly on the rump and off she go running.

He pick up the bucket of milk and smile and start to humming
a tune that Belle is sho' she don't know.
But it's something about the sound in his throat
make her go to rocking her hips back and forth to the tune.
Then little Mega come up and say, "Can somebody help me tie my shoes?"
"Here, let me help this beautiful little lady," A.D. say.
He pick her up on his shoulder and he bounce her and play
a game with her where he spin her around
then he act like he gon' let her fall down to the ground.
The baby laugh and she laugh. Belle say, "I can't remember the day
when my baby sister done had somebody take the time out to play
with her. Can't remember the last time that she laugh."
Then Belle reach down and stroke the yellow squash by the shaft.
She stroke it real gentle. A.D. say, "And what about you?
Big sisters need to take time out to laugh and play too."
"What I got to laugh about? My Mama is gone.
What you speck me to do? Tap my foot? Sang a song?"
"Miz Izzie I ain't meant to show you no disrespect.
It's just I ain't never seen a woman crying like that.
Silent, soundless. Like you think you don't deserve it.
Like it's wrong, somehow, for you to feel what you feeling.
It don't take long for sadness like that to eat you up inside.
You need to let out your feelings. Quit trying to hide
behind that mask of strength spread all over your face."
Belle say, "I don't mean to cry. It's just it's been a long day."

Belle papa had told her bout a hour ago
that he was fixing to marry a woman by the name of Ceola.
Miz Ceola a lady that go to Mt. Zion.
Belle say, "It take me by surprise. That's why I was crying.
My Mama ain't barely cold good in the ground
and already he is bringing a new woman around."
"Maybe he thinking of you."
Belle say, "What you mean?"
A.D. say, "With 14 children, a man need a woman to help cook and to clean."

"What you thank I done done? Mama been sick for 12 years."

"Well, maybe that's exactly what your daddy he fear.
Maybe he don't want you to take care of his children all your life.
Maybe he think you oughta be some lucky man's wife
and have babies of your own."
Belle say, "You reckon?"
A.D. say, "Yes, I do. Now just hold on for a second
and think about it like that. See if you can't see."
"Well, I hope Papa don't thank that woman gon' be a mama to me.
I done had me a mama. Bout as good as they come."
"How long you say she was sick?"
"Pret' near her whole life long.
Then she have too many babies. And too soon right together.
The man that I marry is gon' have to know I ain't never
gon' do that to my body. He gon' have to love me for me.
And not just cause I'm some kind of baby-making machine."
"Well, I don't know you and I can see that you better than that."
Belle say, "You don't see nothing about me, in fact."
"I see that you hurting. I see that you sad.
And when your daddy bring that woman home, I can see you gon' be mad.
I can see you ain't never gon' even give her a chance.
And I can see by your walk that you sho' like to dance."
"Dance! I ain't never..."
"Well, you should. Come with me
down to the Toe Jam this Sat'day. Just once. Let me see
how it feel, how it smell to have your hair in my face.
And don't say no right just yet. You ain't got to answer today.
And you let Miz Ceola help you. I know she a nice enuf woman."
"I can't talk to you no more. I got a cake in the oven.
A wedding cake for Papa and for his new bride."
"Well, maybe I'm wrong. Seem like you taking it in stride."
"I done lived long enuf on this earth for to know
that I ain't got no kinda choice in which way the wind blow."
"You ain't but, what? Seventeen? How you get so old?"
Then Belle laugh and she say, "How you get so bold?"

"Can I call on you Miz Izzie after things done settled down some?"
"I ain't going nowhere, so you take a notion to come
I thank I would like that," Belle say and she smile.
A.D. walk away. Humming that song all the while.

When A.D. look Belle in the face on that day that he meet her,
he decide right then and there that what this little girl need
is some fun in her life. So while they was courting,
he take her to the jook joint a few times to go dancing.
Mostly they go to the Toe Jam. It ain't nothing but a shack
back off in the woods with a whiskey still in the back.
Grinning his mischievous grin, breathing in the rainwater
Belle use to wash her thick, wild hair with,
A.D. hold her close to him on the dance floor.
Her big breasts fold into his body somewhere just below
his chest. Her hips they roll caty-corner
to the rhythm of the music. Belle would stand close up under
him and wrap her legs thru his like she was threading a needle
while they was moving in rhythm to the sound of the music.
They match beat for beat the throb in the bass.
He look down at her. And she look up in his face.
They feet trace slow steps in the dirt for a floor.
A.D. nature rise in tune to the old guitar.
It was during they first dance that A.D. fall in love.
Knew then he had to have her, this woman call Belle.
Had to feel her open and naked. Her hair wild, her breasts bare.
"I love you, woman," A.D. sing into her ear.

Belle throw her head back and laugh way back down in her throat.
"Love me? A.D., what you feeling down there ain't
got nothing to do with no love." Then she laugh so hard
that tears roll down her face. A.D. just keep singing his song.
"Then let me get to know you, Baby Belle, Baby Belle.
Just let me get to know my Baby Belle," A.D. sing in her ear.
He got a voice that sound so sweet and so clear.

The kind that make women legs buckle and make them want to hear
they name in his mouth like that forever and ever.
"It take time to get to know a person, A.D.
You got some time, you thank, to spend with me?"
Izzie Belle say this into her bottle of pop and she laugh.
Her eye got a twinkle that bounce off of the glass.
"You clear up yo' dance card then next time we'll see
if you serious or if you is just playing with me.
Right now you got enuf worries dodging them daggers over there
them girls eyes is throwing." Then Belle really laugh
at A.D. hard.
"Them girls don't mean nothing."
"Well, I ain't trying to take nothing from no other woman."
"You ain't taking nothing. I'm giving it to you for free."
"Do them women know that? The ones who looking at me
like I done stole something?"
"Don't you worry bout that."
"I ain't worried bout nothing. We ain't serious like that.
I just come to the jook joint to see what it's about.
Now you willing to do something with me that I want?"
"Anything. You just name it," A.D. smile his wide smile.
"Come to church with me tomorrow and praise Jesus a while."
"I ain't really one who set no store in no church."
"And I ain't one who dance and go to jook joints and such.
But I done it for you. Now you do this thang for me.
You can dance but can you praise God? That's what I want to see.
Know this, A.D. I am the Good Lord's anointed.
And God don't like ugly. And ain't too particular about pretty.
I ain't the one to be played with. You can leave me alone.
If your intentions ain't in honor, then you can just take me on home.
I ain't one to be trifled with. You got enuf women for that.
Don't you play with me." A.D. he just laugh.
That seem to break up the tension that hang onto the words
that Belle speak in the air. Then she put her coat on
and she walk toward the door. A.D. grab her hand

when he walk her home, holding it all the way there.

Her hair was shining by the light of a chestnut moon.
And all the while they walking, A.D. humming that tune.
"What's that song you keep humming?" Belle she finally ask.
"It's the song that your hair make."
"You is one crazy man."
"Just crazy bout you." They walk up to her door.
"I ain't never hated leaving a woman so bad before.
You think you can give me just one little kiss?"
And, tho it was against her normal standards, that's just what Belle did.
She kiss him under the light of the slim crescent moon.
And she felt so lightheaded, she thought she might swoon
from the touch of his lips. Gentle like a caress.
And she know for sho' now this the man that she'd marry.
That night she let visions of they life dance in her head.
She even dream of the time when he would take her to bed.
She was so sure of herself. But she make one mistake.
If you meet in a garden, you better look round for the snake.

When she look in his face now what she see she call simple.
Can't be man enuf to just own up to what he done.
Her mouth fill with bile and she take out a tissue
to spit the foul taste of him from out of her mouth.
The lamp on the nightstand cast a shadow cross the room.
He standing on the other side, at his side of the bed
with the flowers in his hand. It is then she see the angel.
And she think, 'No Lord; not this angel again.'
She done seen angels all her life standing behind some people.
The people who God want to have in her life.
Every time, seem like, that she had decided to leave him,
that stupid old angel would show up at his side.
That wasn't something that she never told to nobody.
People think you crazy making life decisions like that.
This the natural world. That's what the Super Saints tell her.

God ain't told you to… Whatever. She let them fill in the blank.
But that angel was not for nothing. She would not second guess that.
She was a tool like a chisel that God hold in His hand.
The angel had been there from the very beginning.
Folks can think what they want, but angels do walk this land.

A.D. still talking and talking. Words in the air look like blackbirds
flapping their wings. Not really going no where.
That's when she realize that she had never really wanted him.
She only wanted to be wanted. And that is just what she got.
He wanted her but he always wanted other women.
He was a man who love women. It is as simple as that.
He loved women with great fanfare. Made them feel like a queen.
That's why so many of the women had wanted him back
over the years. It become part of their existence.
So every few years the yellow flowers would show up.
But they had built them a life. He was a good enuf provider.
So she accepted what was and bought another thing for the house.
She had learned from her mama that what a woman want is security.
A house and a car. Nice linoleum. Thick drapes.
That's what love was to her. The taxes paid on time.
They didn't have no mortgage and they had 20 acres.
They own everything outright. Pecan trees and a orchard.
It is her bank book in her purse that always make her feel safe.
But she forget to ask God for a little bit of common decency.
Just to go to the store without another woman in her face
showing her something that A.D. had bought for her,
or the place of his birth mark, the style of underwear he choose.
The smell of another woman on the upholstery of his Mercury.
The seat belt pulled tighter than her hips ever was.

Divorce is not God's way. Plus don't nobody know about the angel.
Don't know how many times that winged woman had block her path.
Stand in between her and her own dignity, seem like.
Her own worthiness. Her own self respect.

How she stand between A.D. and his life fill with freedom.

Belle know she can live a good life by herself,

but she ain't gon' let him have the easy way out of they marriage.

Long as she got chir'en to feed, A.D. gon' be there.

And when she can't take it no more, the angel come stand in front of her

like the angel did in Eden, blocking the path.

She guess she done lived this life for too long for her to do something different.

Cause no matter how bad she want to leave, God always tell her to just stand.

She had thought for a long time that God send her to save him.

But when the Lord send YOU a message, it is to you that He speak.

And this all because she just wanted to be wanted.

She realize now that it was too small a request for her to seek.

It was too trifling a thing to ask. She had played herself cheap.

But folks look at her and see the life they always wanted.

Like the house and the car make up for the cheating somehow.

God send you the desires of your heart. So be careful what you ask for.

Don't nobody know about the lies that always come with the flowers.

She put the vase in the middle of the dining room table.

All her church friends remark about what a good man that she have,

still bringing her flowers after all these years of marriage.

The grass is always greener, the flowers always bloom prettier

in somebody's else yard than they seem to bloom in your own.

That is the great truth that she wanted to tell them,

but she accept her friends compliments and just keep her mouth closed.

When he hand her the flowers, somehow that always make him seem smaller

even tho he 6 foot and 4 inches at 55 years of age.

They been together now for over 35 years.

He still have to tilt his head and he always have to bend

down enuf to get into his big black fancy Mercury.

His daddy always tell him a woman like a nice car.

Belle don't care about that. But he a good enuf man.

She got to believe that. Cause if he ain't, what do that say about her?

Just then her favorite song come on on the radio.
Seem like the DJ usually play it as she falling asleep
when the radio turned down real soft and real low
so she have to be real quiet in order to hear it.
Billie Holiday singing about a man who don't love her.
She say the words wrap around her like a blanket of smoke.
She get up off the bed so she can go over to Francis.
She need to talk to her friend. Right now that is what she need most.

4
STANDING IN THE NEED OF PRAYER

When Belle go over to Francis house,
she walk in the door with her head in her hand.
Francis say, "If you gon' stay with that man – and you know that you is –
you just need to accept that he is a ho' and
have a sip of this Crown Royal. That's what I would do.
I could care less where Dave go and put his old ass dick.
That's the thing about you. You keep on believing
that A.D. gon' change. And he keep showing you
that he ain't."
"But I done prayed on this," Belle she say.
"It is God that keep telling me that I need to stay.
Cause what I care about walking off and leaving A.D.,
I care less about than about what I am cooking today."

"Come on, take a seat so we can have us a bitch session.
Let's grab that niggah 'tween our teeth and gone tear him apart.
Cause he don't care enough about you to even understand
that he keep tearing the pieces of your po' little heart

into little bitty slivers. Goddamn niggah that he is."
"He is that," Belle say. "Yes, Lord, low down and no count."
"The day gon' come soon enuf – and you mark my words, you don't believe me –
that that no 'count niggah ain't gon' be able to get his dick up."
"Girl, I know that's right. Speak the truth and shame the devil."
"And don't start me on them Super Saints over at Good News Gospel Temple.
Walking around like he holy. Like he is leading a flock.
A bunch of whores and backstabbers. That's all that they are."

See, that is why Belle always like talking to Francis.
She put everything out there. Always on her side.
With Francis, she don't have to worry about what she gon' think about her
being, as Belle is, a prominent minister's wife.
They spend all that nite tearing A.D. to pieces,
laughing about how he think he so fine,
about how he love to have his suits fit him just so,
about the whorish woman who tailor his suits all the time.

When they thru with A.D., Belle tell Francis about Quinton.
About him reporting on the radio, talking about the protests.
Francis tell her, "I'm sho' is proud of that boy."
Belle say, "I'm just hoping that my chile don't get hisself killed."
"Where is yo' faith? Tell me that Miz First Lady.
Do you believe or don't you that God hold you in His hand?
And if He holding you, He holding onto that boy."
Belle say, "I don't never know what the Lord gon' do in this world.
What I know is that the Bible say that thou shalt not tempt the Lord God.
Even the Lord Jesus Christ didn't just throw hisself down
from off of that mountain when the devil tell him to.
Let us not be foolish, brethren. That's what it say in His word.
And you know that the Lord didn't make no bigger fool than Quinton.
He jump in head first. And he don't remember to pray.
He thank he can talk hisself out of any and everythang.
But the Lord ain't said that. The Lord did not say
that no harm will come to His chosen people.

And if you read yo' Bible you know that is the truth.
He down there reporting on all them Ku Klux Klansmen
and you don't never know what them white people will do."

Belle look at the clock and say, "Turn on the radio.
We ought to be able to hear him at this time of nite."
Francis get up off the couch. She staggering a little.
She turn the radio on and her and Belle watch it like
it is television when they hear Quinton's voice coming from out of it.
He say, "After months of relentless protests and negotiations,
city leaders in Birmingham are re-opening the parks tomorrow
that have been closed for months rather than integrate them.
White business leaders in the downtown area
are opening back up to white and Negro citizens too.
They have lost millions of dollars since the boycotts began.
The Southern Christian Leadership Conference and Martin Luther King, too,
are still working on plans for the March on Washington
for Jobs and Freedom that is happening next month.
We will keep you updated on this national demonstration."
Francis say to Belle again, "I'm so proud of that boy."
"Right on!" he say. "This is Quinton Delacortes Anderson
reporting to you from here in Birmingham
for WOKJ, your Civil Rights news station."
"I'm just so worried about him," Belle she say again.

"Girl, the Lord got that boy. I don't worry about that.
I worry much more about that crazy fool, Cleophas.
You done heard from him?"
"He call me yesterday.
He probably drunk as a skunk somewhere celebrating
his birthday. You know that it is today.
When he was growing up, I call him my little birthday present
since his birthday happen the day before mine.
He probably gon' be hung over all day long tomorrow,"
Belle say and she get up and go into the kitchen

to get a Pepsi Cola from out of the Frigidaire.
She take a swig and she belch when she come back and sit down.
"Well, I plan to be hung over all nite long my own self,
so I ain't the one to judge," Francis say. "When he coming to town?"
"I don't know," Belle say. "You know he is working.
That is one thing about Cleo. He gon' always have a good job.
God take care of fools and babies." Francis just nod.
"How do he like it out there in California?"
"He seem to like it just fine. He been there long enuf.
I don't thank he could live here after Lil Man get killed.
Not after watching him get hit by that ice cream truck."

"What you want for your birthday?"
"You already giving me a party.
I thank that is already more than enuf."
"Well, you know I would give you the whole world if I could."
"I know you would," Belle say, standing up.
"I don't know what in the world I would ever do without you."
"You ain't got to worry about that, not for a real long time."
Belle get up and grab her shawl off the chair.
"Let me get on out of here," Belle say and she smile.
"Let me get a cup of sugar for my coffee in the morning.
I don't know what I was thinking. Don't know how I run out."
"It ain't nothing but A.D. over there driving you crazy.
Get that 5 pound bag of sugar in the cabinet there out.
I made some cinnamon rolls. Take a pan of them with you.
I made extra today at the school cafeteria."
"Thank you kindly, M'am," Belle she say to Francis.
And when she walk home last night, Belle feeling a little mo' better.

5
THE PARTY

When Mama come home from work today, we all eat 'til we bust.
The chicken and ribs. Sissy make potato salad.
She make it with relish and mustard the same way Mama do.
After dinner Mama go over again and visit with Miz Francis.
I am going over to Miz Francis house myself in a minute
to get her house ready for my mama's birthday party.
Well, I think she was having the party anyway,
but she make it extra special to celebrate my mama.
Every time when Miz Francis have one of her parties,
she have me and Jewel be the hostess and we always set the table.
She put out all her fancy plates and stemware glasses.
She also put out the full silver tea set with all of the fancy
matching silverware. When I go over Jewel's house,
I'm gon' help her get things ready and set everything up.
I know that she have a lot of stuff to still do.
I tell Sissy I'm going and then I run out the house.

I run up under the carport at Jewel and Miz Francis.

It is shaded and cool, a welcome relief from the sun.
I feel something heavy in the air that I can't name besides the heat.
Like the weather fixing to change. The weather do that in Uz.
Miz Francis and Mama ain't nowhere to be seen
and Miz Francis car is not up under the carport.
That mean Mama and Miz Francis done gone off somewhere.
I cannot imagine where they could have gone.
And Jewel is not in the kitchen like I would have thought,
so I walk thru the living room trying to see where she at.
She sitting in her bedroom at the front end of the hall.
I can tell when I look at her that something is the matter.

"What's wrong, Jewel?" I ask. Jewel my very best friend.
"Mama make me sick," she answer me back.
"What she do this time?" I ask her with a sigh.
Jewel mama is one of Uz two only drunks.
Miz Francis have the kind of house that you can eat off the floors
and making sure it stay like that is mostly Jewel's main job.
She use to have to take care of her granddaddy too
until he died. He had the dementia.
"Mama been fussing at me since she came home today.
Over nothing. She been drinking. You know how she is when she drunk.
I'm so glad Maw Belle came over and took her somewhere.
She was driving me crazy before they left the house."
"What you got to do? I came over to help you."
"I'm getting ready to go and polish the silverware."
Miz Francis have butter knives, salad forks, along with soup spoons
and she also have two silver tea and coffee urns that
me and Jewel have to polish before every one of her parties.
"You want me to help you?" I just want her to smile.
Jewel skin color is dark chocolate, just like her hair,
which look like waves of music falling halfway down her spine.
Big blasts of thunder start to shaking the house.
We go in the living room and pull the wooden box out
where Miz Francis keep all of the silver.

Then just like that, the storm over and the sun come back out.

The house have to be sparkling for the 4th of July party.
Miz Francis she have one each and every year.
Even Mr. Dave come out from out the back bedroom
and take off his uniform. That's how special it is.
Most of the folks at the party is people Miz Francis work with
or the people she meet at the club on Ninth Street.
Don't hardly nobody in Uz go to none of Miz Francis parties
except for my mama. Folks in Uz think
that the wife of the pastor of a fair size Baptist Church
shouldn't be caught dead at one of Miz Francis evil parties.
Folks drink out in the open. But my Mama go every year.
And she let me be hostess. That is what me and Jewel's next job is
whenever we finally get thru with all of this cleaning.
Every year Miz Francis buy us new matching dresses
and white gloves that's got pearls that touch the vein of our wrists.
Miz Francis always buy us the prettiest outfits.

Jewel walk over to the china cabinet. She reach up to the top.
She don't get a chair. And she always do that.
The coffee and tea urns is on top of a wide swirled silver platter.
She yank the platter wrong or something and the urns both fall off.
They fall to the floor with a crash. One first, then the other.
Jewel stand there frozen, her hands still up in the air.
We both watch in horror as the handles fall off the urns in slow motion.
We both catch our breath. Jewel mama gon' kill her.
That silver tea set is Miz Francis crowning glory.
All the storm clouds come back and crowd into the dining room.
Ain't nobody else in Uz got a full silver serving set.
Not with silver punch bowls and ladles and spoons.
Miz Francis done had it ever since I done knowed her.
She bring it with her when her and Jewel first move to Uz.
I think it might be pass down in the family or something.
Beside the car and the house, it is the most expensive thing that they own.

Jewel burst into tears. And tears well up in my own eyes.

I just look at her helpless. "Jewel, please please don't cry."

"Mama gon' kill me."

I tell her, "Yeah. Yeah I know it."

She breaking my heart. "If you just stop crying, we can try

to see if it's something we can do to fix this."

I try to think what my Mama would do in this situation.

Mama known to work miracles with household stuff that get broke.

She always saying necessary is the mother of invention.

"Pet milk!" I scream. Jewel look at me like I'm crazy.

But it's something my mama use to glue everything.

If the pieces don't shatter, she can usually put it back together.

And Pet milk dry invisible, real clear and real clean.

We pour the Pet milk in a bowl and I dip in the ends of the handle,

then I press the handle to the tea pot and see if it will stick.

It work like magic. Just like I hoped that it would.

So Jewel hand me the other handle so that I can stick it

onto the coffee urn. This just might work!

"We have to just let it dry," I turn and I say to Jewel.

I dip the ends of the handle and stick it on the other side of the pot.

And we both almost start to crying when it fall off again.

I dip the handle again and I stick it back on.

It just won't stay. Now what is we gonna do?

Jewel stop breathing again. And then she say,

"Well, let's just put it back on the cabinet. We'll just pray she won't use it."

It ain't a chance in hell. That is our first job as a hostess.

To put the coffee and tea and the silver punch bowl on the table

after we set the table with a white linen tablecloth

and lay out the place settings like the Queen of England is coming.

That was the first thing Miz Francis taught us. How to set a proper table.

Water glasses and wine glasses, salad forks and soup spoons.

And the first order of business is to offer all the guests tea and coffee.

There is a order to everything in the way that it's done.

I know where the forks, knives, spoons and the glasses all go,
but sometimes I get it backwards because of me being left-handed.
"Put everything back on the platter," Jewel she say to me.
 "We'll turn the broken side by the wall. Maybe Mama won't notice."
This time she get a chair. She take the platters down first.
Then I hand her the coffee urn that have the handle still broken.
She place it careful so it is next to the wall.
Then I hand her the tea urn, hoping that the handle stay on it.
They still need time to dry. Right now it will fall off
if we so much as touch it. Then Jewel she say,
"We got to clean up this house like President Kennedy is coming."
And that's what we do. Go thru that house like a tornado.
You could take a spoon and eat out of every one of the corners.
We hand wax the wood floors and wash all of the windows.
We set the table up with Miz Francis' big crystal glass vases
then we pick flowers out the yard and we put them all over.
Flowers on every table. Especially on top of the china cabinet.
When Miz Francis come home, she full of nothing but praise.
She say we have done such a fine job of cleaning
that she glad that she bought us the most expensive things.

"Mandy," Miz Francis say, "Belle say she'll see you at the party."
Then she go in her room and she start getting dressed.
Mr. Dave come home and put on a shirt and a tie.
Me and Jewel put on our dresses. They is covered with lace.
Her dress is white with yellow lace. Mine is yellow with white.
Then the guests start to coming, and we serve the coldest drinks first.
We give everybody a cup of the lemon lime frappe.
Mama come over when she get dressed and sit and laugh in a corner
with a man that keep putting his hand on her knee.
They talking like they done knowed each other for ever
but this is a man that I ain't never seen.
Miz Francis keep whispering in her ear. And my mama she shush her
every time she come and say something to them and keep laughing.
The man look like he is in on whatever secret they got.

Miz Francis keep putting records on the hifi in the corner,
B.B. King, Louie Armstrong, and some Johnny Mathis.
"Oh, yeah baby," Miz Francis say every time she change a record.
And then she roll her little butt round and round in a circle.
Mama laugh out loud every time and she snap her fingers,
but she don't never get up out of her chair and go dance like Miz Francis.

Then Mama ask for some coffee. And me and Jewel both stare.
Miz Francis say, "Jewel and Mandy, y'all forgot to put the urns out."
"Yes, m'am" we say together. And then Jewel go get a chair
and stand on it so she can pass the tea and coffee urns down.
Jewel hand Miz Francis the flowers that is hiding the teapot.
She talking to somebody on the other side of the room.
She got a cigarette 'tween her teeth and a drink in one hand.
She grab the urn by the handle and soon as she do, it go blam!

Seem like the music stop. Dinah Washington was singing,
backed up by none other than Count Basie's band.
But I couldn't hear nothing but Miz Francis screaming.
"Y'all done broke my damn urn. You little bitches. Goddamn!"
She turn and start cussing at us. Everybody at the party
reach and grab her by the hand or her arms and her legs.
One lady say, "Francis, them damn teapots ain't nothing
to get yourself worked up about. Quit yelling at them damn girls."
Me and Jewel don't say nothing. We just go get the coffee
that we already got made in the kitchen for now.
Then the music start again. Everybody go back to laughing and talking.
But I'm not feeling so good so I just go back to my house.

Me and Sissy got twin beds last year. She seem so far away.
I wish that I could snuggle up under her like
I use to do when we slept in the same bed together.
Then she move under the covers and she reach her hand out
and I grab hers across the space between our twin beds.
She use to do that when we first stop sleeping together.

Seem like she always know exactly when I need her.
She say, "Mandy, did Mama enjoy her party?"
"Seem like it," I say. She say, "You are home early.
I thought sure that you would have stayed the whole nite
like you usually do after Miz Francis' parties."
"I was," I say, "but I didn't feel like it."

"Is something wrong?" Sissy raise up and she ask me.
"I don't feel good," I say. "And Miz Francis cussed us out.
And Mama spent all nite long talking to some man in a corner.
This been one of the worst days in my whole life."
"Well, you sure look cute. I like how you did your hair."
She scoot over in her bed. "Why did Miz Francis cuss you out?
Want to sleep with me? You can if you want to."
I explain to her about us dropping the silver teapot.
"I thought you said I was too old for us to sleep together."
"You are, plus it's hot. But I want you to feel better."
"Thank you, Sissy," I say as I jump into her bed.
Thank God this day finally over.
And I fall asleep as soon as the pillow touch my head.

6
SUNDAY COMING

Jewel scratch on my window screen the next day. Early on Saturday morning.
I ask did she get a whipping. She shake her head and she frown.
She say she didn't get in trouble cause we had did such a good job
of preparing for the party, Miz Francis wasn't gon' whip our behind.
But then Jewel tell me that her mama still drinking
and she won't let Jewel leave they house or do nothing.
She sneak over my house after Miz Francis fall asleep.
Jewel ask did my mama ask me about what had happen.
I ain't talked to Mama yet, but I know she gon' ask me.
I dread that conversation. I know what Mama gon' say.
Something about me not being careful about other people's property
and how she the one who gon' end up being the one have to pay
for something I done while I was just being careless.
I can hear my mama and my daddy back off in the kitchen.
Jewel say she better go home before Miz Francis wake up
cause all her mama need is just one more excuse to gone kill her.

But Mama don't ask me nothing about it. Her and daddy still fussing.
Sound like he come over to Miz Francis after I had went home
and seen her in the corner with that man hand on her knee.
I just hear Mama say, "What you trying to ask me, A.D.?"
Daddy say, "I ain't asking nothing."
Mama say, "That's what I thought."
Then she took some kinda receipt and she threw it at him.
After that he just got quiet and didn't say nothing to her no more.
I don't know what that's about. And, of course, I can't ask them.

All of us sit together and watch a special on television that evening
where they show pictures of segregation signs being tore down and removed.
And they interview some of the children who had participate in the demonstrations.
One girl said, "God don't even want us" when it had started to rain
after they took all the children and loaded them into the stockades
at the County Fair Grounds where coloreds could not usually go.
In Alabama, colored folks could only go to Fair Park on the last Saturday.
And even then they would have to wait until after 10 o'clock.

Watching the special start Mama and Daddy to fussing again.
Mama still mad at Rev. King and all the rest of the preachers
who use the children when they do the Children's Crusade.
"But, Belle," Daddy say, "look what it's done accomplished.
That racist mayor been kicked out and segregation is over.
That old cracker, Bull Connor, done got fired from his job.
Rev. King did a lot of good when he wrote that letter from jail."
Mama say, "White folks is crazy. This not over. Mark my words.
Them white folks in Birmingham gon' make all them colored folks pay.
This all the excuse that they need to start blowing thangs up.
When these white folks do anything just cause the Supreme Court say?
That town didn't get the name of Bombingham cause of nothing."

And then Mama tell me take Daddy's handkerchiefs off the line
where she done washed them and starched them and made them white as the sun.
This something I have to do every Saturday evening.

While I go to the clothesline, Daddy go get his Bible from
off of the bookshelf. I'm glad Mama's birthday is over.
She act like she have a good time last nite at the party,
and she still ain't ask me about breaking Miz Francis silver tea set.
I guess she gon' wait and ask me about that later on.

Me and Daddy got a routine that we do every Saturday.
It is my very favorite time that I look forward to every week.
When Daddy go get his Bible, I get my Bible story books out.
After I finish the ironing, my Daddy and me
have this thing that we do to get ready for Sunday.
"You ready, Mandy?" my daddy he always ask me.
"What story you doing?" I always ask Daddy,
then I go get the story book that I am gon' need.

Then I start to reading from my book of Bible stories
while Daddy is sitting in the big dining room chair
getting his sermon ready for church service tomorrow.
The story I'm reading always about the same thing.
Me and my daddy do this every Saturday.
He start finishing up his sermon right after we finish our dinner.
But first I have to iron all his handkerchiefs.
Most times I have to iron about 20
that he go thru while he is preaching his sermon.
I count them down every Sunday when he is in the pulpit preaching.
Just as soon as my daddy he start to sweating,
his stack of handkerchiefs they start to shrinking.
The way he wipe his face with one each time
and then throw the damp handkerchief off to the side
is part of a rhythm that my daddy got
as part of his regular sanctified preaching style.

After I get thru ironing all of his handkerchiefs,
I go sit with my daddy in the dining room.
"What your sermon about tomorrow?" I always ask him.

Then he kiss me on my jaw that look just like his.
Daddy tell me he is going to preach about Esther
so I find her story in my Bible Stories book.
The picture it show is of a woman who is dressed
in beautiful clothes holding her hand out.
A king with a crown sitting upon his head
is holding out his staff to the beautiful lady.
They almost look like white people. Almost but not quite.
I like these particular Bible stories books because they
have people in them who look like me sometime
when I turn to look at the illustrations.
Well, not look like me but almost the same color.
And they have all color people on the bright blue cover.
All the other Bible stories books that I have
got people who is white and most of them is blond.
This Esther have dark hair. And her eyes is brown.
Another thing I like is that the illustrations is in color.
When I get thru reading I go back over to Daddy.
He always turn and set his pen and paper down
and place his finger in his spot in the Bible.
He kiss me again. He do that a lot.
"All right," he say, "tell me about the story."
That is what my daddy he always say.
Sometimes I might get the story wrong,
but I'm pretty sure that I got the message right today.

I say, "The story is really about this man name Mordecai.
To me Esther is almost like a secondary character."
"Is that so?" my daddy smile and ask me.
"Yeah. Seem like she got caught up in her uncle's business.
Cause Esther was minding her own self business.
She was perfectly happy with the life that she had
until her uncle he came and got her."
"All right. So tell me the story," my daddy say to me again.
I climb up onto my daddy's wide lap.

This is my very favorite place that I love to be.
He grunt as he position me on his long legs.
"You getting too big." Daddy always say that to me.

I say, "The King had a wife who made him mad
cause she didn't come when he told her to
cause she was having a party with some of her friends.
So he banished her and started looking to
find another woman who would come whenever he called.
And he asked his assistant whose name was Haman
to help him find the right kind of woman.
And this Hebrew man name Mordecai overheard him say it.
And since Mordecai had him a beautiful niece,
he figured he should throw her name into the pot.
And since Mordecai worked right in the palace,
he got the folks he worked with to hook Esther up
and dress her in the stuff that the King like best.
Showered her in all the King's favorite perfume.
So when the King was picking over all of the women,
he smelled Esther before she even walked in the room
and he picked her out to be his newly crowned queen.
Stay in the harem where the king keep all of his women.
The king didn't know that Esther was a Jew
and so he crowned her the new Queen of Persia.

"Well, Haman and Mordecai happen to meet up somewhere,
and Haman commanded Mordecai to kneel and bow down.
But them Hebrews don't bow down to nobody except God,
and when Mordecai wouldn't, Haman got real mad
and decided he was gon' kill off all the Jews."
(See things like this I just do not understand.
That's how white people always do Negroes now too.
One Negro do something and every Negro is bad.)
"But the killing got to be done on a particular day,"
I tell Daddy. "So Haman had his wizards and prophets and whatnot

to come up with the exact perfect date.
And them people choose the date by casting lots.

"The picture they showed at the beginning of the story
was of Queen Esther holding out her jeweled hand
to the King. And the King didn't strike her down and kill her.
He told beautiful Queen Esther to come right on in.
And it wasn't like Esther was even in love with the man.
She just was doing what her uncle had told her.
So she went to the King and she flounced around
until she got him to take a look at
the document that Haman had made him sign.
The miracle was that Esther did not get killed,"
I tell my daddy. "Cause back then nobody
couldn't just walk into the office to go see the King.

"When the King found out that Haman had tricked him
and made him sign something he didn't understand,
the King lynched Haman on the very same tree
that he had built for Mordecai and
all the Jews. So God protected His people.
And He use the young girl, Esther, to pull it off."
That's the story I tell that nite to my Daddy.
He listen to everything I say real hard
and then he say, "That was the perfect story.
I want you to preach it tomorrow at church."
"Me preach the sermon? I can't do that."
"Yes, you can," my daddy answer me back.
"You just stand in the pulpit and tell the Bible story
the same way that you just told it to me."
"For real?" I say.
"For real," Daddy answer.
And that is how it came to be
that I preach my first sermon in Daddy's pulpit
after one of the worst days I done had in this world.

Mama fix my hair in a ball. I think I look real sophisticated
just like my daddy do when he preach the Word of the Lord.

I guess you know I was real excited.
This the first grown thing that I done ever done.
Daddy even give me a new handkerchief
that is sparkling white with lace sewed all around it.
When I walk up to the big wooden podium,
Deacon Jones put a stand behind the lectern.
I step up on the wooden block
so I don't have no trouble seeing over
the pulpit. I look straight at the audience faces.
I bow my head and start with a prayer
the same way that my daddy he always do.
The whole congregation say a big "A-man!"

And then I tell the story of Esther
just like I tell it to Daddy in the dining room.
I end my talk by saying that
what I learned is that the Living God
who rose on Easter Sunday morning
in the form of His Son name Jesus Christ
always knew what would happen to His chosen people
way before Haman even thought about casting lots.
The whole congregation stand on they feet.
"Aman! Aman!" the congregation call.
I use my handkerchief to dab the sweat
off of my top lip while I am preaching my sermon.

Then Daddy take over and put the 'whoop' on it.
He say, "It's just like what is happening down in Birmingham.
Mordecai was a outsider like they call Rev. King
when they lock him up back in April in that Birmingham jail.
And that king in the Bible is just like the Supreme Court
who refuse to be tricked by this dark evil system

of segregation that everybody call Jim Crow.
And Jim Crow is gon' die on that same tree just like
Haman did." He tell the congregation,
"Esther was born into the world for a time such as this.
To marry that King and save God's chosen people.
And what is to say that each and every one of us ain't been
born in this moment for such a time as this too.
Even tho you just as scared as that young Esther was
when she held her hand out to the Egyptian king,
you can't let fear freeze your heart and then stop you from
doing your duty to God and to His chosen people.
Jim Crow got to go," my daddy yell out.
"Jim Crow got to go!" Miz Ella Mae start to shouting.
"Cause we God's chosen people just like it say in the Bible
about the Jews and all. Because all of us Negroes
have borne the brunt of oppression just like all of the Jews."
I think the church really like my sermon about Esther.
My Daddy smile at me a lot. And I smile back at him too.

When we get home from church that evening,
my Daddy sit me on his lap without me even asking.
Then he grab my hands and tell me he proud of me.
And then he sing me a song. And I just can't stop laughing.

> *A-a-man*
> *Aman*
> *Aman*

7
LEST THOU BE JUDGED

"If I can but touch the hem of His garment,"
Daddy preach the next Sunday standing in the pulpit,
"I will be made whole." All of the congregation
is screaming and shouting like they having a fit.
"If the woman who have the issue of blood –
with 12 years of the *same* problem – can reach out her hand,
then why can't you?" he say to the people.
And the whole congregation start to shouting again.

We starting off 12 days of revival.
With 12 different preachers. My daddy the first.
We usually just have one week of revival,
but God told Daddy this time that he need to do something different.
And usually we don't have but one preacher for revival.
And Daddy don't usually preach on none of the nights.
Daddy say God told him the preachers he wanted.
So for the next twelve days I got to be at the church.
That's the thing I hate about being the baby of the family.

Wherever Mama and Daddy at, that's where I got to be.
Maybe I can get them to let me stay with Sammie sometime.
I'm sitting with Sammie and her sister. Her name is Smokey.

Sammie Lee my best friend over in Little Rock
except for Geneva Johnson. She my best friend too.
Geneva granddaddy is the president of the Deacon Board
so him and my daddy always have work to do
together to keep the church running smooth about money.
She live with her grandmama and her granddaddy.
I can't remember never once even meeting her mama
even tho Geneva tell me all the time that I done met her.
Sammie Lee mama is on the Usher Board.
Her mama name is Miz Priscilla.
Miz Johnson and Miz Priscilla is the only two people
my mama ever let me stay with beside Jewel and Miz Francis.

Since my daddy church is over in Little Rock
and not in North Little Rock where we live at
I have my best Uz friends and my best Little Rock friends.
They all know each other but we don't interact much.
My best friends in Uz is Jewel and Carol Jane and Red.
Carol Jane and Red is sisters. They last name is Montgomery.
Carol Jane real dark and Red is real light skin
and both of them got real long hair just like me.
Sammie Lee is what my mama call a real fast girl
but for some reason my mama she still really like her.
She say Sammie don't make trouble for nobody but herself.
Her sister Smokey is about two years older.

Sister Miller is shouting. Me and Sammie Lee laughing.
She shout like a baseball player that's just winding up his pitch.
Then she stop in the middle of the wind-up movement she doing
and she scream real loud. I don't like her one bit.
She is always telling my mama something bad about me.

Something I'm wearing that she don't think I should wear.
One time I wore some fishnet stockings to church
and I overheard her telling my mama that I look like a whore.
My Mama say something back to her, but I cannot hear it
cause Mama's back turn to me. Plus she got on a hat.
When I ask her later on what she say to Sister Miller,
she tell me stay out of grown folks bizness and quit being so fast.

"Some of you have been bound," Daddy start in again
after the congregation done sit down in they seats,
"like that woman in the Bible with the issue of blood.
Did you ever notice from the text in the Bible that we
don't even know her name? All we know is her problem.
Some of us is like that. Our problems so big
that they come to define us. I done heard y'all say it.
That unwed mother. That drug addict. That illegitimate child."

It's two girls in our church with illegitimate children.
And Miz Ozella Davis is married to the drug addict.
The whole church be gossiping about them all the time.
They even ask my daddy to have a put-them-out-the-church meeting.
But Daddy just blessed both the babies and gave Miz Ozella
the benevolent offering. Now the Super Saints is mad.
One of the unwed mothers is Sammie Lee sister Smokey.
Now everybody acting like they want my Daddy
to treat her just like he ain't never knowed the girl.
Like he didn't baptize her. Like having this baby done turned her into some kind of devil.
The Super Saints in our church can list every kind of sin,
but they ain't nearly so Christian when it come to forgiveness.

Folks ain't hollering and shouting so much now neither.
Now folks done got quiet. Cause my Daddy stepping on toes.
Cause so many in this church done changed somebody's name to they problem.
Daddy talking now like he mad. Real soft and real low.
Sister Miller just grunt. Not a amen or nothing.

Let Sister Miller tell it, she was born without sin.
But Mama say she done knowed her since she was a young woman.
And she done got too old now to do anything but raise hell.
Of course, she didn't say this to me. I heard her tell Miz Priscilla.
Miz Priscilla just laugh and say, "Girl, don't you know."
Then my mama say, "If she say anything else about Mandy,
I'm gon' slap her in the face." I'm so shocked I can't move.
I ain't never heard my mama take up for me with nobody.
I always thought she agreed with every bad thing folks said.
It is usually my Daddy that take up for people.
Judge not, Daddy say, lest thou wilt be judged.

"The Bible say that the woman touched the hem of His garment.
That mean she was down on the ground in the dust and the grime.
I can see Jesus now with all the important men around Him.
The ones arguing about who is gon' sit on which side
of God in heaven. And here come this lowly little woman.
Face to the ground. Unnoticed because of the press
of people that Jesus had at His side.
He didn't even pay her no attention until she touched the hem of His dress.
And then Jesus said, 'Wait. Somebody done touched me.
I can feel that my virtue has gone out in the crowd.'
And the important men who had not taken of His virtue,
who walked beside Him every day, not one of them had decide
to take of this gift that Jesus had to offer.
How often do we take the gift right next to us for granted?
How often could we have had the power of another person's gifts
and didn't even think it a gift cause it was offered so easy?"
Now the people in the congregation done really start to squirming.
Daddy wipe his face with a handkerchief. One that I iron myself.
He done use at least 15 of the 20 handkerchiefs I iron.
That's how I can tell that his sermon is just about to be finished.

And then Daddy say, "Sometime you got to be at your lowest
before you step back and let God do what it is He do best.

The Bible say that woman had spent all of her life savings.
She had gone to the doctors and they couldn't give her no help.
So she didn't have nothing to lose, crawling on the ground to see Jesus.
Even tho Jewish law said because she had the issue of blood
that she was unclean. She shouldn't have even touched Jesus.
But instead Jesus said, "Woman thy faith made thee whole."
Now people is shouting and standing up on they feet.
Daddy waving his handkerchief in the air like a banner.
Miz Ozella and Sammie Lee sister both got tears in they eyes
and both of them is standing and they got both they hands up.
"God's power is able to heal and resurrect you.
To turn you around and stand you back up on your feet.
God don't never see nobody who is past His redemption.
Who is past His forgiveness. Sometimes *in spite* of the church."
Sister Miller is starting to look real uncomfortable.
Daddy's sermons is like that. If you have done something wrong,
it always seem like he preaching directly at you.
I don't know how he do that. I guess that's why they call it the Word of the Lord.

"Some of you have been bound." I see Smokey is crying.
Her baby in her lap. She got him dressed up so cute.
"But the devil is a lie!" Daddy scream at the congregation.
"You are never alone. God can always touch you
and heal your body. Heal your sin sick spirit.
Somebody's gon' touch Him today and He gon' set you free.
I open the doors of the church," my Daddy say then.
"If you want God's forgiveness for your judgments then He
is ready and willing to bear your afflictions."
Smokey hand her baby to Sammie and she jump out of her seat.
She walk down the aisle to the chair by the deacons.
She is crying unashamed. Her tears flowing free.
Daddy say, "We as a people have been bound like that woman.
We ain't got nothing to lose we so sick and broke down.
Why not take a chance on a man they call Jesus?"
He go take Smokey's hand and lead her down the aisle.

"Why not take a chance on this thing that's call freedom?
Do you believe God can heal a nation as sin sick as this?
But, Preacher, you say, how can God ever heal them
if they do not even believe they sick in the first place?
You leave that to God! Just remember that woman
crawling down on the ground in the dirt and the grime.
Her faith made her whole! Not the doctor's diagnosis.
It is faith in God that will lead every one of us out.
And I'm not saying that all the protests and all the demonstrations
ain't got nothing to do with the changes being made.
But our people done marched for a hundred generations.
Been marching and protesting ever since we was slaves.
It is faith in God that can heal a sin sick nation.
Only God can change a Klansman's hateful heart.
We done seen that the laws changing don't make one bit of difference.
But first I ask that you take the time out to start
by looking at your own heart. Look inside your own self.
I imagine that woman with the issue of blood
had took the time to clean up her problems with her own neighbors
before she dare to touch Jesus. Before she dare to ask God
to heal her. You can't change others if your own heart is dirty.
God say cast the mote out your own eye before you take it out of your brother's.
If you ready to change your own self, come on down to the altar.
God is waiting for you with hands outstretched in forgiveness."

Then something incredible happen. Sister Miller go get the baby.
She raise up real slow and she get up off the pew.
She take the baby from Sammie and she walk straight up to the altar.
She stand up there beside Smokey. She say, "Baby, God forgives you."
Everybody start to shouting. Daddy walk back out the pulpit
and go stand beside Smokey. Two other people done came and sat down in the front.
Daddy extend to both of them the Right Hand of Fellowship,
but before he do that, he wrap Smokey up in his arms.
And just like that, I can see the great power in forgiveness.

Sister Miller hug Smokey. Smokey burst into tears.
And then Miz Ozella she come down to the altar
and Sister Miller grab her and wrap her up in her arms.

In all the years that I done been at this church,
I ain't never seen Sister Miller hug nobody before.
She always sit apart. Like she better than everybody.
Making wrinkles in her forehead when she look at folks down her nose.
She hug the other two people who join church this morning.
These is people I done seen, but not people I know.
I don't think Sister Miller know who these people is either.
But that don't make her no difference. She wrap them both in her arms.
Even tho she is crying, she got a smile on her face.
The wrinkles in her forehead seem to disappear too.
Her nose ain't all crinkled from looking down it in blame.
She look totally different when she ain't judging you.

Then everybody start to hugging everybody.
The whole church on they feet with somebody else in they arms.
I seen people who I know ain't spoke to each other for years
come right down to the altar wrapped up in each other's arms.
I don't know what Daddy say that make such a difference this time,
what miracle happen that made God touch her heart,
but I can see for myself that Sister Miller done been changed.
And I know then that forgiveness is something that come straight from God.

I look over at Mama. She sitting in her seat rocking
back and forth, back and forth like she is filled with the Spirit.
I wonder what it is that she is thinking about.
And I am also wondering if church gon' ever be ended.
And then I see my mama get up and walk up to the pulpit.
I ain't never seen my mama do nothing like this before.
Daddy come from where he at behind the big wooden lectern
and my mama fold my daddy up in both of her arms.
Daddy got tears that is streaming straight down on his face.

His lips is moving. Almost like he praying.
Him and my mama standing at the front of the church
in front of everybody just hugging and swaying.

I don't know exactly what I'm suppose to think about this,
but I guess it's all right since both of them looking happy.
My mama's eyes is dry. Like they always is.
She ain't the kind of person to just cry in the public.
Not like my daddy. He cry all the time.
Seem like all of the men in our family do.
It is something I done seen all of my life.
I guess that's why I cry all the time too.
All of us do. Except for my mama.
She don't understand, she say, why a man be sniffling
and slinging snot like he is some kind of weak woman.
Daddy say it don't make a man weak just cause he show his emotion.
It actually work good for him since he is a preacher.
He will cry whenever the Holy Spirit hit him.
And when he start to crying, folks always start to shouting.
So I guess that's a good thing for his preaching business.

Daddy say the benediction holding onto Mama's hand.
They looking at each other with them googly eyes.
"May the Lord bless you and keep you," my daddy say then.
The whole congregation got some great big smiles
upon they faces. Like they all is happy
to see the Pastor and the First Lady acting like they in love.
I don't know why it would make them one bit of difference.
But I ain't seen my mama look this happy for a long
time. Maybe now they will stop arguing and fussing.
Maybe we can even stop for some ice cream while we on the ride home
from church. Since everybody is acting so happy.
It's a place we all love cause they got the best ice cream cones.
"While we are absent one from another,"
my Daddy say. "Let the church say amen."

And then Curtis play the recessional music
and Daddy walk down the aisle to the door holding onto Mama hand.

8
ITTA BENA

We all file out the church and go get in the car.
Sissy and Lucky is sitting in the back.
Sissy holding Jake Jr. who keep reaching for me.
It always seem like I'm the one who Jake Jr. like best.
Jake and Dara going out to a restaurant for dinner.
Mama say she just do not understand
how they can spend they money on foolishness like that
when for the same money, she say, they can
feed the whole family. Mama say, "That's just selfish."
Daddy say, "It's they money. They can spend it like they want."
I ask if we can go to the malt stand and get us some ice cream
and Daddy say yes before Mama can say no.

The car radio is on and Rev. Jasmine talking about
a town down in Mississippi that is call Itta Bena.
It has been a lot of stuff that's going on down there
that have to do with Negro voter registration.
Rev. Jasmine the DJ that come on on Sundays.

He say, "I have never before seen people work with such courage
as these Negroes from this small town in Mississippi,
in spite of the threats of violence and lynching.
Silas McGee is leading the efforts down there
of the Student Non-Violent Coordinating Committee
working with students from up north and the local
young people as part of the Mississippi Summer Project."

Since June, white folks from up north and Negroes
done been holding a memorial drive for voter registration
in honor of Medgar Evers, the NAACP President,
who got killed when a white man came and assassinated
him last month in the driveway of his house
in front of his wife and his two children.
One reason was cause he had reopened the case
of Emmett Till who was killed for talking to a white woman.
Plus he had been working to get colored folks to register
for the Mississippi Freedom Democratic Party.
So some colored in Itta Bena decide to hold a mass meeting
at a little church call Hopewell Missionary Baptist.
They want to start they own Democratic Party
because the Mississippi Dixiecrats
ain't nothing but a bunch of white supremacists.
Most was registered members of the Ku Klux Klan.

Rev. Jasmine is interviewing a woman from that meeting.
She say, "The Ku Klux Klan had gotten into their cars
and threw a tear gas bomb up under the church
while they drove their cars around and around
in a circle around the church. Of course everybody was scared.
But the man who put the meeting together,
Silas McGee, the one who works with SNCC,
brought us all out of that church with the whole congregation singing!
And then he led all of us on a march,
even tho the white folks threw rocks and bottles at us,

and even ran us into a ditch.
But instead of the police arresting the Ku Klux
Klan, quite naturally they arrested the Civil Rights protestors.
They locked 45 colored people up in jail that night.
And those people have been on the prison farm ever since
because SNCC doesn't have the money to bail them out."

Rev. Jasmine ask everybody to send in a donation
for the protestors that are locked up on the prison farm.
"The next week," Rev. Jasmine say, "200 more people showed up
and they put 13 more colored people in jail.
They have all been working on a chain gang ever since."
He say one colored woman that they got locked up
is 75 years old – older than my mama.
They talking about her on the radio now.

Rev. Jasmine start to interview the old woman's daughter.
Her daughter – I did not hear her name –
say they got her mama outdoors working in this heat.
She say they got her mama working on a prison chain gang.
That just do not make a bit of sense to me.
When I hear things like that I always think
that the whole wide world is done gone totally crazy.
White folks mad at Negroes cause they ain't gon' take it
no more. Cause they thinking that things have got to change.
The woman's daughter is talking about their strategy.
She say, "My mama is willing to be locked up
and work in the hot sun if it's going to help our people."
This is something about Negroes that always make me feel proud,
no matter what it is that the white folks say.
Because when I hear things like this woman that is on the radio,
it make me think that Negroes is going to be ok.

Rev. Jasmine say, "It's important we support the people SNCC is organizing
for the voter registration drive down in Mississippi

because they threw all the colored people's votes out last time.
So even though this vote is probably going to just be symbolic,
Negroes will vote anyway. Of course, white folks don't like it.
But whether they are counted or not, it is still important to vote."
My mama and daddy vote in every election.
All they have to do is to pay a poll tax.

"They are electing the governor in Mississippi.
The Lt. Governor, Paul Johnson, is running for that office.
With Gov. Ross Burnett, he blocked James Meredith
when he tried to register to go to the University of Mississippi."
Of course, Johnson is for segregation.
He is always saying that NAACP stands for
niggers, alligators, apes, and coons.
And he say that the P it stand for possums.

Daddy say, "I'm so proud of all them people
cause they fighting the white system trying to make a stand."
They trying to do a voter registration in Little Rock too.
But a lot of the preachers done been too scared
to let SNCC have the meetings in they churches.
They scared the Ku Klux Klan gon' attack them too.
Mama say, "Them white folks ain't gon' stand
for colored folks to have the same thing they do.
As long as coloreds stay in they place
white folks don't seem to have no problem."
It's the same way that I feel every time
my Daddy get a present from Governor Orville Faubus.

Gov. Orville Faubus he really like my daddy.
He take a picture every year with all the janitors.
And he always give my daddy some money
for Good News Gospel Temple every year at Christmas.
This is the same man who everybody know
stood on the doorsteps at Central High

and wouldn't let them nine little colored children in
when they tried to integrate the school that time.
But now Central High School is integrated,
although it's still only a few coloreds who even go there.
So Gov. Faubus hate coloreds but he love my daddy
as long as my daddy stay in his place.

Mama say she don't see no reason for folks to get killed
when they know they votes ain't gon' count no way.
Daddy tell her he gon' let the protestors come
and use our church. My mama say,
"We just got that church building paid for, A.D.
Now you gon' let white folks come and burn it down?"
Daddy say, "This don't have nothing to do with no white folks."
Mama turn to the window, her face pulled in a frown.
Last year we had the burn-the-mortgage ceremony
when we paid off everything that we owed on the church
from the special collection money we saved in the building fund.
Now the church is paid for free and clear.

Seem like I can feel some storm clouds rolling
into our car. And we been doing so good.
We pull into the malt stand and Daddy go get the ice cream.
I ask my mama if she think I could
have this ice cream when we have my birthday party.
They have soft lemon ice cream right out the machine.
Mama say, "You don't want me to make you lemon from scratch?"
I can't say no to that. She make the best ice cream
in the whole entire state of Arkansas.
Ask anybody and they will agree.
"What else we gon' have for my birthday party?"
"What else you want?" my mama ask me.
Sissy say, "Since this is the last time that I'm going to be home,
I think we should make this birthday something special."
Well, she ain't gon' get no argument from me.

Sissy and Mama always give me the best birthday parties.
My birthday is at the very end of July
so it is less than two weeks away.
This year my birthday fall on a Wednesday
and since Mama is gon' have to work all that day,
we gon' have my birthday party in the evening
after she get home from work.
Sissy say, "Maybe this year we can all get manicures
and pretend we Dorothy Dandridge. Mandy, what you think of that?"
Mama say, "I don't know why they need to get they nails did up
like they is getting ready to go out to some club."
Sissy say, "I just think it's time Mandy gets treated like a young lady."
"Please, Mama," I say. But she don't say nothing.

When we get in the house, the telephone is ringing.
Mama pick it up. Then she start to laugh and scream.
It is my brother, Quinton, calling.
He say this summer he mostly staying in Birmingham.
He move right after he graduated. Mama was mad
that he didn't stay at home and go to school.
But he said he'd been in Arkansas all his life.
His name on the radio is DJ Qool.
He don't call too regular. Cause he always be busy.
So Mama is real happy to hear from him today.
Cause I don't think he called her on her birthday.
Sometimes I think she love Quinton the best
cause no matter what he do, she don't never fuss at him.
Not like she do with me at the drop of a hat.
If I told her that I wasn't going to go to college,
my Mama would throw a natural born fit.

Mama she finally hand the phone to Daddy
so he can talk to Quinton too.
Daddy stop in the middle of a sentence.
He say, "Now Quint you be careful with all this stuff you doing."

And then he listen to Quinton again.
He quiet with the phone up to his ear.
I hear Mama stop rattling the pans in the kitchen
where she done been warming up Sunday dinner.
"Un-huh. Un-huh," my Daddy say.
He just keep listening. Quinton doing all of the talking.
I ask Daddy if I can talk to Quinton.
Daddy say, "Hush now. I am trying to listen."

Mama come out the kitchen and stand in the doorway
between the dining room and living room where we got the phone.
She wiping her hands on her favorite dish towel
and she done also put her favorite apron on.
"You be careful now, boy. What you doing is important.
But you my son. That's what I'm concerned about."
Then he listen again to something Quinton is saying.
Then Daddy say, "She right here," and he hand me the phone.
I ask Quinton to dedicate a song to me on the radio.
He ask me what it is that I want to hear.
I say, "*Fingertips* by Little Stevie Wonder."
"I will do it this Saturday nite. Now you be sure to listen in,"
Quint say to me. I ask, "You like it in Birmingham?"
He say, "Yeah, I like it a lot." And then he ask me
if I want to come and stay later this summer in Jackson.
He say he will talk to Mama. I can't stop grinning!

Daddy and Mama done went back in the kitchen.
They talking real low so I cannot hear.
I tell Mama I'm gon' go and see Carol Jane and Red 'nem
since I know she really want to get rid of me
so she can talk about what Quinton was telling my daddy.
She tell me come back when it is time for dinner.
And she tell me don't eat over Miz Montgomery 'nem's house.
I can hear they voices rise as I close the door behind me.

9
IT'S MY BIRTHDAY!

Sissy get the nail polish and stuff for my birthday like she promise.
And she convince Mama to let me have the manicure party.
It seem like that should make this a good day for me
but I done got too excited and now my head done start hurting.
This birthday party suppose to be my very best one ever.
Mama cook me my favorite four tier chocolate cake.
And she make homemade lemon ice cream just like what I wanted
with frozen peaches to put over it, little bits of ice
still floating in the juice where it start to defrost.
And I know what it is that my daddy gon' get me.
He is going to take me and all of my friends
to the rodeo Saturday. I love when he do that.

When we go to the rodeo my Daddy always go
to see my Uncle Thaddeus and his prize-winning hogs.
They almost as big as his Shetland pony.
He always win some blue ribbons. He also raise hunting dogs.
Uncle Thaddeus is married to Mama sister Aint Ree.

They live Down Home, deep down in the country.
I love to go to they house to stay
with my favorite cousin. Her name is Marlene.

Sissy spend all day getting ready for my party.
She put a big long table out on the front porch.
It's a folding table we get from the church.
She cover it with a red and white checker tablecloth.
Then she put little red plastic baskets on it
and she fill them up with M&Ms and peanuts
that each person will get when they come to the party.
Don't nobody else have things like that
when they have they birthdays. It's just like the ones
that Mama put out for her white ladies parties.
Sissy pour the custard into the ice cream freezer
and me and Jewel, we both take turns
cranking it until the ice cream is ready.
I cannot wait until it is hard and set.
Every so often Sissy come out on the porch
and put some rock salt around the edges.
"This my last party I'm going to do for you,"
Sissy tell me as she put out the red and white napkins.
I still don't know what I am going to do
when it's time for Sissy to go off to college.
When me and Jewel can't turn the crank no more,
Sissy take the ice cream container from out the wooden bucket
and put it in the big deep freezer.
Mama already move stuff around so it will fit in
cause my Mama deep freezer is always full.
One shelf have nothing but my frozen peaches.
But Mama cook and can anything so you can't always tell
when you pull things out what it is that you eating.

Daddy get home from work before Mama do
and take the ice cream out of the freezer.

Mama white lady drive up in the yard
and drop her off about 30 minutes later.
Her white lady have a present for me.
Mama make me open it on the front porch.
She always make her white ladies stay outside.
She say they don't need to see the inside of our house.
Miz Donahue buy me a cute short set
and two pairs of cute little baby doll pajamas.
One pair is full of ruffles and lace.
The other pair is covered with little bitty red cherries.

My daddy is quieter than he usually be.
He ain't came out of the house to play.
He always take part in everything.
He love to play all kinds of games.
It's strange to see him running out in the yard
or down on the floor when we play pick up sticks
because he stand so big and tall.
But when he play he like a little kid.
He fold his body and settle down on the floor
like a giant tree that is such a great height
that the branches and leaves would strain at the sky
and even the very roots would block out the sunlight.
He is a bear of a man, standing tall as he is
before he even put on his shoes – which is size 13.
A big brown cuddly bear. That's what he is to me.
I feel safe and protected whenever I am with him.

Pick up sticks is our game. The one we all get on the floor for.
We play a lot after dinner, after the dishes is done.
Mama always sit on the couch picking turnips or green beans.
And Mama is usually the onliest one
who do not join our game. The rest of us fight for places.
There are four colors of sticks, and so only four of us can play.
Lucky seem like he always the first to call out a color

cause he play sports and think he always the greatest
at everything. We all love to play Daddy.
He is always the biggest competitor.
And each of us want to be the one to bring him down.
You would think that his hands – as big as the paws on a grizzly –
would be a disadvantage. But he use them like claws
to pick the sticks up with grace and dexterity.
How he wrap his fingers around the sticks is a thing to behold.
I ask him do he want to play before everybody come home
but he say no. He is kinda sweating.
And he say he ain't really feeling good.
He tell me to go and get my mama
and then he head into the bathroom.

I start to the back on my way to the kitchen.
But just then, I hear a crash come from down the hall.
I scream and I say, "Mama, come here quick!"
as I turn and see Daddy laying on the bathroom floor.
Part of him is stretched out in the hallway.
His head on the floor laying by the commode.
Mama come down the hallway toward me running.
Sissy is following right behind her. Her hands is folded
across her chest like she scared or is hurting.
I'm so scared that I do not know what to do.
It look like a tree done fell down inside of our house.
Mama scream at Lucky, "Hurry! I need you to
go get the car and drive your daddy to the hospital."
Even tho she is older, Sissy ain't got her license yet.
By now my mama done made it to my daddy
and she holding his head cradled in her lap.

"A.D," she say. She call him over and over.
I finally see his lashes flutter and his eyes open up.
Lucky done found the keys and already pulled the Mercury
in front of the door. Him and Mama sit Daddy up.

Mama ask, "A.D., do you thank you can walk?"
"I think so," he say. His voice sound real weak.
The voice that come out his mouth do not sound like my daddy.
Mama and Lucky get him into the back seat
of the car. Me and Sissy watch them all leave
and then both of us sit down on the porch steps.
Carol Jane and Red come walking up just then
with Jewel and Mabel Ann and Brenda Nell
to start my birthday party. They look at the car and they ask,
"What happen to Rev. Anderson?" I can't hardly talk.
I tell them," I am not going to have no party."
And then I run in my room and shut my door up.

I hear Sissy on the porch passing out the party baskets.
She let all the kids have one that keep showing up.
Jewel come and knock on my bedroom door
but I can't even open the door up for her.
I don't know what's happening with my Daddy.
Please God! That's all that I want to know.
I just lay on my bed praying and crying.
I ain't never seen my Daddy fall on the floor before
and it ain't nothing I never thought I would see.
Not my Daddy. He is strong as a tree.
After Sissy finally send all the children away
she come in the room and lay down on my bed with me.
"Just keep on praying," Sissy she tell me.
"God is going to make sure that Daddy is all right."
"How you know?" I look at Sissy.
She cannot look me in the eye.

Just then the phone ring in the living room.
We both jump up. Sissy get there first.
Mama tell us that they bringing Daddy home
after the doctors get thru running all these tests.
Me and Sissy dance around and we hug each other.

We put all of the party stuff that's left out away.
I just got the best birthday present ever.
My daddy coming home.
Thank you God! is all I can say.

10
ANGELIC TROUBLEMAKERS

Now Mama is planning a big birthday party for Daddy
when his birthday come. It is in September.
When he get home when he come back from the hospital,
he have to stay in bed for a week. The doctors told him
he had some kind of problem cause his heart is too big.
He can't even preach at the church for the next four Sundays.
The Pastor's Aid Society usually plan all the celebrations for Daddy,
including his birthday and the Pastor's Anniversary.
That's my favorite thing that they do at Good News Gospel Temple.
It is a week of celebrations for Mama and Daddy
and they give them all the money they take up all that week,
and Mama always give me the change from out of all the collections.
Most times it be about forty or fifty dollars!
And I get to keep the whole thing for myself
to spend it on whatever I want to spend it on.
This the time I like being the baby of the family the best.
I don't get to go stay with my brother, Quinton, in Jackson
because he too busy running back and forth across the south

covering all the protests and demonstrations
before the March on Washington for Jobs and Freedom this month.
He been interviewing all the Big Six Freedom Rights Negro leaders,
including John Lewis, James Farmer, and Martin Luther King.
He said Rev. King had ask him to work for his organization,
but Quinton had told him no because he could not take his gun.
He say he told Rev. King, "If some cracker come up to me
and try to do me some harm, I'm gon' shoot him dead in his face."
So Rev. King had told him it was best for him to stay a DJ.
He say, "Quinton, you know that violence does not have a place
in the Movement." John Lewis feel that exact same way too.
That's why he been elected Chairman of the National SNCC.
A. Philip Randolph the one who started this whole march thing going.
He the Pullman Porter Union national labor leader,
and seem like all colored people just LOVE the Pullman Porters.
That is one of the best jobs that a colored man can get.
They the ones who snuck Emmett Till's body home to Chicago
after them white men in Mississippi had tortured and killed him.

Daddy say, "Randolph been trying to do this march to Washington
seem like to me for pretty near twenty some years.
He the one made President Franklin Delano Roosevelt
investigate discrimination in federal union jobs back then.
And that's the only reason Rudolph called off the march when
he first wanted to do it back in 1941.
That man don't never give up when he put his mind to do something
and now he got them other organizations, SCLC and CORE,
to work with him too. This gon' be something to see.
They say 100,000 Negroes is planning to come."
Quinton say folks already starting to march from the deep south already.
He know cause some of them have already spent the nite at his house.

Bayard Rustin, who is doing most of all the organizing,
had been on the radio. He done sent out a call
for people to let marchers stay with them across the country.

Cause the people is poor and most of them can't afford
to ride trains and buses, so people is actually walking
from Florida, Mississippi, and other places down south.
Mama say, "I ain't never heard of nothing like it.
Somebody get out on the road without no food in they mouth
going to something that ain't gon' make one bit of difference no way."
Daddy say, "We gon' let people stay in our own church basement
and we serving them food at least twice a day."
"I don't understand, A.D., what it is that you thanking,"
"Negroes done gone from protests to a whole new revolution.
If President Kennedy hisself can back this Washington march
and support our Negro leaders, I don't know why I can't."
Mama just shake her head but she don't open her mouth.

Daddy really seem to like President John F. Kennedy.
My mama don't trust him. I think it's cause he a Catholic.
People say he can't make no decisions without talking first to the Pope,
but my daddy say them people who think that is just plain old ignorant.
President Kennedy was not too excited about the March at first
cause, after the Children's Crusade, he been pushing for a Civil Rights Act
and he was scared that some violence is going to break out in D.C.
"That would be all that I need," President Kennedy said,
"to get the Democrats that are from those deep southern states
to dig in their heels against forced integration."
And when the Big Six had a meeting in his office last month,
John Lewis said later you could tell by his expression
that he didn't want no March. "I think we're gonna have problems,"
the President said when they present him with they Poor People's March plan.
"We want success in Congress, not a show at the Capitol."
But the Negro leaders gon' hold the march regardless of what the President said.
So when President Kennedy saw that he was not gon' stop nothing,
he say, if you can't beat 'em, join 'em, and he lend a helping hand
and do everything he can to make the march a success.
But he make sure his office can always cut off the microphone – just in case.

"And that Bayard Rustin," Mama she say to Daddy,
one nite when they think I cannot hear them talking,
"is one of them funny men, ain't he?" she whisper under her breath.
Daddy say, "You sound just like that redneck Senator Strom Thurmond."
Strom Thurmond call Bayard Rustin a commie pinko nigger faggot
and make it seem like him and Rev. King is sleeping together in bed
just cause Rev. King and the other leaders won't deny or disown him.
A. Philip Randolph stand in front of the white reporters and he said,
"We have absolute faith in Bayard Rustin's fine character,
and we have absolute faith in his ability too."
Daddy say, "If Randolph and Roy Wilkins and Whitney Young believe in him,
then me believing in him is the least I can do."
Bayard Rustin had said what the Negro need most
is a community of what he call angelic troublemakers.
That's people with the patience of a saint or a angel
so they can put up with being beat and still uphold nonviolence.

When the March finally happen on August the 28th,
Rev. King's speech was definitely the best thing of the day.
His subject was "I Have A Dream" and he talk about colored and white children
getting together and playing like it ain't nothing one day.
"That man sho' can preach," Mama she say to the television.
Seem like everybody in Uz come and watch it at our house.
It ain't like people in Uz ain't got they own TV set,
but everybody want to be together, to dream together somehow.
And it turn out over 200,000 Negro marchers show up!
Quinton was right there with them. We even seen him on the news.
And it was not one bit of violence. It's white folks that do that to us anyway,
so I don't know why President Kennedy was so crazy worried about it.
My sister Vernell watch it with us. She bring over her children
so Twinkie and Lulu and Grady Jr. sit on the floor with me
and eat the popcorn balls that my mama make for all us kids.
Vernell say out of everybody, she like John Lewis's speech.
After the march was over and the Negro leaders meet with the President,
John Lewis said President Kennedy act like he was some kind of proud daddy.

And he promise them again he gon' pass the Civil Rights Act.
Mama say, "We gon' see," as she walk back in the kitchen.

When Mama ask me what kind of party I want to have for my daddy
when his birthday come, I tell her I want a hayride
so all the children in Little Rock can come out to our house in Uz.
The children at my daddy's church act like he they daddy, not mine.
They will get a big long truck and put some hay bales up in it
and then all the kids from the church will ride in the truck in the back.
Mama usually do this once every year anyway
so everybody at the church can see where they Pastor live at
since we don't live in Little Rock. It is always lots of fun.
It ain't usually for Daddy's birthday, but since this year done been so hard,
Mama say we ought to take time out to celebrate his life.
She say this with a funny smile at the corner of her mouth.

My daddy birthday is on September the 15th,
and this year his birthday it happen to fall on a Sunday.
So Mama say he gon' let church out a little early that day
and everybody can follow us home in a kind of caravan or something.
Mama been cooking like crazy for the last two weeks.
She done made six pies and four different kinds of cakes.
Plus Aint Ree give her two cakes from Down Home
that she take out of her freezer that's wrapped up in wax paper.
Look like Mama done fried every chicken in the state
plus she make corn on the cob seem like by the bushel basket
and potato salad by the ton, plus the cooker full of green beans
that she done cooked after she pick them from out of her garden.
On the day of Daddy birthday, we all get to church early.
I ain't got to stay home cause Aint Ree come for the day
and she stay at the house to get everything ready
so the party will be ready to start when we get home from church.

Seem like we was just finishing up with our Sunday School lesson
and was getting ready for the part where all the classes meet up

and talk about the moral of the story that we learn that morning
when Miz Cella Mae run in and scream, "They done blowed that church up!"
A waterfall of tears is gushing from out of her eyes
and she ain't finish fixing her hair in the style that she wear.
"What church? What you mean?" Mama run over and grab her.
One of the Altar Club ladies come and bring her a glass
of water. She sit down on the first pew in the front
where the Mother's Board sit every Sunday at church.
Miz Cella Mae say, "They bomb the Sixteenth Street Baptist Church."
And then she start to crying so hard she can't hardly talk.
By now, Daddy done brought his television from out of his office.
It is a small black and white set that Deacon Taylor give him
from somebody who didn't pick it up in his store where he fix them.
Daddy sit it on the offering table and I go plug it in.

Walter Cronkite is interrupting whatever program that is on.
I don't know what it is cause I don't watch TV on Sunday morning.
They showing pictures of the church with the stain glass windows blowed out
and it's two cars that's been damaged and trash all over the ground.
They is carrying a body out covered up on a stretcher.
It's some colored men carrying it who got they Sunday clothes on
and they behind a rope tied between two telephone poles or something
that separate them and the firemen from the rest of the crowd.
Walter Cronkite say, "On Sunday morning Sept. 15, 1963,
a dynamite bomb exploded at the 16th Street Baptist Church
in Birmingham, Alabama, killing four Negro children
and injuring many others. The names of the dead girls are
Addie Mae Collins, Cynthia Wesley, Carole Robertson, and Denise McNair.
Our correspondent, Gene Patterson, is there on the ground.
Gene, what can you tell us about what is happening there now?"
Another white man come on the screen. He got some dark frame glasses on.

"A Negro mother wept in the street Sunday morning
in front of a Baptist Church in Birmingham.
In her hand she held a shoe, one shoe, from the foot of her dead child.

We hold that shoe with her. Every one of us in the white South
holds that small shoe in his hand. It is much too late now
to blame the sick criminals who handled the dynamite.
The FBI and the police can deal with that kind.
The charge against them is simple. They killed four children.
Only we can trace the truth, Southerner – you and I.
We're the ones who broke those four children's bodies.
We hold that shoe in our hand, Southerner. Let us all see it straight,
and look at the blood on it. Let us compare it with the unworthy speeches
of Southern public men who have continuously traduced the Negro with hate;
match it with the spectacle of shrilling children whose parents and teachers
turned them free to spit epithets at small huddles of Negro school children
for a week before this Sunday who lived in Birmingham;
hold up the shoe and look beyond it to the state house in Montgomery
where the official attitudes of Alabama have been spoken in heat and in anger.

Tears running down all of our faces as thick as molasses
as we watch the television. Walter Cronkite come back on.
He say something, but I can't seem to hear his voice no more.
Seem like a fog done covered the world and all my hearing is gone.
They show pictures of the little girls who was in the church that morning.
They was just using the bathroom after they Sunday School service was done,
waiting for the worship service to start upstairs in a few minutes
and in the twinkling of a eye, all they lives was all over.
Denise McNair and Cynthia Wesley look like they could be kin to me.
Addie Mae Collins hair kind of nappy and she wear some cat frame glasses.
Carole Robertson more light skin than all the rest of the girls is
and she got them Chinaman eyes like they got in Red 'nem's family.
Miz Inez start to singing, and that get the church service started.
Daddy turn off the TV and move slow up into the pulpit.
He join in the singing, his voice strong with him leading
the congregation in the moan that he let loose from his lips.

> *Calver-ryyy   Cal-ver-ry*
> *Calver-ryyy   Cal-ver-ry*

Calver-ryyy   Cal-ver-ry
Surely He died on Calvery

Seem like the caravan to our house turn into a funeral procession.
Everybody kinda quiet in the back of the truck
until Sammie Lee start acting crazy and get everybody to talking.
So all of us is pretty much laughing by the time we get to the house.
That was two months ago. Everything done went back to normal.
Since he couldn't take me to the rodeo, Daddy say he will take me to the zoo
and to Fair Park. They close the weekend before Thanksgiving.
But since he busy that weekend, Daddy taking off work early tomorrow too.

Mama tell my daddy to watch us close when we go to Fair Park tomorrow.
She say coloreds done made the white folks mad with all these marches and demonstrations.
"If a child cannot be safe in church, where can she go?" Mama ask.
"I got a bad feeling about tomorrow. Now they done start to kill little girls."
My daddy say that it is Governor George Wallace
who is stirring things up with his mean hateful speech.
He say, "If the governor can outright call us niggers and get away with it
in this fine Christian nation, then what do you expect?"
President Kennedy talking even more about the civil rights legislation
after them four little girls get killed. Mama say, "It ain't no law you can pass
that is gon' change people's hearts and make them finally love colored people.
No law that's gon' cause them children to get they life back."

When I go to school this morning, I can't hardly sit still.
It's a good thing that we having a light day at school cause today
it is so hard for me to concentrate and I can't hardly pay attention.
At recess and lunch I been talking to Carol Jane and Red
and Mabel Ann and Jewel about what we gon' do tomorrow.
All the rides we gon' go on. I like to ride the ferris wheel
and the little train that take you on the tracks all thru the park.
Twinkie and Lulu going too. And my friend Brenda Nell.
Our teachers is watching a trip that President Kennedy
is taking with his wife down off in Dallas, Texas.

The teachers is watching it in the teacher's lounge.
They taking turns going in and out watching the television.
Jackie Kennedy is making this her first official trip
since her baby died. His name was Patrick.
Mrs. Kennedy always be cleaner than the Arkansas board of health
with her pretty pink suit and her matching hat.
Yesterday they was visiting in San Antonio.
I think I might have a cousin who live out there.
And Vice President Johnson and his wife, Lady Bird,
is traveling with the Kennedys riding in another car.

Now my daddy done got mad at President Kennedy
cause he still ain't introduced the Civil Rights Bill
that say Negroes have the same rights as white people do.
But Quinton still love the President and he say that he will
do anything to get President Kennedy elected again
when he run for office again next year in November.
He say the president will introduce the Bill when he win his second term.
Quinton say he doing that because he is too scared
that the white people in the South won't come out and vote for him
if he sign something that make Negroes like they is equal to whites.
My daddy say, "President Kennedy ain't nothing but a coward
and I done started to believe he ain't gon' introduce the Bill the next time
either." Him and Quinton was just arguing about it
when Quint come and visit us on his way home to Jackson.
Mama done told them they can't even talk about politics no more
because she is tired of hearing them always arguing and fussing,
even tho I think it's Mama that make Daddy mad at the President.
She the one who done always said that he ain't no count
and I believe she done made my daddy think like she do.
I just know I am tired of all of them fussing about it.

Today the President go to Dallas. It had been raining but now it's not.
So they was riding in they convertible and the Secret Service had let down the top.
My sixth grade teacher – her name Miz Lewis – she reporting every step of the trip.

Seem like she like President Kennedy too. She say this is a historic event.
I don't remember why this trip is more important than any other one
that the president been on since it ain't got to do with us Negroes.
Except if we have a test, I know this trip is gon' be on it.
Miz Lewis always do that. Show us something irrelevant and then test us on it.
When we come back into our class after the lunch recess is over,
all the teachers done gathered together sitting in the teacher's lounge.
And it seem like I can hear somebody in there that is crying.
Not one teacher is in they classroom. It ain't nobody around.
Quite natural, all of us kids is wondering what in the world done happen.
All of a sudden, we can hear Miz Randall come on the intercom
and tell us all to take our seats and pay attention and be quiet
because she say she have a important announcement that is about to come on.
Miz Lewis come into our classroom. Her eyes is red and filled with tears.
"What's wrong, Miz Lewis?" we all ask her. Just then on the intercom we can hear
Miz Randall, the principal, clearing her throat like she been crying too.
"John F. Kennedy has just been shot." I can hear kids scream in another room.
"President Kennedy has been taken to Parkland Hospital in Dallas
for treatment of his gun wounds. Other reports are still coming in.
I'm asking teachers to keep all the children in their classrooms
as we await the news reports as they come on the television."
She have her own television in the office. I want to go in the teacher's lounge
but I know that I can't cause the teachers be in there smoking.
Miz Lewis say, "Children, let us all bow our heads now and pray."
She pray that the president don't die. Then we all say A-man.

What is wrong with the world? That is what I am thinking.
I ask Miz Lewis, "Who would do something to the President like that?"
She say, "All that I know is that they are looking for a white man
but they don't know who that white man is as of yet."
All of us kids have got about a hundred million questions.
Miz Lewis tell us, "Governor Connally has been shot along with him too,
but it looks like the governor is going to be all right."
Then we hear the crackle of the intercom coming into the room.
Miz Randall say, "The president is dead according to Walter Cronkite on television."

Well, if Walter Cronkite say it, you know that it is the truth.
Everybody in the classroom seem like they all start to crying
all at once. Except for me. I'm just sitting there in shock.

After all the praying that I did for my Daddy when he was sick,
I can't pray no more. I used up all my bargains with God
when I promised him my life that day that my Daddy fell.
Miz Lewis say, "The man who shot him is the devil and he's going to go straight to hell."
All I want is to talk to Daddy. I ask Miz Lewis to use the phone.
I ain't never called my daddy at work but I need to hear the sound of his voice.
Miz Randall come on the intercom. She say the buses coming to take us home.
She say, "Line up in a orderly fashion and proceed in silence to the front door
where the buses are waiting." When I go into the hall,
most of the kids is crying loud. Don't n'an one of them know
the man so I don't know why they acting like they daddy dead.
I didn't even cry that loud when my own daddy fell
on my birthday. But seem like it's always one or two kids
that get all emotional over everything. You know one of them is Mabel Ann.

I get in the line with the other kids who take our bus home to Uz.
Ain't nobody talking or really saying nothing. Everybody wiping they eyes and nose.
Me and Jewel start holding hands when we get on the seat we share,
but we don't say nothing to each other. Everybody on the bus just seem to stare
out of the windows. When they let all of us off
seem like all our mamas is at the bus stop standing there waiting on us.
I don't know how everybody mamas got home so fast that particular day.
My mama wrap her arms around me, and that is where I want to stay.
That's when I cry. I ask her have she heard anything from Daddy.
She say he is on his way home. He went to the church first to make sure
everything was all right there. He thought somebody might break windows out or something.
I don't know why anybody would want to do anything to our church.
I ask Mama, "He coming home now?" My mama purse her lips into a line.
She tell me ain't no need for crying. And then my Daddy pull into the yard.
And I run fast as my feet will take me and go and jump right into his arms.

11
'TIL DEATH DO US PART

I start to follow my daddy wherever he go.
I always like to go with him, but now even more
I don't never want to let him out of my sight
cause it seem like to me if a President can die,
then anybody can. I don't know what God will do.
I feel scared all the time. I think the whole country do too.
Cause that same week after President Kennedy was killed
by a white man by the name of Lee Harvey Oswald,
another white man come and shoot that white man too.
It was a man that go by the name of Jack Ruby.

We was at church that Sunday, just starting service
when Deacon Taylor run in and start to shouting,
"They done shot the man who killed the President!"
My ears would not take in what Deacon Taylor was saying.
I thought for sho' it had to be some kind of mistake.
Miz Angel Lea was doing the announcements and she take
a break in the middle of what she is reading.

Daddy stand up in the pulpit and say, "Deacon, what you saying?"
Deacon Taylor say, "Somebody just shot Lee Harvey Oswald
as the police was taking him out to the car
to carry him to the courthouse for the hearing this morning."
Everybody in the church start to talking all at once.

Some gangster who own a nightclub in Dallas
had shot the man who kill President Kennedy.
There was police all around. That didn't make no difference.
Jack Ruby come out of the crowd of reporters
who was covering the trial that was about to start
and just walked right up to Lee Harvey Oswald
and shot him with a pistol one time in the stomach.
And like President Kennedy, they took him to Parkland
Hospital where he died later of his bullet wound.
Folks was clapping they hands when they told the crowd the news.
They got film of the whole thing on television.
I just think again the world done really went crazy
if you can shoot somebody on live TV.
Ever since then I like to have my daddy close to me.

That's been two months ago since all of that happen
and seem like things done went back to normal.
Well, as normal as things get in this crazy country
while Negroes is still out there fighting for our freedom.
A lot of the Civil Rights leaders done been arguing about
what is the best way to keep fighting in the South
for change in America. Some of the young people want
to keep doing boycotts and protests and stuff.
John Lewis and SNCC is for direct confrontation,
but Rev. King and the Southern Christian Leadership Conference
believe changing laws is how things gon' get better.
Daddy say, "Well, they did just pass the 24th Amendment
that make it illegal to charge a poll tax."
Quinton say, "And the 24th Amendment wouldn't have never been passed

if it wasn't for young folks putting their lives on the line
sitting in at counters and doing Freedom Rides."

Quinton had been part of the Freedom Rides two years ago.
That was his first time doing his eyewitness reports.
He had told the radio station he was gon' go with the students
who was challenging segregation in the south in bus stations
on the interstate bus system. The law had already been passed
that said it was illegal for the bus station lunch counters and
the bus companies to separate passengers based on they race.
It was right after Quinton first start to work at WOKJ.
But, like Mama always say, the law hadn't made no difference.
I remember real clear that Mother's Day morning.
We had the radio on listening to his first national broadcast
from outside the bus with the Freedom Riders on it.

The daffodils was dancing in the front yard like tornadoes.
Red roses climbing, wild, to the roof of our house.
That Mother's Day was alive with hope and with morning
'cept for the slash that was running across my mama's mouth.
Mama was kneading the dough for the biscuits for breakfast.
All of Uz was listening to the radio that day.
Waiting for Quinton's smooth deep voice to come thru the airwaves
and talk about the Freedom Riders. Colored folks and whites
riding buses down South from Washington D.C. to New Orleans.
All of them is students. My mama say,
"This how these chir'en choose to spend they spring vacation?
They ought to be home with they mamas."
Then she whip the dough like it's the thing made her mad.

The sun was shining that day like a bag full of diamonds,
coming thru the dining room window in long, shiny strands.
What Mama really mad about is that Quinton is with them.
His job on the radio is to report everything
that go on. We hadn't heard nothing from him so far that morning.

Mama keep sucking her teeth. And saying, "Hmmpfh, hmmpfh. Hmmpfh, hmmpfh."
Ain't nothing we done to try to make her happy
on her special day done worked out at all.
Not the handkerchiefs I bought with my babysitting money.
Not the earrings from Sissy. Not the perfume from Jake.
Not one thing that we plan done made her one bit of difference.
Not even the new dress that Daddy buy her for Mother's Day.
Daddy already at church. Jake had drove him
to Little Rock, and then he come back for us.
Daddy wanted to be at Sunday School on time,
and the rest of us was being slow so he had just left all of us.

Sissy say, "Let me cook the biscuits for you, Mama.
You're supposed to take it easy today."
Mama say, "Sissy, you know I don't let nobody cook my biscuits.
Wash that pan out there for me. Mandy, you gone out and play."
That's when I know something up. Cause this is a Sunday morning.
I don't play outside on a Sunday. Never did. Never have.
Sissy done comb my hair but I ain't even got dressed yet.
I ain't done nothing this morning but brush my teeth and wash my face.
We don't do nothing but get ready for church on Sunday morning
so Mama must wanna say something to Sissy she don't want me to hear.
So I go out the front door and run around to the back
and sit outside the kitchen window. The only thing about that
is that Cud'n Thetta can see me if she laying in her bed.
And that's the only place she be at. So she gon' tell Mama where I am.
But, 'til then, I'm gon' sit here and be quiet as a mouse.
Sissy see me thru the screen, but she don't open up her mouth.

"What Quinton say when he call on the telephone this morning?"
"He didn't talk to me long. He said things have started going bad."
"What kind of bad? He say anythang else?"
"No, he just said to listen to the radio." I feel a spider on my leg.
I brush it off real quick. It run thru the grass like a monster,
legs spreading all over, every which away all at once.

The grass so green and sparkling, seem like it's been sprinkle with sunshine.
Strange how things can be so beautiful and so scary all at once.
Mama voice been heavy with sanctified songs all that morning.
Her voice carry out the window.

> *Hear my humble cry*
> *Whilst on others thou art calling*
> *Do not pass me by*

The Freedom Riders had been riding on the Greyhound and the Trailways.
Eleven days they been together, whites and coloreds on the same seat.
Today they was suppose to finally get to Alabama.
When they get to a bus station, they always go in to eat
at the white lunch counter. They hadn't had no trouble
'til they got to South Carolina. That's where John Lewis was beat.
He the one who introduce Quinton to Martin Luther King Jr.
And Rev. King hook Quinton up with this new eyewitness report.
Mama say he a fool. "Don't he know white folks is crazy?
They care less bout a colored man than bout the dirt on they feet."
But Quinton is a grown man, so it ain't nothing she can do about it.
She just keep the radio tuned to his station. Mama yell, "Mandy! Come and eat!"

I go round the front like I ain't been listening to nothing
and walk thru the front door just as cool as you please.
Mama say, "Mandy when I tell you to do something, I mean it.
And don't start lying and make it worse. You got grass on your knees
where you been sitting by the window. Wash yo' hands. Quit being hardheaded.
I got enuf to think about without worrying about you today."
I start walking down the hall on the way to the bathroom.
Then Quinton's voice come on the radio and we all freeze where we at.

"The Greyhound bus just pulled into the Anniston station.
It's the stop before Birmingham. And there is a mob of white men outside.
They are screaming profanities and breaking out the back window of the bus."
Then we hear a big explosion. Then, "Let's burn them niggers alive."

Quinton start to sound like his voice full of panic.
He say, "The bus is on fire! The bus is on fire!
The gas tank just exploded. The mob has started to flee.
The Freedom Riders and other passengers are all trapped inside.
And I can hear breaking glass. Wait! I see
the door is now open. The riders are pouring outside.
They are gasping for air. Some of them are falling to the ground.
I can hear moans for water. And there is no one to help.
Wait. I see a little white girl coming through the crowd
with some water. She just walked over to a Negro woman
and put a towel on her face. Now she's giving her a glass.
This is a child of maybe 12 or 13.
She is the only one who is helping. She is moving from place to place.
She is giving every Negro she encounters a glass of water.
When she is sure they're all right, she then moves on to the next."
Mama say, "Amazing Grace!"
Quinton say, "This is amazing.
This little child has surely saved a life today.
The mob is starting to come back in the direction of the bus.
Someone just hit a Negro man on the ground with a club.
The Negro is using the towel that the little girl gave him
to wipe his face. His face is covered with blood."
Then the radio go silent. We all look at one another.
Then Mama start to singing. Her voice sound like a sigh.

> *I'm calling you, Saviour*
> *Blessed Saviour*
> *Hear my humble cry*
> *Whilst on others thou are calling*
> *Do not pass my chile by*

Her voice break at the end. She stand there looking at the radio.
You can tell that she scared. Don't nobody know what to say.
We all huddle around the radio to hear what happen to Quinton.
Don't know if he got hit. Don't know if he safe.

Mama say, "Let's sit down to eat." So we all take our places.
Uncle Jesse come out his bedroom and go fix him a plate.
Ain't none of the rest of us hungry. Uncle Jesse take his plate back to the bedroom.
Sissy sit down at the table and start to pull on her bangs.
Lucky suck his two fingers. He always do that when he nervous
or whenever he scared. That's bout the only way that you know.
I start to crying. "Mama, what happen to Quinton?"
Mama say, "Ain't nothing happen to Quinton. He fine. I just know it.
Eat yo' breakfast so you can start getting ready."
"I don't want to go to church. Not 'til I'm sho' my brother is safe."
Sissy say, "Don't you worry." But she ain't looking at me.
Her eyes is all watery. And she looking down at her plate.
I watch a tear drop into Sissy's tomato preserves.
When I touch it with my finger, she smile a sad smile
then she reach over and kiss me on the top of my forehead.
"Pray, Mandy," she say. "You just pray real hard."

The radio done fill the whole room with its silence.
Not even the diamond colored sun can lift the despair in the room.
Everything in me is screaming that the white mob done got Quinton.
I can see it in my mind. He all bloody and wounded.
The radio start to crackle. Now we can all hear the static
like it is something under water trying to make its presence known.
We all hold our breath waiting to hear Quinton speak.
"Our sound engineer has been wounded," Quint say,
and all our breath explode like a bomb.
"As if on cue," Quinton say, "the white mob all dispersed.
Rev. Shuttlesworth has shown up with some members of his church.
There are about 5 cars. Each one of them are filled
with the dozen or so Freedom Riders. Tho some are wounded, they are all well
enough to walk on their own. We are moving away.
We will bring you more breaking news later on today.
Right now, we are all going to Rev. Shuttlesworth's church.
Looks like the Freedom Rides are over. These students are hurt
and have all decided they cannot continue this trip.

There has been talk from some corners that there are replacements here,
but I cannot confirm that. Stay tuned for more breaking news.
We will be reporting next from Birmingham, the next stop on the tour.
What a day this has been! These young students have stood strong.
I wish to all of you out there a pleasant Mother's Day morning.
This is Quinton Delacortes Anderson for WOKJ,
your Civil Rights news station."
"God sho' is good," my mama say.

> *I'm calling you, Saviour*
> *Blessed Saviour*
> *Hear my humble cry*
> *Whilst on others thou are calling*
> *Do not pass me by*

The whole church singing that song that Mama sung that Sunday morning.
Daddy he getting ready to say the benediction
when all of a sudden he start to swaying
back and forth a little like he having trouble standing.
He on his feet in the pulpit holding up both his hands
to bless the congregation at the end of the service.
"The Lord bless you and keep you," my daddy say next.
Then I hear Miz Cella Mae cry out, "Somebody catch him!"
And then my Daddy stumble back two steps in the pulpit.
Deacon Taylor jump up from his seat, and he start to run
up to the podium where my Daddy is standing.
Miz Inez scream, "Catch him! Catch him! Don't let him fall!"

Then all of the deacons get up off the front bench.
I cannot understand exactly just what is happening.
The Pastor's Aid Society bring some water and wash cloths.
Mama get up from her seat and she go up in the pulpit
too. She start to moving everybody.
"Y'all need to give him some air," I hear Mama say.
The deacons done got him back in his pastor chair.

Rev. Long stand up and he start to say
the benediction again so everybody can leave and go home.
Deacon Jones gone in the office so he can call a ambulance.
That's when I finally figure out that my Daddy sick again.
I run out the church. I can't watch nothing else.
Sammie Lee run out of the front door behind me.
I open the door of Daddy's car and fall into the front seat.
Sammie crawl in too and she sit there beside me.
We wait in the car together until we see
the ambulance pull up and put Daddy in the back.
I hear somebody say that he had a heart attack.
Mama climb into the back of the ambulance with him.
And I don't never see my daddy alive never again.

Somehow I end up later that day in the car with Grady,
who is married to my oldest sister Vernell.
I remember her picking up the phone in our living room after we got home
and falling to the floor when she hear that my daddy is dead.
I kinda remember some people coming in and out of our house
bringing a whole lot of food for the family to eat.
I remember when Sissy and Quinton come home.
I remember Cleophas coming from Los Angeles the next day.
He driving all my aunties. I remember Dr. Parkland coming
to our house like he do whenever my headaches is real bad.
He bring some medicine for me to take.
He say he bring it cause he hear that my daddy is dead.

I don't remember nothing else until the day of the funeral.
That's when I end up with my mama in the front of the church.
We at the first funeral we have at our church in Little Rock.
We have another one Down Home schedule for the next day.
The funeral line start at the front of the church
and wrap around the sidewalk all the way to the back.
We dressed in my Daddy's two favorite colors,
so we is all dressed in red and black.

That is how we always do at all our funerals,
dress in the colors that the dearly departed
wore the most when they was alive.
Daddy wearing his church robe that's the exact same color.
It is the one that he loved the best.
It has even got a small raggedy tear
just at the shoulder of his preacher robe
where the red velvet done come aloose right there.

Daddy's oldest sister, Aint Pankie, say she do not want her brother
to be buried in no worn out old raggedy robe.
But Mama say that is the one that he wore the most often,
more than any of his other ones, and so she chose
to bury him in that. "Let him wear it in glory.
The Lord will recognize him in it when he get there
cause he bout wore that robe almost every Sunday morning."
Aint Pankie get mad about it, but Mama she don't care.

My four aunties all come up behind my Mama
after Daddy's children and they spouses we all take our places.
The aunties fall in the line right after all of us,
black hats and veils hiding all they faces
that is swollen and wet from the tears they crying.
Each and every one of them is acting dignified.
We ain't a hollering and screaming kind of family,
at least not in the public most times.
After the aunties and they husbands is all lined up,
next in line come all the grandchildren
except for the babies sitting on they mamas laps.
They mamas trying to keep they dresses from wrinkling
cause everybody clean as the Board of Health.
Everybody done bought a new black dress.
And we all got on some kind of red accessory
like a red scarf or a red and black hat.
All of us girls got on bright red corsages.

My dress is a red and black checkered print.
Aint Pankie bought it when we went to Jack Fine's.
It's the most expensive dress that I ever got.
And it's got a matching red and black checkered coat.
Mama tie a red ribbon around my head
and let my hair fall down my back.
I would think I'm cute if I wasn't so sad.

We all file in the church behind the casket.
It is shiny black with a red rose on the side
and its got the Masonic symbol on the top,
the silver Mason emblem covering the wide
top of the coffin. It is really beautiful.
It remind me of my daddy's car.
Curtis play the processional on the organ
as we march into the church, our legs and arms
moving in rhythm to the upbeat music.
That's another thing about a Anderson funeral.
There ain't never no dirges or feel sad music
cause my daddy's life deserve a celebration.

Mama she don't seem to cry or nothing.
I can't stop crying. I ask her, "Why
ain't you crying cause Daddy dead?
Ain't you gon' miss him as much as I
do?" She say she done seen way too much in this life.
"I done cried so many tears, maybe they all dried up.
Quite natural I am sad about it.
Cause it's done always been A.D. and Belle.
But the good Lord tell me a long time ago
about this life I'm gon' have to live.
That's it's gon' have a whole lot of sadness.
And I done seen that come true time and time again.
But you cry just as much as you want to, Mandy.
Don't let nobody tell you when it's enuf.

That's something you get to decide for yo'self."
So I cry into her chest while she hold me in her arms.

II
THE ANGEL

12
A HUNGRY GOD

My Mama sit down at the head of the table,
close her eyes to say the grace, bow her head and start to cry.
Ain't n'an one of us who is sitting at the table
done never seen a tear fall from out my Mama eyes.
My brothers and my sisters all look shame-face at the bacon.
My nieces and my nephews open eyes wide with fear.
Mama reach down and grab the hem of her apron
and use the corner of the fabric to wipe away her tears.
"Lord, I thank you fo' the food we bout to receive," Mama pray,
her voice all thick and clog with snot,
"and for the nourishment of our bodies."
My stomach tied up in a knot.

The dirty gray sunshine coming thru the dining room window
match the gray that's showing in my Mama hair.
If it's done been there before, I ain't never notice.
Seem like it come in all at once.
       once my Daddy was dead

I turn my head and look up toward heaven.
My eyes follow Mama's prayer up thru the ceiling.
I wonder if it's really a God up there.
   Wonder what my Daddy is really feeling?

Vernell she look around the table
to see where she gon' lay the blame.
Anything at all happen with my Mama,
she always seem to find my name
in her mouth. I can tell by her look
she gon' try her best to gimme some trouble.
And let me tell you right here and now –
whatever she bring me, I'm gon' give her back double.

My Mama she is the mother of ten children.
But it ain't but seven of of us that's left.
All but two is at the table.
Plus they children. And my Uncle Jesse.
My brother Quinton he coming by later.
He move back to Little Rock. He is living in sin
with a woman who got a whole bunch of children.
She go by the name of L'il Wren.
L'il Wren play the piano with her elbows for The Five Blind Boys
and wear leopard-skin shoes that cost seventy-five dollars.
'Til they get married, they can't stay at our house.
Mama say she don't care how much L'il Wren shout and holler
and carry on in church. So Quinton he gon' come by later on.
Probably won't even stay for dinner.
My oldest brother Cleophus still living in California.
Out of everybody in the family, Cleo is the real sinner.

Why she sit there we all wonder.
And why she cry? But we don't say a word.
Why she sit in Daddy chair?
My heart it flutter like a bird.

But, I don't say nothing. And don't nobody else neither.
We just wait for Mama to bless the table.
The burden on my heart this morning
seem more to bear than I am able.
Mama seat always been on my daddy's right side.
Cause Daddy he always sit at the head.
Mama always sit like a disciple, her place assured.
Now she sitting in the chair where my daddy sit at.
Mama face is full of fear and trembling
like she serving up The Last Supper of Christ.
Vernell four children look at all the food we having.
They probably looking round for the rice
cause that's all they mama and daddy feed them.
Mama say that's why they all got the worms.
They stay at our house when Vernell and Grady is fighting.
I wash everything when they leave to get rid of they germs.
Mama say that hurt they feelings. LuLu (she they oldest girl)
start to scratch. Soon she be bloody.
Sometime she just sit for hours and twirl
and twirl her plaits around her fingers.
Sometime she suck 'em like they made out of candy.
I reach over and grab LuLu by the hand.
I whisper, "Everything is gon' be okay."

"In Jesus name and for His sake, we pray," Mama say.
Seem like I can see her words float up thru the roof.
"A-man" all of us say as one.
We raise our heads. Then Mama stand up and stamp her foot.
Her left foot seem like it move on its own power,
guiding her cross the living room and on toward the front door.
She step like she marching straight to Zion
straight cross our old worn linoleum floor.
Mama stop at the door and turn around for a minute.
She hold us all within her gaze.
She wipe her nose again on her apron,

the one she wear on special days.
See today is Easter. Mama look at us like we a package
and she don't know just where to send it.
Then she straighten that curve sorrow done put in her back.
She say, "It sho' gon' take mo' than this to bend me."

Then Mama she close the front door behind her.
The twelve of us just sit and stare,
our heads bent low over the smothered potatoes.
The smell of sweet onion gravy hang heavy in the air.
For one long minute, don't nobody say nothing.
    Say nothing.
    Not nothing.
    Not one little word.
I feel again within my chest that thing that flutter like a bird.

I can hear Rev. Ike preaching on the radio.
His voice is smooth and sweet as honey.
I touch the tears left on my mama's plate.
Rev. Ike asking people to send him some money.
Do you want to be heeeaaaled?
Do you want to be saaaaved!!!!???
He'll send you a prayer cloth in the mail.
My mama say on Judgement Day,
Rev. Ike is gon' go straight to hell.

I put her tears up to my lips.
Mix with the tomato preserves, they look like blood.
They taste sweet like sugar to my mouth,
sprinkle with a mother's love.
A light rain fall from out the sky
despite a sun that shine bright in the heavens.
"The devil beating his wife," I say.
Everybody look at me. All eleven
pairs of bright brown eyes that sit in the same shape head

stare at me like I'm the one they all think is odd.
The thunder that rumble cross the sky outside
sound like the empty stomach of a hungry God.

Between Rev. Ike preaching and asking for money,
talking like he know The Good Lord real personal,
Rev. Jasmine come on the radio
and talk about the Civil Rights marchers.
All the marchers dress in they Sunday best.
All the men got on they wide brim hats.
And the women all got on they Easter bonnets.
I see them on the radio inside my head.
We been watching them on the television all week long
ever since they kill that boy in Selma.
That's when people start coming from everywhere.
The boy registering folks to vote name was Jimmie Lee Jackson.
I know somebody with that same name
so I think it could have been my friend who died.
They gon' march from Selma all the way to Montgomery.
That is a long way. It is 54 miles.

Everybody listen close when Rev. Jasmine come on.
Already it sound like it's gon' be a disaster.
And it's something about Rev. Ike voice on the radio
that is making my heart start to beat a little faster.
I don't know why that would be so.
I listen to Rev. Ike every Sunday.
But today he seem to be talking right to me.
Somehow, I know today is gon' be different.
How different I could not have even imagine.
It's strange how things work out that way.
How one thing can happen and everything can change.
So I just hope, whatever happen, the Lord will just lead me today.

13
MY DADDY DEAD

Mama she come back home that Sunday
for us to all get to the church on time.
She don't say nothing about where she went to.
I think she probably went to Miz Francis house.
She put on her princey slip and her stockings.
And then she go put her makeup on.
Just then Quinton he pull up in the yard.
He stay outside and just blow on the horn.

When we drive to church that morning,
all of us is in
Quinton's new pink Pontiac.
The one with the back light fins.
The radio is full of static.
All the windows rolled up and closed.
I feel like I got on some kind of armor
instead of my new Easter clothes.
I'm sitting between Quint and Mama

in the middle of the front seat.
My nieces Twinkie and LuLu sitting in the back
directly in back of me.
On each side of them sit Lucky and Sissy
so we can't let the windows down
cause Sissy say the wind gon' blow her hair.
And she ain't walking in church looking like no clown.
She say with this new hairstyle
she need every strand to stay in place.
Her hair is comb like one of them Beatles.
Comb to the front. Down in her face.
Sissy come home this week for spring break from college.
She come home more often since Daddy died.
She always doing stuff to make me happy.
She say she miss my big wide smile.

The air in the car is hot and clammy
from everybody taking up the air to breathe.
Ever so often Twinkie cough
and her sister LuLu start to sneeze.
"Mama," I say, "Can't we open up the window?"
I like Sissy and all, but my head bout to blow.
Mama say, "Mandy, don't start worrying me bout them windows.
And don't let me have to tell you that no mo'."
I don't know why it is Sissy hair
mean more to Mama than my breath.
I got another sick headache.
And I hurt down in my neck.
My eyes is watering like I'm seeing things.
And my stomach it is churning.
And I got a smell in the back of my nose
that smell just like a house is burning.

All of us got on two-piece suits.
Mama's is the color of a deep dark rose.

And she got on a hat that's the exact same color
with a veil that reach down to her nose.
Mama's sister Aint Ree make the hat Mama wearing.
Mama she make the suit.
Her hat cocked so her silver widow peak show
where it's done greyed down to the roots.
All the hats that Mama wear lately
done had some kind of veil on them.
Until today, she been dressing in black.
But, today, she say we gon' all start to live.
I thought living was what we had been doing.
Every day and all the while.
But today, somehow, is suppose to be different.
I can see it in the way my Mama smile.

The radio blaring to be heard over the static.
In between the church songs they been
talking about them colored marchers
crossing over the Edmund Pettus Bridge.
They done started out from Selma, Alabama.
Mama reach over me to turn the knob and say,
"I can tell by the noise that's in this static
that this gon' be a real bad day."
Ever so often, I look over at Quinton.
His face wear something look like a smile.
I'm trying to look anywhere but the highway
cause I'm getting sicker with every mile.
 "Can't we at least crack a window, Mama?"
I'm gon' die anyway so I ask her again.
"Mandy, hush up," Mama say.
Then she lean across me as she bend
over even more closer to hear the radio better.
I want to tell her to get up. But what can I do?
So I just sit there like a dummy.
Feel like her elbow gon' go straight thru

the big bone in my leg. But do Mama care?
She just continue to use my thigh
like, to her, it ain't nothing no more than a armrest.
I feel like I'm about to cry.

Mama say, "God gon' make things better for coloreds
by and by. Up in the sky."
Quint say, "But colored folks is tired of waiting."
Mama say, "Tired ain't no reason for folks to die."
Quint say, "It's time for Negroes to stand up for themselves
and help God on this path to freedom."
Mama say, "And them white folks on that bridge is saying
if you can't join 'em, then you might as well beat 'em.
And don't go blaspheming, Quinton Delacortes,
the Holy Name Of The Lord."
"I ain't blaspheming nothing, Mama.
I'm just repeating what God say in His word."

I think when they get to the other side of the bridge,
they gon' kneel down and pray to God above
and sing the Civil Rights National Anthem.
It's a song that's call "We Shall Overcome."
Everywhere you go and all on the radio,
seem like colored folks is singing the song's refrain.
Rev. Jasmine is playing it on the radio.
I feel a storm inside my brain.

Quint say, "Colored people trying to change the world
and all the bad things going on in it."
Maybe things is changing somewhere up North,
but far in the world as I can see in it,
everything going on the same way it was.
And folks in Uz don't see nothing wrong with it.
Colored folks in Uz still get up off they seats
and let the white folks sit down in them.

I done been raise that way all of my life.
It ain't even been nothing I done never found
time to think or worry about.
In Uz, children get up to let *everybody* sit down.

Quinton say, "Mandy now you pay close attention
cause you watching history fixing to be made."
Mama said, "Hush talking to that chile bout that foolishness.
Long as I live on this side of the grave
this one chile of mine who ain't gon' be caught up in this mess.
Grown folk ought to know better, but the chir'en they don't.
And long as God leave breath in me
you can be sho' n'an 'nother one of my chir'en won't
get mix up in this Civvie Rights mess."
She hold my head close to her breast.
"People marching cause they tired," Quint say,
"of being treated like they something less.
Ain't your children suppose to have
the same things that God bless the white children with?"
Mama say, "Quinton, that's what y'all don't see.
God done bless me with His breath.
He bless me when He woke me up this morning
dress and clothe in my right mind.
God blessing me in spite of white folks.
Been blessing me. All the time.
And you couldn't pay me to sit behind that counter
up to Franklin Department Store.
I done seen that man stand behind that counter
pick up some food from off the floor
and put it back on them white folks plate.
Just as nasty as he can be.
So why I want to eat behind white folks?
You tell me what that's gon' gain me."
Quint say, "Mama, that ain't the point..."
"That's the point exactly far as I can see.

The Bible say wherever you is,
content is what you spose to be.
Quint say, "Mama, you know being second class citizens
is not what the apostle meant.
You can look all thru the Bible.
Moses came cause the people were not content.
Didn't in the Bible God return
His chosen people's captivity?
God mean His people to be whole.
God mean His people to be free."

"Shush! Shush!" Mama say.
Rev. Jasmine, the DJ, he done start to talk again
about them Negroes down to Selma
and they walk across that bridge.
It seem like we ain't gon' never get to church.
Never get out this car and this long, stuffy ride.
Quinton exit on Ninth Street off the freeway.
My eyes watering with tears and I feel like crying.

Ninth Street in Little Rock is a whole different world.
Colored women dress up and go to smoky clubs
and dance with some other woman's husband.
At the Lucky Lady, you can play the numbers and bet on the dogs.
Most people live in apartments on this part of Ninth Street
and they don't wake up in time to send they children to church.
Even thru the closed windows, I can hear the games they playing.
One group of heathen children standing out on they stoop
in front of one of the apartment buildings.
They playing a game I play sometime with Jewel or Brenda Nell.
Sometime we play it after school in the yard.
It's a game that's call Aint Dinah Dead.
        'Aint Dinah dead,' the leader call.
        'How she die?' the others say.
        'O she died like this,' the leader call.

Then she twist her body all kinds of ways
to show what Dinah looked like when she died.

'O she died like this,' the other children say.
And the one who can't do like the leader the worse
got to be "It" the next time we play.

I can hear the game the heathen children playing
ringing over and over inside my head.
We finally get to the church and I jump out the car.
I bend over and breathe in great big gulps of air.
Sissy say, "Mandy, are you all right?"
"No, Sissy. I been sick this whole long ride."
Then Mama walk up. She grab me by my arm
and pull me over to the side.
She say, "Mandy, I ain't fo' none of yo' foolishness.
I particular ain't fo' n'an one of yo' fits."
"I can't help it," I tell Mama.
"My head is hurting and I'm feeling sick."

Just then Sammie Lee walk up.
"Y'all better hurry up," she say.
I look at Mama thru the fog in my head.
Curtis done already start to play
the processional music. Since today is Easter,
ain't none of us gon' wear our robes.
That way all of us that's in the choir
can show off our new Easter clothes.
My head is pounding. I can't hardly walk.
Sammie reach and pull me by the arm.
We rush into the choir room and take our places
just as Curtis play the last opening chords.
The song of the heathen children still ringing in my head
so I keep messing up the beat.
I'm dipping and stepping when I ought to be swaying
and I feel real shaky on my feet.

When I finally walk thru the door into the sanctuary,
the very first thing that catch my eye
is the Pastor's chair that belong to my daddy.
I catch my breath. And I start to cry.
They done took the black mourning cloth from off my Daddy chair!
This is just not suppose to be.
And if it was suppose to happen,
seem like somebody coulda at least told me!
I still cannot believe my eyes.
When a Pastor die, they drape his chair in black
for a mourning period of one whole year.
My Daddy ain't been dead for three months yet.

The whole church stand up with the choir.
Over the organ, you can hear the sound of shuffling feet.
I look over at the pew where my Mama sit at.
She will not even so much as look at me
cause she know she wrong for how this happen.
She coulda at least gave me some kind of warning.
Now I know why she sit in Daddy chair
when she say the blessing at breakfast this morning.
Ain't nobody never sit in my Daddy chair.
His place done always been at the head of the table.
He wasn't the kind of man who was gon' miss a meal.
I thought Mama cried cause she finally missed him this morning.
But what she really was saying, I see now,
is that this the day when Daddy no longer have a place.
Not at our table. And not at our church.
The only place my Daddy got now is a grave
down in the ground up under the earth.
Ain't nothing left of him now but his rotting body.
When I close my eyes I can see, like yesterday,
the pallbearers as they tenderly carry his body
out of the church after the second funeral Down Home.
I can hear the gravediggers scooping dirt from out the ground.

Tears is running down my face.
I look at Mama. And she frown.

All I can hear in my head is the heathen children's song
and the game they was playing about Aint Dinah dead.
You know how sometime you hear a song
and can't seem to get it from out your head?
That's what it's like for me this morning.
Rev. Long say, "Today we celebrating Jesus being raised from the dead.
And now it's time for us to pause in the program
so the children can get they speeches said."
Miz Angel Lea get up from off the front pew.
She the Mistress of Ceremony for the Easter program.
"Er-rer," Miz Angel Lea clear her throat.
 "Can the church give us another A-man?"
"A-man," the congregation say.
"Speak thru her, Lord," Miz Caroline groan.
Miz Angel Lea ask the choir for a "A" and "B" selection.
The music from the organ sound like a moan.

Curtis start to play "Just As I Am."
He raise his hands and the choir stand up.
Everybody, that is, except for me.
At first, I can't even move. Feel like I'm stuck.
I can hear the kids in the audience out there laughing.
I look at Mama and I can tell she mad
cause I'm embarrassing her in the public.
Sammie Lee she grab me by the hand
and pull me to my feet real slow.
My mouth open and close when it's suppose to happen
but I can't remember the words to the song.
Seem like everything around me starting to turn hazy.

"Sang, Bessie," Miz Caroline say.
"Sang the song." The church all on they feet.

When the choir finish singing and everybody sit down,
Sammie Lee have to pull me to my seat.
"The first selection is by little Miss Cora Lee Sanders,"
Miz Angel Lea say. "Come on, baby, and say your speech."
Cora Lee mama push her to the front of the church.
Cora Lee can't be no more than three
and she shame-face in front of the congregation.
"Say your speech, baby," Miz Sanders say.
Cora Lee mutter something and run back to her seat.
"A-man! A-man!" the church all laugh.

"And the next selection is a special treat.
Miss Amanda Denise Anderson will bring us her own unique rendition
of that great Negro sermon by James Weldon Johnson.
That timeless standard called, "The Creation."
The whole church applaud. They been waiting for this
cause I done done The Creation before.
But, when I stand up in the choir stand,
my feet feel like they ain't quite touching the floor.
Last year for the Christmas program, I did this speech.
Everybody say it was the best thing they done ever seen.
I walk slow to take my place in front of the pulpit.
My head is bowed. And I'm feeling mean.

The first line go, 'And God stepped out…'
so I turn away from the audience so when I turn around
I can step out like I'm as mysterious as God.
I ball my hands into a fist and I open my mouth.
But what come out is,
       "My Daddy dead
       How he die?
       O, he died like this…"
I hadn't intended to say them words.
Seem like something just come over me.
And, if that wasn't bad enuf,

I act it out for the whole church to see.

I clutch my chest just like Daddy did
on that Sunday when he had his heart attack
after he had just finished up his sermon.
I show the whole church how my daddy act.
I flail my arms out to the sides,
and step back two steps like I am about to fall.
That Sunday when Daddy had his attack in the pulpit,
the church rose as one and, as one, they had called
out, "Catch him! Catch him! Somebody catch him!"
I act that out too. My mama looking real embarrassed
like she cannot believe what she is seeing.
I can't believe it neither but I can't help myself.

The whole church is in confusion.
"Hush! Hush!" Miz Caroline cry out.
I slowly come from out the fog
and realize it's now that I'm hearing her shout.
My ears is ringing in my head.
Miz Cella Mae running up and down the aisles.
Everybody else looking over at my mama
to see what she gon' do about her youngest child.
Seem like I can see everybody's reaction,
all of a sudden and all at once.
For the first time since Daddy died, I can really see.
Not just what's on people's face. But what's in they hearts.

Mama's gray streak shining in the sunlight
and the rays is bouncing from off her hair.
The sunbeams shining thru the stained glass window
bounce off her head and into the air.
Her face is twist in perfect agony.
The tears she cried this morning done start to flow again.
She allow them to run free down her face

and she fix her mouth in a bitter grin.
Then Mama open her mouth wide and she holler.
It's a high-pitch mewling put you in mind of a cat.
The birds outside fly into the windows.
The ushers run to where my Mama is at
and fan her with some fans from Ruffin and Jarrett funeral home.
A sorrow so deep, so wide seem like she need to share it.
The sound Mama make come from high in her throat.
The birds outside can't seem to bear it.

Everybody looking at her like she uncovering they shame.
The whole congregation is crying in they seats.
One thing I can say about what's happening with Mama
is that it's done took all the attention from off of me.
So I run down the aisle and out the front door.
I'm too tired to cry. And I'm too sick to sing.
Besides that, I'm just about sick and tired of crying.
Seem like crying is all I done been
doing ever since my Daddy died.
My heart is tired from missing my Daddy.
And I'm tired of people treating him like he ain't never lived.
Inside the church, I can hear Sister Sadie
starting up a old Dr. Watts hymn.
I can still hear Mama in betwixt the singing.
Her voice sound like something I ain't never heard.
Sorta like a small animal that has been wounded
or like a little baby bird that's been stepped on
but not crushed hard enuf for it to die.
Sissy get out of her seat and come stand beside her.
She wrap her arms around Mama and try to wipe her eyes.

I run out the church into the parking lot.
I lift my hair to get some air on my neck.
I go round the back to the back of the church
and lean my head against the cool red brick.

My stomach rumble from deep in my gut.
My mouth it start to fill up with spit.
"Help me, Jesus. Help me, God."
The prayer bubble up from off my lips.
Seem like the whole wide world is spinning.
I feel myself falling to the ground.
And then, just like that! In the blink of a eye,
I feel myself being lifted up by the neck and turned around.
I see a woman bright as the sunlight.
I turn to the presence at my side.
Her garment is of a bright, shiny material
that put you in mind of a beautiful bride.
She dressed in a flowing, clingy gauze-like fabric.
And on her head, she wear a crown
that's sprinkled with the moon and stars.
The angel look me up and down.
She say, "God's ways are not our ways. Nor are His thoughts our thoughts."
"What do that mean?" I ask. But the angel do not say.
She already disappearing in front of my eyes.
Her last words is, "Mandy, don't forget to pray."

This don't look like the angel I seen in my bedroom.
She is not all covered up in flames.
I seen her clear when she stand beside me
and that other angel don't speak my name.
I'm so scared, I'm seeing double.
All I can do is stand and stare
off into space with my mouth open.
When Sammie come out, I'm still standing there.
I walk to the car with Sammie holding me up.
The wind feel like fingers playing in my hair.
I keep reaching up and touching the back of my neck
like I think I'm gon' find a hand back there.
Mama standing by the car talking to Brother Green.
She look at me with what feel like shame.

Her hat done come off and her hair hanging loose.
And I decide right then that she the one to blame
for all the pain that I been feeling.
Cause she won't sit down and talk to me.
If I ain't the baby girl of the Pastor no more,
then I need to decide who I'm gon' be.
How come everybody else get to decide my life?
Mama mad at me. But I'm mad too.
Cause she don't even think enuf about my feelings
to tell me what the deacons had decide to do.

Mama look at me and her eyes say it all.
I'm gon' have to pay for what I did in church.
She look like she totally disgusted with me.
Like she sorry she ever took the time out to birth
a daughter that act as bad as me.
She motion for me to get in the car.
I get in the back seat by the door this time.
I grab the handle and roll the window down as far
as it will go. The air cool on my face.
At least, for the ride home, I'm gon' get to breathe.
I know I'm gon' be in big trouble with Mama
but I wish that she could, for once, just see me for me
and not just as the baby of the Anderson family.
This role we play don't work no more.
How can I ever be the same after losing my daddy?
And how can she not see that? I lean my head against the door.

I keep hearing the words and the voice of the angel
ringing over and over, all thru my head.
"His ways not our ways. Nor is His thoughts our thoughts."
Then I remember the other words that the angel said.
On the radio they say it was bad for the marchers.
Bloody Sunday they calling this Easter day.
Many Negroes was injured. Maybe some even dead.

So, I bow my head.
And I begin to pray.

14
BLOODY SUNDAY

"You seen a angel?" That's what Mama say
after I tell her what had happen to me.
One thing I can say about my Mama
is when you talk about spirits, she listen very closely.
"She call yo' name? What she say to you?"
She stop mid-step, her arm raised up.
She was just getting ready to whip me good,
but when I say this, it make her stop.
"She say God's ways is not our ways
and His thoughts is not our thoughts."
This conversation working good for me
cause she ain't gon' hit me if I can keep her talking.
"It was a woman?" Mama say.
"What she look like?" she ask me then.
"She was wearing a crown made out of the moon and stars.
I guess you could say that she look like a queen."

Soon as we get home from church,
Mama start right in with fussing at me.
She tell me to go outside and get a switch.
"And don't get one off that little plum tree."
I ask her the words that come out of my heart.
"Why you didn't tell me?" That's all I keep saying.
But every time I open up my mouth,
Mama just go to fussing and praying.
"But why you didn't tell me, Mama,
that they was gon' put Daddy's chair on some kind of display?"
"Wasn't no display. And it wasn't none of a chile's bizness.
And the reason I didn't tell you is cause of how you acting today.
Mandy, I believe sometime you done lost yo' na'tral mind.
And sometime I thank you is sho' 'nuff crazy."
"I wouldn't have acted like that if I had knowed about it!"
"You woulda acted worse. And you woulda started sooner.
I don't know why it is, Amanda Denise,
you thank you kin act like whatsoever you please.
You ain't gon' make it in the world like that.
White folks is gon' knock you to yo' knees."
I know she thinking about the television.
They been showing them marchers on the Edmund Pettus Bridge.
Folks got trampled. Tear gas was everywhere.
And I think at least one person got killed.
"I just don't understand colored people,"
Mama kept saying all of the way home.
"You can't never give colored folks enuf.
I ain't seen nothing like this as long as I been born."

"I'm going, Mama," Quint had said
when he heard Rev. King speak on the radio.
"You going where? Down to Selma, Alabama?
Now what you think you going down there for?"
"I'm going to march when they cross that bridge again.
I can't just sit back and just do nothing."

136 *Keep A'Livin'*

"And get yo'self blowed up like them girls
did in that church that Sunday morning?"
Bombingham. That's why they call it that.
They bomb a colored person's house almost every week.
So many colored people done got killed in Alabama
that I can't even hardly remember.
That's when my mama first start acting so scared for me.
When they bomb that church with the four little girls in it.
She shake her head and just keep on saying
if you ain't safe in church then the world is gone crazy.

"See, this why I don't set no store by this mess.
Why the chir'en caught up in this grown folks test?
I hope you ain't really planning to do this, Quinton.
I done lost my husband. I can't lose my chir'en.
How many more places gon' be bombed? How many more people hurt?
And that NAACP always want to use the church.
That Daisy Bates come right to our door.
She ain't never set foot in our church before.
But when they want to integrate that high school, they all come round.
They need to run Daisy Bates right out of this town.
I don't put no store in all this mess."
Her hands was shaking. Quinton said,
"Mama, didn't nobody want them children hurt.
But how you expect to make a mark
on anything if you ain't willing to die?
And Daisy Bates did integrate Central High."
"All them girls was doing was going to Sunday School
where they is spose to learn about the Golden Rule.
Learn about Jesus and His marvelous works.
Don't no mother send her chir'en to church
to have them killed. Boy, is you crazy?
I bet I bet' not never see you – never –
having no rallies and such up in our church."
"I know you feel like that, Mama. But I can't just hush

up about it," Quinton said.
He look at the floor like he feel real bad.

Since Quinton got back home, Mama done got even worse.
Mad all the time. Her and Quinton keep fussing
about the meetings that he keep going to.
Quinton he join SNCC, the young people's movement.
He say, "Mandy look. These the shoes one woman was wearing
on one of the marches." They got holes in the bottom.
Some members of SNCC done started feeling non-violence
ain't the way to go. Quint say, "I'm sick and tired
of turning the other cheek while I'm getting beat up side the head."
But SNCC believe in non-violence, and since Quinton did
join the organization in Little Rock,
he have to follow they rules whether he want to or not.

A lot of people done start to feel this way.
Like non-violence is out of date.
It's done worked so far. Got the Civil Rights Bill signed.
President Johnson couldn't wait after President Kennedy died
to sign that paperwork into law.
I wouldn't have never believed it. But I saw
it on television with my very own eyes.
It say Negro people have the same rights now
as white people do. We can go where they go.
Eat where they eat. Go into they stores.
White people is still fuming mad about that.
But I guess voting don't count in the Civil Rights Act
cause they killed that boy down off in Selma
when all he was doing was trying to register
some colored people just so they could vote.
And a white man come and slit his throat.
So I know that Mama got a right to be scared.
Thank God ain't nothing happening in Arkansas like that.
And all of this is going thru Mama's head.

So she in my face after church just screaming and yelling.
It's Quinton who she is mad at really.
But he is grown. So she can't do nothing.

"What the angel crown look like? Did she have long plaits?"
"Well, yeah, she did now that I think back.
Her crown made of stars and a light like a jewel.
How you know these things?"
"Cause I seen her too."
"You seen her when? You seen her where?"
"Don't matter when. Don't matter where."
"It matter to me Mama. Don't you see?
You can't keep keeping all this stuff from me."
"Don't tell me, Mandy, what I can't do.
I still ain't near bout thru with you.
Gone get that switch. I'm gon' make you mind.
And every time you don't, I'm gon' whip yo' behind."

I done decide today that I don't care
if Mama beat me 'til I'm sick.
I'm gon' go outside to the biggest tree
and pick off it the biggest stick
that I can find. Just let her beat me.
I don't much care no more what my Mama do.
Cause today I done finally figured out
that if I can take a whipping, it ain't much else she can do.
Sometime I think my mama hate me.
How you hit somebody you suppose to love?
My daddy didn't not once never whip me.
It make me miss him even more.

I jump off the porch and pull a limb off the tree.
Just then I look up and see Carol Jane and Nikki.
They coming from over to Carol Jane 'nem house.
When they see me in the yard, they both start to whispering.

I don't want them to see me, but it ain't no use.

Carol Jane and Nikki both raise they hand and wave.

I keep on walking across the yard.

"Hey, Mandy," Carol Jane she say.

"You look like you been crying," Carol Jane say with a frown.

She look straight in my eyes. She know me too well.

"I don't want to talk about it,"

I say with a sigh. But she ask me again,

"What did you do?"

"I didn't do nothing."

Carol Jane look at me again out the corner of her eye.

"So why Maw Belle getting ready to whip you?"

In Uz, everybody mama whip they children. That ain't no surprise.

"Tell me why you getting a whipping."

"Cause I messed up on my Easter speech."

"You getting a whipping for that?!!" both of them ask together.

"Well, what I did was actually worse than that.

I showed the whole church what was on my mind."

"What you mean by that?" Nikki she say.

"It don't really matter. Let me get this switch in the house

cause its gon' be worse if Mama have to ask me again."

Nikki say, "You look like you gon' break down and cry in a minute."

I wipe my eyes real fast on my dress sleeve.

Look like she can see straight to my insides.

"I don't really care what my mama do to me."

"You look like you care," Nikki say. "And like you hurting too.

Well, I guess I'm gon' have to just care for you then.

I'm gon' pray for God to send you a miracle.

And you gon' get one too. Just wait. You'll see."

Then Nikki hug me around my neck.

She got a crooked little smile upon her face.

I'm surprised cause I don't really know her like that.

Then her and Carol Jane walk on down the highway.

This all feel like it is a sign or something
I think as I walk back toward the house.
My feet is dragging across the yard
and my head feel like it's about to bust.
So I pray, "Lord if you let me get out of this whipping,
I'll be real good. I'll do whatever you say.
I will love everybody. Just make Mama don't whip me."
Then I feel something warm in the seat of my pants.

"My period done started." I hand Mama the switch.
A look of disappointment dart cross her eye.
She mad cause she can't whip me now.
The look is there for just a second. But I see it and start to cry.
Mama think I'm crying cause my period done started.
I cry long helpless sobs that reach from down in my gut.
Mama hold me in her arms and just let me wail.
She stroke my head and I cry 'til I'm weak.
When I'm quiet, she say, "You ain't a girl no mo', Mandy.
That blood 'tween yo' legs mean you's a woman today.
That ain't nothing to be shamed about nor sad.
It explain a whole lot about how you been acting today.
Sometime fo' it happen, you feel bad about thangs.
It got something to do with the pull of the moon.
It'll pass soon enuf. Now gone clean yourself up.
And stand up real slow less'n you make yo'self swoon."
I go down the hall into the bathroom.
I take the Kotex from out of the drawer
where I been showed that Mama and Sissy keep 'em.
I take it out the blue box along with the elastic holder.
I can hear Mama shoes flapping down the hall.
She come in the bathroom. "You all right?" she ask.
She rub my belly and and put her hand on my forehead.
"Tell me about the angel. Please, Mama," I ask.

Cause of the blood, I can't set the table.
Mama send me to her room and I lay cross her bed.
She come into the room and she crawl up beside me.
I rest my head in the crook of her neck.
Mama's bed done always been a special place.
A magic place that can heal your soul.
Whenever I'm having one of my headaches,
it is to this safe place that I always come.
I can smell the Avon talcum powder
that she put between her breasts to keep them from chafing.
It help when the weather is damp like today.
I'm surprised to feel that her whole body is shaking
like it's something inside trying to make its way out.
Her top lip get a tick like she about to cry.
She lay cross the bed and pick the lint from the bedspread.
She get a faraway look in the corner of her eye.

"I love you," I whisper to the fold of soft skin
that lay wrinkled on the back of my Mama's thick neck.
"I love you too, baby," she say to me.
She never move her eyes from the ball of lint.
"Mandy, this here a story only a woman should hear.
It ain't nothing a little girl got no right to know.
When the angel come, it mean thangs stirred up some.
It mean that a change is gon' come for sho'."
"What kind of change, Mama?"
"Hush up and listen."
I get quiet cause I'm scared she won't talk no more.
She look at me like she is afraid to answer.
I can tell she scared. But I just don't know
why. "Last time I cried like I did today
was the day Clyde die. The day he left this world.
That was the first time that I seen the angel.
But first the dark angels come. They come a-twisting and whirling."

A dark cloud seem like it cover her face.
She twist on the bed and her eyes start to get wet.
She shiver like a goose done walked cross her grave
or maybe she see something bad inside of her head.
I done heard Mama tell bout how Clyde die a lot.
He my oldest brother. He die way before I was born.
But she ain't said nothing about no angel before today
so I look careful at her face to see what she got to say.
Mama say, "When she come, you done been chose to do a mission.
You kin tell her from other angels cause she always have plaits.
She done come to all the chosen women in this family."
"Chose to do what, Mama?"
"Whatsoever God like."

15
THE DARK ANGELS

O my God!
O my sweet Jesus!
Belle pray to God laying on her bed crying.
She alone that nite, tossing and turning,
a dream world dancing inside of her eyes.
The house was black dark and she fill up with terror.
Her skin feel hot against the chill, damp sheets.
A legion of angels dance right into her bedroom.
She watch as they dance straight up to her roof.

Whirling and twirling, the dark angels they come,
with hair like flame and eyes blacker than hell
like so many loose women drunk on the wine of lust and of madness.
They reaching for her. Calling her into they dance.
Round and round her bed they go.
She feel a line of sweat roll down the trench of her back.
She start praying to the Good Lord Up Above,
pleading with her Saviour, asking Him for His help.

Dear God Up In Heaven, Belle call out His name,
Look down from above on a po' retch like me.
Come down from Heaven. Hear me, dear Lord.
Look down on thine handmaid in grace and mercy.

She was so scared she could have died laying there,
her heart beating so fast she can almost see it in her chest.
She watch as the haints look down from the ceiling,
watch while they mock all her words, all her prayers.
Laugh like old women who sit on a mourners bench
come to show her heart for the whole world to see.
She pray that nite like a Old Testament prophet.
Cause she can feel something bad is getting ready to be.

The words bubble up from some wellspring of faith
and she knew what was happening was a message but she
was so cold and so scared on that frightful nite.
Forgive her, dear Lord, but she just cannot see.
It was the darkest hour of the morning that come just fo' day
when Jesus come and roll all of yo' burdens away.
The nite was so black it was evil with dark.
The Devil angels hold a message. And she better get it right.
But she didn't. And she done had to live with that fact.
His servant know His voice. That's what it say in the Bible.
Listen while I tell you about this dream that Belle have.
About the nite when her life it change forever.

Sweet, sweet Jesus! her cry go past evil to God,
darkness and desolation done come here to this place.
Fear and trembling have done come down upon me.
Turn it from me, Lord. She roll onto her face.
The sheets on the bed was both clammy and cold.
She could feel the rough cotton, and it was scratching her some.
She reach out her hand to A.D. side of the bed,
reaching for him first, before she reach out to God.

A.D. wasn't there, but Jesus grab onto her hand,
His voice a gentle stream. He say Obey Only Me.
But soon as the words come from out of His mouth,
from out of the darkness, mean old Satan appear.
It was a dream. But then again it wasn't.
She seen the things that she seen just as clear as the day.
She seen the Devil when he walk into her room that nite.
He come right at her. Laughing like he was playing.

He wearing a cape that fling out when he walk.
His body change shape as he throw it that way and this.
Sometime he look like a woman. Sometime he look like a man.
Another time he turn around, and Satan look just like a fish.
Whatever he turn into, it was always beautiful.
Preachers act like the Devil got a pitch fork and tails,
but he don't. She don't expect the Devil to look like any and every thang,
but the Devil subject to show up and look just like a lamb.
Like he wouldn't hurt nobody. That's what he want you to think.
And he don't, I guess. He let you hurt yo'self.
And all the while you think you ain't hurting nobody,
thinking the only thing you doing is protecting yo'self.

The hair on His head was the moon and the stars.
His mouth was perfect, and shape just like a bow.
He was chilling. And beautiful. And dark. And cold.
And in his mouth you could see all the lies ever told.
But they didn't look like no lies. They look just like the truth.
Like something you want really bad to believe.
Like Sandy Claus coming early on Christmas morning
or the promise of something better come New Year's Eve.
The Devil had a place in her heart that day
and he look at her close like she his own special prize.
He knew her heart was just as cold as his was,
and she could tell that he knew it when he looked in her eyes.
It had to do with A.D. That's all I'm gon' say.

Her heart was harden. And it had a right fo' to be.
But a hard heart is the Devil favorite playground
and his favorite game to play is self pity.

Jesus say to her, Daughter, now you go on.
Turn away from this evil. Go forward. Walk on.
Do not look back, I charge thee. No matter what thou shalt hear.
I will protect thee from harm. Trust me, child. Do not fear.
Then the Devil come between them and he twirl her around,
lift her up off the ground and fill the air up with sin.
She can tell it was sin by the way that it smell.
A smell put you in mind of a old paper mill.
In the dream she start to walk down the road like she warn.
She could hear Jesus and the Devil. And she could still smell that smell.
She was scared as could be. Cause it sound like, you see,
that The Lord was the one getting the worse part of the deal.
Jesus's voice was getting weaker and weaker
'til He was pretty much groaning like He was in misery and pain.
She moan out loud on her bed, the sheets wrapped up all around her.
Then she heard Jesus say, Help me. She hear that clear as the day.
Help me, He said. She hear it above
all the other sounds that was coming from behind her that nite.
Slimy, snotty, bloodthirsty sounds.
And it sound like The Good Lord was the one losing the fight.

She had never thought about Jesus losing a battle,
never thought the Devil could beat Him in a one to one match.
Thought His Heavenly Father would send down a legion of angels or something.
One word from God, and the whole host of Heaven dispatched.
That's what the Bible said. And fo' that nite, she believed it.
Never once had a doubt never entered her mind
until that nite alone on her bed tossing and turning,
while a legion of angels circle right over her head.
She was fill up with a fear that is too great to be named.
It is called Uncertainty in The Lord Up Above.

Kathya Alexander   **147**

It's that same fruit that growed on the tree in the garden.
Eve took a bite out of doubt instead of eating from the tree that's call Love.

Faltering faith is a knowledge that is as old as Eden.
Look like to Belle, in her mind, she knew just what to do.
The Good Lord needed her to help Him fight this battle.
I guess more folks than A.D. can be a big fool.
She always shake her head at this part of the story
like she shaking loose a sound ringing long after the words is said.
That was the beginning of how thangs go bad that nite.
Helping God instead of waiting like The Good Lord had said.
She turn round and face a cloud so thick and so full of evil
that she thought she would choke. She rub her eyes and her arms.
Then she call out and say – she remember it clear as day –
she say to Jesus, My Savior, wait. Here I come, Lord.

Just then evil blacker than a Arkansas swamp
start to swirl round and round her bed on that nite.
And in the dream, she turn and go back to help The Good Lord.
She turn back! Yes she did. To help The Lord in His fight.
A thousand creatures come forth from out of the cloud.
They have heads like a dragon and fire spout out of they mouth.
They dance round and lick at her with tongues that's like fire.
They was seeking her weakest place. And they found it in her heart.
She try to scream out in her sleep but no sound would come out,
just a gagging kinda noise that was dry, hoarse and low.
She had to come out of the dream or else she knew she would die.
She couldn't breathe. The dark angel's breath was almost making her choke.

With some strength she did not know that she even possess,
she broke free from the dream and she took a deep breath.
Her head was still foggy and her chest hurt her bad.
But when she looked up at the ceiling, the dark angels still there.
Fear was sucking all the air out the room
and sorrow was clutching her heart like a vise.

She sit up in the bed and wrap the quilt round her body.
The nite air had turn cold. It was January the ninth.
She turn toward the door and see a figure in the darkness.
It look somewhat familiar, but she didn't know who it was.
It wasn't tall enuf for A.D. And the boys was all sleep
so she thought she was dreaming, sleep and wake mixed up like they was.
The figure turn and walk on back down the hallway.
She could see the back in retreat, but she see it like thru fog.
All the dark angels twirled as one on the ceiling
then they followed the figure on back down the hall.

When she come back to herself, she see the dark angels is just lightning,
searing purple thru the grey, thick clouds gathering outside.
Thunder was rolling cross the sky like a chariot
like God up in Heaven was out taking a ride.
Far away in the distance, storm clouds they come rolling.
Sound like hearse wheels she remember. She grab the hairs on her arm
that was standing on end. The hair inside her nose was stinging.
She reach for the covers and fling them back just as hard as she could.

It was then that she knew. The house was on fire.
It was burning down round her just sho' as here she was.
While she was sitting there stupid, watching lights in the sky.
Then she heard a sound, a sound not of this world,
a sound that would change her life forever, in fact.
The noise come with the lightning. The sound it make, it go, 'Craaaaack!'
It was the sound the Devil made with his cloak when he walk
or the sound a star make when it blink out and go dark.
It's a sound that she know she will never forget,
the sound that God make just before He make the world stop.
Everything seem like it start to move in slow motion
and she hear a voice inside her, seem like whispering again.

Don't go! Don't go! gnaw at the pit of her stomach.
But she do not follow her first mind. And that is why Clyde is dead.

Kathya Alexander **149**

Always follow yo' first mind. She learn that lesson that nite.
She learned it too late, but learn it she did.
If she had only listened, not gone running like she was crazy,
her chile would be here now. But run is what she did.
Sometime in this world, you have just got to stand,
not go running round like you crazy. That's what change her whole world.

She feel round in the darkness for some shoes to put on
but she can only find one. She slide it onto her foot.
She touch the floor with her hands to see if she could feel the other house shoe.
She never seed it again. But she did feel the boot
that she had threw at A.D. It was up under the bed.
They had been fussing before he left the house that nite.
He was supposed to help Clyde with some homework he had.
And Belle threw the boot at A.D. during their fight.
She put the boot on her foot, slipped the other one in the slide.
Then she was overtook by a sadness greater than any she'd known.
Her foot went to tingling and her leg buckle a little,
like having that boot on her foot had made her heart turn to stone.

She clump down the hall in a slide and a boot,
trying to outrun the fear that was gripping her soul.
She wasn't paying attention to nothing, didn't care what she had on her feet.
She wasn't concerned about nothing except to get down that hall
to get to her babies, to get them out of the house.
She was so scared by now that she had started to run.
It takes a long time to tell you about how this thing happen,
but everythang happen so fast. Really just a few seconds.
She felt 'long side the wall 'til she got to the steps
that lead to the loft where the boys is all sleep.
When she open the door, smoke hit her smack dab in the face.
Flames was dancing around like the dark angels she'd seen.
The lightning bolt musta hit this here room direct.
She remember that thought coming into her head.
The wall furtherest from the window where the boys sleep was aflame.

She run over to the bed and she call out they name.
They was all under the covers. Wasn't no heat in the loft
so they slept covered up from they heads to they feet.
She shook the covers, trying to keep the panic out of her voice.
Get up, y'all. Get out now! Cleo, Clyde, Azra Lee!

She could still smell they toe jam. She could still smell they sweat.
Little stinky boy smells. Even thru the fire and the smoke,
she could smell they aliveness. Azra Lee wake up crying.
Get up, y'all, right now! Y'all get out of the house,
she scream over her shoulder. She don't never look back.
Clyde would get them all out. Clyde would know what to do.
Clyde was the kinda child who you could depend on to do right.
She had always depended on him. And she did this nite too.

She didn't never look back.
She didn't never look back.
Just run down the steps to the kitchen so she could wake up the girls.
They was sleep on the roll'way bed in front of the stove.
Both of them have a head full of those crinkly, little curls.
She grab both of them girls by the hem of they garment
and she near about drag them both outside to the yard.
These was children somewhat use to getting woke up in the nite.
Sometimes for tornados or other really bad storms,
she would wake them up and put them all down in the root cellar.
That nite she scoop them both up and run out thru the back door.
It feel like forever, but it probably took less than a minute.
She could hear the boys footsteps overhead in the loft.
Something ain't right, a voice scream in her head at her.
She could hear it just like somebody was standing right at her ear.
Then she hear the door slam on the other side of the house,
and she knew Clyde had got his brothers all out of the loft.
Cause she trust that chile like she trust her own life.

As the oldest, he the only chile out the five she had time to know.
The rest come so fast, they start to all meld together
into one big skin knee, one snotty runny nose.
That's what being a mother is about. And she love all her children
the same. But somehow her and Clyde formed they own special bond.
He was smart as a whip. And Lord, wasn't that chile brave!
He would try to protect her just like he was a little man.
He talk in full sentences fo' he was even one year old.
She carried him tied in swaddling cloth for I know a good year.
A.D. say she gon' spoil him. They had argued about that.
If she knew then what she know now, she woulda carried him forever.
She woulda carried him on her back for the rest of his life.
She had to stop and take a breath. She let it out in a sigh.
Her leg shaking a little. She starting to shudder all over
and one single tear run from out of her eye.
Something nibble at Belle brain like a old mangy dog when
hot foam from they mouth spew way up in the air.
Something keep on trying to tell her that something ain't right,
but she got her mind made up. And she thought that she knew
where all of her chir'en was at on that cold wintry nite.

Like I say, that nite everything happen so quick.
She got up from that bed and just started to do, not to think.
See she knew she didn't have nary a second to waste
cause she could hear the fire like a voice, and it was whispering her name.
It spread like it wasn't no earthly way that it coulda.
Considering the weather and all, it moved more quick than it shoulda.
She could hear the boys on the side steps as they run off the porch
from the steps that lead around to the north side of the house.
The kitchen door was the one that was closest to to her.
The front door lead west into nite black as pain.
It was a dark like she ain't never seen it before nor since.
She couldn't even see Cici and Vernell 'nem little faces,
and she was holding both of them in the crook of her arms.
Even with the fire that was dancing from off of the roof,

she was blinded by darkness that felt like it could harm,
like there was a danger inside it that she just couldn't see yet.

Lord knows she was scared, her body tight from the fear,
and it wasn't the dark that scared her the most, don't you see,
cause she knew that house and every inch of that land.
The thing scaring her most was the thing nibbling inside her head.
She grab onto the girls tighter and they both start to cry.
It was like something had came and took ahold of her mind.
She was starting to fix on it when all the air seem to stop.
Then lightning come and hit the house once again on the roof.
It stop her in her tracks. Then she hear the door go, Blam! Blam!
Two times. Real quick. Where the dining room was at.
Something about the sound was telling her that thangs ain't right,
but she ain't following her first mind on that long awful nite.
Another streak of lightning light up the sky.
Cici and Vernell still in the fold of her arms.
She stand there holding them with her mouth wide open,
the hair on they heads now looking like a crown of thorns.

She gather the girls even closer up to her.
They was both holding her tight. Silent tears run out they eyes.
She stand there watching the tears making creases on they faces
by the light of the streak of lightning that fill up the sky.
It pretty near light up the dark with a brightness like daylight.
The heavens had something in them that she ain't never seen since.
It wasn't the stuff of this world. Fire and blackness, stars and moonlight.
And under it all, she knew it was something she ain't seeing.
She running with the girls now. The house going up like tinder.
Like a big explosion almost, sparks crackling the skies like they bombs.
Seem like everything go in slow motion while the fire fill up the nite.
Look like Judgement Day and the Crucifixion all roll up into one.
Everything happening now, in Belle's eyes, like slow motion.
The house was still standing but the whole roof was in flames.
When she come to herself, she running toward the front door,

running and cussing A.D. like goddamn is his name.

Not one time since she married him had A.D. been around
at the times when she really most needed him to be.
She thinking and running and holding Cici and Vernell,
carrying them cause they ain't got no shoes on they po' little feet.
That make her even madder at A.D. That's all she was thinking.
Not about the boys at all. Cause she knew Clyde had them.
She had heard the door slam. So she thinking how they all standing
out here in they nite clothes and A.D. laid up somewhere.
She was hotter at him than from the heat of the flames,
sweat running like a river sticking her nightgown to her back.
Her clothes was clinging to her arms and her breasts.
Then Cleo and Azra Lee run up. Cleo say, Mama, where is Clyde at?

Them words hang in the air like a echo on a mountain.
It's funny how a few words can sometime change your whole life.
Seem like if something gon' destroy you, tear out the substance in yo' soul,
it would be enuf words to really fill up yo' mouth.
Clyde!
O, dear God!
Ain't he with you?
What you mean?
She grab Cleo by the collar, the girls still in her arms.
She squeeze his little neck so hard it's a wonder she didn't break it.
Cleo! she scream. Cleo, where is yo' brother?
He can't hardly breathe. You choking me, Cleo whisper.
I will do more than choke you. You tell me now what I'm asking.
She was crazy, I guess. Don't know why she yell at that chile.
Of all the things they go thru that nite, it's that one single act
that shame her most now. But that nite she wasn't thinking
about the chile in front of her. All she could think about
during that one long minute with fire dancing all around her,
was her chile who she knew was still shut up in that house.

I don't know where he at. He wasn't in the bed, Mama.
What do you mean you don't know? Belle eyes crazy with fear.
Cleo moan and gasp for breath. He croak, I don't know, Mama!
Mama, please! Let me go! Please Mama, I'm scared.
She let loose of her hold to the crook of his neck.
What you mean? He didn't come up with y'all to the bed?
Azra Lee start to crying and pulling at his mama.
Said he was gon' wait up for Daddy. Or something like that.
Cleo say this like he scared. And I guess you couldn't blame him.
She was crazy. She was scared. Her heart filled up with such fear.
She push the Chir'en Who Live out onto the road that use to run
side the house where the tractors go out to the fields.
She turn around with her heart closing off the breath in her mouth.
She run back in the front door. Flames was leaping and dancing.
The fire had eat up the back part of the house
and was starting on the side. All the while, her heart groping
for some kind of understanding. Where my son at? What happened?
Then she hear a small sound. She turn to the other side of the room.
Fire was everywhere except for where Clyde was standing.
Her name in his mouth cut thru her like a wound.

Maaa-muhhhhhhh!
Clyde! she call as she race toward her chile.
But the flames they stop her right dead in her tracks.
Mama coming! she scream. She try her hardest to reach him.
Lord know she tried. But the fire was fighting her back.
It fight her, I tell you. She done tried to explain that to people.
'Course that make folk think she crazy. But I believe that she know.
That fire was holding her back. She could see Clyde in front of her.
He was standing in a circle of safety, his face lit like a halo,
and between them stood the flames. They was like a thing alive
that had fingers and arms, had a face and a nose.
It was a thing with a brain standing between her and her baby.
Every time she reach for him, the thing would touch her just so
and burn her hairs and skin. And she ain't even got a scar.

Ain't even got that. Least she could have had something to show
for how hard she worked to try to get to that chile.
God know she tried. Her and God. Them two know.

She run out the house. Run round on the side.
Thought maybe she could get to him if she went thru another door.
Her heart racing so bad, hitting her chest wall so hard,
that to this day that space in her chest is still sore.
Out the corner of her eye, she can see Sister Lou
pull the other chir'en out the road. She they closest neighbor to the west.
The chir'en was all screaming like somebody was killing 'em.
Lou hold Azra Lee. Vernell bury her face in her dress.
Belle musta crossed that yard in less than 10 seconds.
She ain't never ran like that, not before and not since,
trying to reach the back door that lead to the kitchen,
all the time praying, Please God let me get my chile out that house.
She run thru the kitchen door. Knock it straight off the hinges.
She can hear Clyde's voice right off. Moaning and crying out in fear.
Mama, where you at? Mama, Mama, Mama, pleeeeaaaseee!
She run smack into a wall of flame that was standing between them.
Then the lightning strike again. Right in the place where Clyde standing.
Seem like it was pointed directly at him. The whole house go up in flames.
The last thing that she see as the house fall down around them
is Clyde mouth. Shape in the form of his Mama name.

The next thing she know, she coming back to herself.
Where Clyde at? These is the very first words that she said.
We got him out, Izzie, Mr. Veezy say to her.
She look at his eyes. And she sho' Clyde is dead.
Where he at, Brother Veezy? she look at him and she say.
Him and King George Overstreet both help her to her feet.
She could see a crowd standing around something laying on the ground.
She manage to stand up but both her knees feel so weak.
She start to scream when she get a look at Clyde body.
He was swole up so bad that it look like he was gon' bust.

She stoop down and she wrap Clyde up in her arms.
When she look again, both her hands is covered in blood and in pus.
His skin was so black, if she hadn't known him she wouldn'tna known him,
wouldn'tna known what this thing was that she held in her arms.
His face look like burnt crackling, his shirt burnt into his skin,
all his fluids seeping out of him and running all down her arm.
It hurt so bad, Mama, Clyde say in a whisper.
These was the last words that her chile ever said.
Sister Lou tell her later that she coudn'tna heard him say that
cause his lungs and mouth and tongue was already burnt up so bad.
Lord, I wish he couldn'tna said it. And I wish she hadn'tna heard.
She done heard them five words ever day she live since.
Use to tear her heart open in the months after the fire.
Heard 'em when she was woke, and specially loud in her sleep.

Just then A.D. come from round the house running.
She look at this man that she marry and she curse him in her heart.
Curse the day he was born and the woman who bore him.
She hated A.D. with every single part
of her body and soul. If Clyde hadn'tna been in her arms,
she would have killed A.D. dead, standing right there in that spot.
But Clyde was bucking and heaving, he was hurting so bad.
If her hate for A.D. hadn't been in it, Clyde's pain would have flat stopped
her heart. She open her mouth to say something to A.D.,
but it was a scream that come tearing from out of her lips.
A.D. had scooped up the other chir'en while he was running.
They was all hanging off of his legs and his hips.

Izzie Belle, what happened? A.D. say to her.
He drop all the chir'en and grab up Clyde in his arms.
He didn't wait for her to answer. I think she was still screaming.
He grab the blanket Louvenia give him and he wrap Clyde body up.
She try to bite A.D.'s legs. They was the closest to her mouth.
She had drop to the ground, her mouth spewing spit and foam.
I can't even 'magine what she look like. But right then it didn't matter.

She wanted to hurt A.D. Wanted to make him hurt like she was.
Somebody had hitch up Old Joe, they horse, to the wagon.
He was a sway back old nag but he was fast and was sho'.
A.D. lift Clyde into the back of the wagon
like he was light as a feather and placed him in the back just so.
She say she will never forget how that sight it look to her,
Clyde with that blanket wrap around him down past his knees.
The blanket had stains that was made from Clyde's body,
pus and blood all together. When she close her eyes, she still see
the picture in her head sometime. Everything get quiet for a minute.
Lou say her eyes was like saucers, a look hanging in them
like she ain't never seen. Sister Lou come up with Cici.
She say, I'm gon' take care of these chir'en. You just gone with A.D.

She climb in the back of the wagon. Her eyes ain't never left Clyde.
Never once did she never turn her head toward A.D.
I'm gon' get these chir'en from out of this cold, Lou say.
You take care of that boy. These other chir'en can stay with me
just as long as you need. Folks was still drawing water
from the well for the fire. Handing buckets hand over hand.
But it wasn't doing no good. It was like they was spitting on it.
The fire was raging like crazy. Like it come straight up from hell.
She open her mouth. Seem like she was trying to thank her.
But what come out of her throat wasn't nothing again but a yell,
so she shut her mouth tight cause she knew if she really started to holler,
she would not ever be able to stop hollering again.
If she'da released it from her throat, that scream woulda went on forever,
so she grab Clyde head off the blanket and place it gentle in her lap.
She look at her baby. That sweet, sweet little boy.
Tears roll out her eyes and fall onto Clyde head.
Where her tears fall on Clyde, seem like his body start to sizzle.
His body that hot. Her tears rise up with the steam.
A.D. holler at the horse and start the wagon to moving.
Her eyes was fill up with water, so she could not really see.

Clyde's eyelids was burnt so bad, they was shut.
His skin look like tar, except it was all black and crisp.
She knew if he lived, he would have surely been blind
and both of his hands was both burned into fists.
She knew he couldn't live. But she could not let him die.
Keeping her chir'en alive is what a mother suppose to do.
So she prayed to God. And she started to singing
about how God can wash his chir'en whiter than snow.

> *Jesus paid it all*
> *All to Him I owe*
> *Sin done left a crimson stain*
> *Oh, but He wash*
> *Yes, Lord He wash*
> *Me whiter than snow*

16
DAY DAWNING NEW

A.D. turn around and he look at Belle then.
He was whipping that po' horse near about next to death,
urging him faster and faster, foam forming in both of they mouths.
A.D. turn and look at his wife and his son and he ask,
What happen, Izzie? Izzie Belle, do you know
exactly what it was that started the fire?
She look at the snot that was freezing under his nose
and at the tears turning to frost in the corner of his eyes.
She fix him in her gaze for one very long minute
then she drop her head again and start back singing to Clyde.
She hated A.D. with every breath that come out of her body.
If it wasn't for him, they wouldn't be sitting here now.
What difference it make how it started? What difference that make at all?
If he'da been in his bed like he shoulda, then he woulda known.
But he wasn't in the bed with her. That was true many a nite.
It was cause of the woman who was name Delta Rose.

She always knew that woman was gon' cause harm to her family.
Always knew that she'd be the death of one of them yet
because she was a white woman. And her daddy a big shot lawyer.
He even worked sometimes with the governor and such.
They'd all grown up together. A.D. was like her pet.
Anything cute about that was a long time ago gone.
Belle told him that woman wasn't nothing but trouble.
Course he'd lied and he said that what they had was all done.
They was the worst kept secret in all of Dudlye County.
Everybody whispered about 'em, both white and black too.
A.D. family was well-liked. And Delta Rose a spoil little white girl.
Her daddy never couldn't do nothing with her. That don't make A.D. no less a fool.
Putting them in danger like that. White men kill a colored
for whole lot less than a rumor about a white girl.
Of course, Belle didn't know this was how the harm was gon' come.
Didn't know this was how the white woman was gon' destroy they whole world.
A.D. swore up and down that wasn't nothing between them.
And Belle didn't have no better sense than to believe what he said.
How could she believe anything else? No colored man would be such a fool
as to mess around with a white woman. And now her son was dead.

Clyde had been waiting on A.D. to help him do his homework.
Belle couldn't do too much to help him with his arithmetic.
He musta fell asleep waiting on his daddy at the dining room table
and must have heard her while she was dreaming and got up to come look
into the bedroom. He must have been the figure she seen
standing at the door and then walking on back down the hall.
But she say to this day she don't think that was Clyde.
But she was so crazy from the dream of the dark angels that come.
And she thought that she knew where all her chir'en was at.
All of them was used to waiting on A.D.
A.D. had told her that he was gon' be at his mama's.
Course she knew when he left that he was lying thru his teeth.
That's why they fought before he left the house that nite.
She had talked to his mama and knew that was a lie.

And she knew in her heart she didn't have it in her to go on
and had told him so. That she was gon' stop trying.
Lordy, Lordy, she sho' learned a lesson that nite
about just what The Good Lord will put His children thru.
You think you done had all that is in you to bear
then God come and throw something even bigger at you.
Clyde death teach her that. And it teach her some more things.
Even tho she don't learn what they all was that nite.
That nite holding her dying chile head in her arms,
she blame it all on A.D. Her hatred like a bright light
shining in the darkness. She want to hurt him like Clyde was hurting.
She throwed daggers from her eyes at the top of A.D. back
trying to find the spot where she knew she could pierce him
at that strawberry birthmark on the back of his neck.
That spot seem like it always would hurt A.D. some.
When she touch him there, she always had to be real gentle.
That was where she trained her eyes. And for one holy instant
she prayed that The Lord send a legion of angels down to earth just to kill him.
Clyde moan again then in the crook of her arm.
Then he start to take these little bitty hitching breaths.
She could hear death rattling way down deep in his lungs.
She could see death struggling to take ahold of his chest.
That baby was gasping for every breath that he took.
A mewling sound was coming from out of his burned up little nose.
She knew that his soul was getting closer to God.
And so she prayed for him to stop hurting. For The Good Lord to take him home.

She done wondered since then if she done the right thang.
She know her heart was not right. Too full of hating A.D.
She wonder now if she had prayed a different prayer on that nite,
wonder how different her life would have turned out to be.
But all she knew when she prayed was that her baby was hurting.
And every breath that he take tear her heart right in two.
The sound he was making was a knife thru her brain.
Not my will, but thine was her prayer unto

The Good Lord above. Her heart had went to her throat.
She can't breathe. Feel like she was gon' die right 'long beside Clyde.
The thunder was still rumbling. The lightning now was just lightning.
She prayed holding her baby and looking up at the sky.
Pain that ripple like river water come from off his burnt skin,
soaking straight thru her clothes and running on down her legs.
His chest hitched up with every breath that he take.
And the smell of his breath was like the smell in the dream
when she dreamed of the devil. Clyde so fat and so bloated
that he look like he was something come out of a UFO.
It pain her to her heart to see her baby like that.
Pained her to her heart. Yes, Lord, it hurt her so.
Then the baby stop breathing. Seem like for one long minute.
And it seem like that's when she can start to breathe once again.
A.D. look back in the wagon. He can hear from the sound
that everything in his whole life is fixing to change.

He start to beating Old Joe, making him run faster and faster.
"Quit beating that horse, A.D. It's over now. Clyde is dead."
Then the chile breathe again. Them hitching breaths like I told you.
A.D. mumble something at her, but she didn't hear what he said.
Seem like he is more determine than ever to run that po' horse
straight into the ground. He was gon' save his chile.
If the horse die, then that was even mo' better.
Both of them want to kill something. Kill anything but Clyde.
Cause if they didn't they would die. She knew just how he feeling.
That thing that want to kill something. Madness scalding like that.
Like if you don't take it and put it somewhere else outside of you,
it will make you go crazy. Belle start to tear at her hair.
A.D. keep beating that horse. They was still at least five miles
from the only hospital that would take a colored chile.
And no matter how hard that horse run, she knew clear as the daybreak
that her chile was good as dead lying there in her arms.
His breathing weaker now. His chest heaving, but silent.
Don't know how that chile live for as long as he done.

Kathya Alexander   **163**

Don't know why he did it. Why he live thru such pain.
I think sometimes it was just so he could feel his mama's arms
around him awhile longer. I like to thank that.
Like to thank he felt something that nite more than the pain.
And Belle got to thank that too or she wouldn'tna been able to live.
She see that hollow-eye look on the face of her son.
She just keep looking at his face. Kissing him over and over.
Was glad for that last breath. For another chance just to feel it.
Folks don't realize that life is breath.
That make people take thangs like a draw-in of breath so for granted.
But if you know it's the last one that you gon' ever hear, ever feel -
specially if it's from someone that you love -
then breath become one of yo' life's greatest treasures.
Gold and silver don't have nothing on it at all.

The sun was just coming up over the trees in the distance.
Seem like that old sun want to kiss Clyde good-bye too.
The boughs was sparkling from a cover of frost on them.
Look like diamonds on long fingers that was flirting with you.
All of a sudden the wagon stop. That's how she know Clyde had stop breathing.
Old Joe pull up short, reared back up on his hind legs.
The sun hit off his hoofs. He was coughing and wheezing.
That horse wasn't never the same after that day.
But then nothing else neither in her life ever was.
You can't lose a chile and then stay like you was.
Cause you done become something you ain't never been before.
You done become the mother of a dead son.

She bend down to kiss him. She know she is still singing.
She got her lips right up close to Clyde's burnt up face.
She cover the baby nose and his mouth with her mouth.
She breathe into his burn body the words of Amazing Grace.

> *Amazing grace! How sweet the sound*
> *That sav'd a wretch like me*

I once was lost, but now am found
Was blind, but now I see.

She look down at Clyde face. It always was the most beautiful
face she done seen. The color of pecan pie.
The kind made with Karo syrup and rich heavy cream.
His skin was real creamy and real smooth just like that.
She hold his body in her arms and rock back and forth, forth and back.
She breathe in the odor of the skin that's still clinging to him.
Mingle, as it was, with the smell of smoke and of death.
But in her mind he was the same Clyde. Her sun. All the life she ever wanted.
I mean, she knew Clyde was dead. Didn't know she could deny it.
Otherwise she woulda. But her mind wouldn't let the thought go.
Her mind kept saying he dead, telling her over and over.
And the pain that it cause! Only God Hisself know.

She tried to block out her hurt and just focus on Clyde.
On this body that was still laying there in her arms.
Tried to make death fit together with everything else she knew about him.
Like his favorite foods. Oatmeal and fried corn.
He love them two foods more than anythang else.
Could eat them both for breakfast, lunch, and then dinner.
He like his oatmeal with sausage crumble up on the top.
Otherwise he wouldn't eat it. A.D. say she spoil him rotten.
I don't know why how she treat Clyde bother A.D. like it do tho.
He say Clyde would become a manchild that's no good.
Now if that ain't the pot calling the kettle black, I sho' don't know what is.
A.D. a fine one to talk the way his own mama treat him.

It hit her then that she would never cook for him again.
That she'd never get another chance to blow a speck of dust out his eye.
Would never daub blood from off of his leg when he fell.
All she had of him now was the time left on this ride.
All that she had was this shell in her arms.
A shell of a body that had once held her sun.

And the shell became precious, pure and cherished in her sight.
The time she had with him become all the time that time was.
She seen every time she ever kissed him goodnight.
Seen every laugh that he laughed and every tear that he cried.
Her tears stream down her face unashame.
Seen the crown of his head on that warm, starry nite
that he was born. She'd looked at him that nite and promised
to protect him. A promise she never once doubted that she would do.
Just keep her chile safe until he become a man on his own.
And she couldn't even do that. She see day dawning new
as she kiss Clyde burnt little hand and tell him that she love him.
And then she kiss his brow. Told him she'd love him all her life.
"Clyde, I want you to know that you was my greatest treasure.
You was the best part of me." She stare straight into the sunlight
and then she wept. Wept like her eyes they was faucets
that God had turned on to wash her sins away.
Great big sobs that took hold and racked her sin-sick body.
Then she look back at her chile. Down on his dead face
and remembered the love that she felt the first time
he wrap his chubby hand around her first two fingers.
Remembered the joy in her knees when he was still a lap baby.
When she come in from the fields, Clyde always be so glad to see her.
And he trust her total. Wasn't nothing he didn't think
that his mama couldn't do. She lift his head from her lap just a little.
She see in his face everything she done lost.
And the biggest loss was her faith. Clyde death make her bitter.

I'm sorry, Clyde, she say. Just you know that I love you.
They was speaking spirit to spirit. And she could hear his words plain.
He say he love her too. And I will never forget you.
And I'll never let no one else never forget.
I thank God for the time He allow me to be with you.
For every lesson you learn me bout love. And bout myself.
And then Clyde say, way down deep in her spirit,
Mama, Daddy is out here all by hisself.

She look up from his body. A.D. walking the horse.
He was hunch over like he sorry. Like he have a right for to be.
She can hear him quietly call on God like he praying.
Like God want to hear anything that he
might have to say. There might be a God in Heaven to forgive him
for the things that he done and didn't do to bring about such a nite.
For being where he was instead of where he wasn't.
For handing her a dead son in return for her life.
She didn't even pause to think about where her and A.D. was going.
They didn't have no home. The fire had destroyed all of that.
All the safety and security she'd spent the last 10 years building,
the fire come along and destroy it in a flash.
That's what happen when you believe in the things of this world.
When you attach your love to anything beside God.
Cause God don't like ugly. And He ain't too particular about pretty.
You can gain the whole world, and then sho' 'nuff lose yo' soul.

A.D. pull the horse and wagon into the front yard.
There was some people out there that was still milling about.
She kept hearing a sound. Didn't know where it come from.
Then she realize it was coming from out of her mouth.
A.D. move the wagon pass the trees at the edge of the property.
That's when she finally seen the remains of the house.
The A-frame was standing. But that's about all.
A few men was carrying water to douse some hot spots
that was still smoldering. They studying the buckets of water.
Guess it give them something to look at beside at her face.
Instead of looking at her. No one looked in her direction.
Everybody head seem to be hanging down in disgrace.
Mamie Jackson was the first to see them ride up.
She reach out and touch her husband arm. His name is Dwight.
Everybody start to murmuring. Mo' heads drop down to the ground.
And all Belle was praying for was the cover of nite.
But the sun was up now. The darkness had past.
The darkness, that is, except what lay in her heart.

I imagine they shame for what they know about A.D.
Cause they all knew where A.D. had not been on that nite.

Mamie climb in the wagon with her and with Clyde.
She grab her hard on the shoulder and she say, Belle, let him go.
Y'all come on and git down, Mamie whisper in her ear.
Let him go. I got him.
She say, Mamie, you sho'?
Yes, Belle, I got him. I'ma hand him to you.
Give him to me now. You go on and git down.
But she couldn't let him go. Mamie tried to pry loose her fingers.
But she still could not seem to let go of her chile.
Mamie couldn't break her grip. Belle could not give him up.
Not to arms that did not know how to hold him just right.
Not to some arms that did not belong to his mama.
She just sat there in the wagon and she cried and she cried.

When she finally climb to the ground, A.D. he rush over at her.
He put out his hand like he was gon' steady her fall.
Belle turn around and look at A.D. like he hit her.
Don't you never touch me! She fairly spat out the words.
This all yo' fault! You kill my chile!
You kill him just as sho' as here I stand.
Don't you never put yo' filthy hands on me again.
You is worse than sorry. You is less than a man!
A.D. snatch back his hand just like she had slap him.
Maybe she did. She don't remember now.
Belle reach for her chile. And Miz Mamie hand him to her.
But that's the last she remember as she fall down to the ground.

17
ANGEL IN THE OUTHOUSE

Mama turn her head now toward the wall in the bedroom.
She say, "I ain't remembered that nite, not the particulars, that is,
in a long, long time. It hurt so bad to remember.
Feel like everythang on me hurt just the way it did then."
She wipe her nose again on the corner of her apron.
It's crusty from all the snot and the tears she cry today.
But she say she got to tell the story. Cause the angel done come
and I need to hear it. She turn to me and she say,
"The next few months pass in sort of a numbness.
Seem like I remember Vernell snatching at me once or twice.
I can't say that I even remember being at Clyde funeral.
Something took hold of my body and took hold of my mind.
It was the angel that give me the strength to go on.
It was her touch on my wrist that lead me out of the pain.
If it wasn't for her, I wouldn't be here today.
The Buffalo Calf Woman.
That was her name."

"What kind of name is that for a angel to have?"
I ask my Mama. She look over at me.
"In the Bible angels have names like Michael and Gabriel."
Mama say, "I will tell you if you just listen to me."
I snuggle back down on the bed where my mama is sitting.
Dark settling outside like a old mangy dog.
Everybody else is eating dinner in the front of the house.
My head hurting like the day when the fire angel come.

Mama say, "It was the pain in my butt that snap me out of it
sho' as the pain in my heart had broke me down.
It's the first clear memory I have after the wagon.
I wake up in a bed and I look all around.
I pass gas then. Real loud and stanking.
I can't remember the last time that I have a b.m.
It all seem kinda funny. Sorta amusing.
Like this pain in my gut can match the pain that I'm in
inside of my mind. Inside of my heart.
I don't know what to do. Don't know where to start.
Don't know if I want to. Don't know if I can.
Don't know if the thing beating in my chest is my heart or my pain
cause feel like my heart done been tore out and left on the floor.
Then all of a sudden, I hear a knock at the door.

"I don't even know what door I'm on the other side of.
I look around the room that I'm in to make sho'.
I'm in Papa bed. I can see that much by looking.
But that's bout the only thang that I can say that I know.
I don't know how I come to be over at Papa's.
Don't know when I got there. Don't remember how long.
Cause all I been doing for these past few grey months
is laying and rocking. Or singing that song.
That song I sung in the wagon with Clyde.
The one about a crimson stain."
She say all this time, she been mad at my daddy bout Clyde,

but she wake up that day feeling like she a part of the blame.
"What you blaming yo'self for?" I ask my mama.
She say real low, "Cause I couldn't save Clyde."
"And what Daddy do?"
"He wasn't at home to help me."
She adjust her self on the bed and lay down on her side.
She say she know she got to get up to get her life back on track
so she sit herself up and she say toward the door,
"Who that out there knocking? Yoo! Come in here to me.
Then the door it swing open and in walk A.D.

"Out of all the people on the other side of the door,
yo' daddy is the last face that I want to see.
Seem like I can smell the smell of Clyde death still upon him.
He step a foot over the door face. And I show him my teeth.
My stomach lurch then. I can hear it rumble.
'Get out, A.D.,' I say. 'Gone now. Leave me alone.
I can't listen to nothing that come from out of yo' mouth.
Ain't nothing to be said. Gone now. Gone on back home.'
I guess I forget all about we ain't got no home to go to.
Don't even cross my mind where him and the chir'en staying at.
I just know that I can't stand to so much as look at his face."
I squirm on the covers when my mama say that.

A.D. mouth open up. Belle look at him like he something
she found on the bottom of a nasty old shoe.
Just stare at him like he a cartoon or something.
Like a booger done ask her to watch what kinda dance it can do.
Then she smell another smell. The smell from the dream.
The smell of the woman, Delta Rose.
Seem like all the hairs on her body stand up and at attention.
All her spit dry up real quick. Like it's done been froze.
Her stomach lurch again, and this time it happen.
She erp her guts out all over the place.
When A.D. run over to the bed to wipe up the vomit,

Belle reach down and grab a handful and wipe it all over his face.
Then she pass out again.

"A pain," she say, "shoot thru my butt
and that make me come back to myself.
I'm still laying in my papa bed.
I smell like I done soil myself.
I still don't know how long I been there,
but I know it must have been a while
cause I can smell the honeysuckle.
It smell so sweet, I almost smile.
I holler out loud from down deep in my pain.
A thousand tiny razors cut thru my gut.
Don't no one come. I am alone.
It seem to me such a comforting thought
that I can just lay there in this bed and die,
alone in my pain with only my grief to help me.
I didn't see how I'd go on long as Clyde was dead
so I lay there praying to go meet my Maker.
I feel empty and all hollowed out inside.
I ain't got nothing left in me to give.
All that is alive inside me is a pain
trying to eat up my insides, my gut and my liver.
Felt like a monster tearing at my body with sharp pointy claws
that was making my belly swell up with the pus.
I can't even think about the Chir'en Who Live,
about what they might need to get from they mama.

"But the mind and the body is a powerful thang.
A thang you can't always count on to control.
It want to live. Even when you don't,
it somehow want you to go on.
And go on you must if it want you to.
I done heard about white folks who laid down and died
cause of thangs like losing some money in the Depression.

Colored folks starve to death and they bodies still survive.
They just keep on walking. Just keep on talking.
Like they got some life still left to give.
But if you look close enuf in them people eyes,
you can tell sometime how they ain't got no mo' life left in them.
That's how it was with me that morning.
I was just laying there waiting for God to take me home,
a stupid smile across my lips."
The frown on my mama's forehead look carve out in stone.

"I prepare in my mind to leave my body,
to join my spirit again with my son.
I close my eyes and say a prayer.
I say, 'I'm ready, Father. Come take me on home'
and I wait for a angel to come down to get me.
I lay there like that for a minute or two
assured with a knowing that God gon' answer my prayer.
With the knowing that livin' just wasn't something I can do.
'God, You know that I hurts too bad.
The way my life is is just too sad.
I can't stay down here without my chile.
I don't even know who I is if I ain't the mother of Clyde.'"

I want to ask her about Cleo and the others,
about what they gon' do if they don't have no mother.
I got tears running down both sides of my face
and it feel like my heart is almost breaking.
"But all that happen was pain. Pain. Pure and simple.
The kind I can't just lay in the bed and ignore.
A fire blazing down the middle of my stomach
like razors again, sharp and sure,
tearing like claws down the insides of my gut.
Much as I want to, I can't just lay there and die.
I throw my legs out of the bed and sit there on the side
erping my guts out, praying and crying."

It feel so real. So in the present.
Even thru her darkness, it get her attention. Quick.
Her stomach heaving. And she throwing up bile,
hot and clear and thick and slick.
The pain was throbbing from the top of her hipbone
and it travel all the way down to the tip of her spine.
She reach out her hand to wipe her mouth
and she think to herself, This hand don't look like mine.
Her hands and arms skinnier than she remember.
Somewhere in the fog she remember some food on a tray
when somebody come and present it to her.
Then she kinda remember somebody taking it away.
"Wonder who been cooking for me?" she ask herself out loud.
Then, somewhere in her mind, she hear Dr. Watts songs being sung.
She remember it like she seen it from somewhere in the clouds.
Seem like she see the face of the Missionary Board,
they clothes and heads wrapped up all in white.
Sisters Lora, Barbara Ann, and Belinda Sue
standing round her bed sanging The Old Rugged Cross.
And she say seem like they sing That's What My God Can Do.

She can sorta remember, somewhere down in the pain,
Cleo standing beside her, Vernell sucking her hair.
They need was so strong, she say she remember,
that it make her want to crawl back inside of herself.
They wanting. They aliveness. It just add to her sorrow.
They was The Chil'ren Who Live when her sun, Clyde, had died.
Whenever they come in the room and she have to see them,
seem like she can see Clyde body float just over they head.
I know she don't remember too much about the burying.
Remember A.D. say some words that don't quite reach her ears.
Spoken words (just like bowel habits)
belong to that time before she have Chil'ren Who Live.

"Then the Real Pain begin. The muscles in my butt drawed up together

while a spasm rip thru my belly like a beast with a knife
doubling me over in a terrible kind of agony
I ain't never experience before nor since in my life.
Up 'til then I been living in another time and place.
A time before I come to be The Mother of a Dead Child.
That other time when I take a child living for granted.
That time, that place, that was before Clyde had died.
But now the pain in my body bring me back to the present.
Sometime, Mandy, I think that's why pain in this world.
Cause if it don't do nothing else, it sho' do get your attention.
Bring you back to yourself. Back to the now and the here."

The only real thing before this pain in her stomach
is the pain that she carry in the bottom of her heart.
And for the past three months, the only sound she done hear
is the sound that her chile make with her name in his mouth.
Clyde calling for his Mama. Telling her how bad he hurt.
Over and over again. The only thing that she say
she would allow herself to hear. A sound like rain and like thunder.
The sound of it ring thru her insides and double her over again.
Her legs creak when she move them. That cause another spasm of pain.
She grab the headboard with both hands and get a whiff under her arms.
She smell like a slut on a good Saturday nite
or like the manure pile that lay just outside of the barn.
Then another pain shoot thru her, straight in the hole in her butt
and it travel all the way up to the pit of her stomach.
She breathe in short shallow breaths. Breathe them out quick and hard,
trying to release the misery that's settled in the bottom of her lungs
during these past three long months. Outside the world just keep on turning.
Winter done turn into the warm days of spring.
The seasons keep changing, the world never stop moving
all the while she done been wrapped up in her cocoon of pain.

"I ain't even notice yet that the flowers done bloom.
Out the window, I can see the sunflowers round the toilet outside.

Three bright yellow soldiers standing watch at the outhouse
like three uniform guards charge to hold up the sky.
The sunflowers and the toilet both grow from the same dirt,
and they both been around long as I can remember.
I reach down under my belly with both of my hands
to see if that will help to relieve some of the pressure.
It don't. But I don't know what else to do with my hands
so I leave them there and look for some shoes for my feet.
But I can't find none. So I walk barefoot to the toilet
in pain so bad that it make me weep.

"The day was real warm for the beginning of springtime.
The odor from the toilet taint the air that day.
The sun burn my eyes and spots of pain jump out in front of them.
And I have to struggle for every step that I take.
A warm breeze was coming from the direction of the outhouse.
My nose register the stink. I ain't been outside in so long.
And I have to stop with every few steps that I take
to try to let out the breath that sit in the bottom of my lungs.
I wonder if I have what it take inside me to make it.
That ole raggedy toilet seem so far, far away.
My lungs done been damage, scarred a little in the fire,
and my stomach cramp up with every step that I take.
About halfway to the outhouse, double over in pain,
I realize don't nobody even know where I was
and I wonder how long I would lay out here in the field
before the sun kill me if I so happen to fall.
But I just keep on walking. One step at a time.
In life, Mandy, sometime, that's just all you can do.
Just take you one step. And then take you another one.
And wait to see when you get there if you know what to do."

Sweat stream down her face. Her whole body is shaking
like something vibrate inside her to a whole 'nother tune.
She turn and look back over her shoulder at the house

to see if anybody done missed her from out of the room.
Ain't nobody around. But she can hear voices in the fields.
It's time for planting. And that's what everybody is doing.
It was a time that Belle woulda been out there herself
plowing and planting to the pull of the moon.
She wonder if she ever will do thangs like that again.
Something simple like holding a bulb in her hand.
Or if this life she living now will stretch out in front of her forever
with her somewhere between the land of the living and the land of the dead.

"When I finally make it to the door of the outhouse,
I pause for a minute and take me a rest.
I lean my head up 'gainst the door of the toilet
and take me some more of them little bitty breaths.
Pain cut thru me with every breath that I take.
My lungs in the back scream out loud with the hurt.
I have to cough a few times to release some of the pressure.
I look down at my feet and see they covered with dirt.
I'm covered head to toe slick in my own sweat.
I stand there real still while I try to catch my breath.
I can feel my heart beating in the pit of my stomach
and the breath in my throat sound like the rattle of death."

The outhouse narrower at the top than it is at the bottom.
The ends splayed out in the dirt like a old raggedy skirt.
The wood is wash gray, the color of a cloudy day,
and the ground round the bottom is always soft and wet.
She can feel the goo ooze up in betwixt her toes,
rich and black from the fertilizer of human manure.
She push the door forward with one hand and go inside.
She take a second to turn back the small piece of wood
nail loose to the door, securing the lock in the slat.
The darkness wrap itself around her like she done step in a tomb.
The cool air a welcome relief from the heat outside.
Her hands go under her dress so she can pull down her bloomers.

It was then that she notice she ain't wearing no draws.
She pass her hand cross her chest and see she ain't wearing no brassiere.
She don't have no recollection of never having got dress.
And the clothes she got on don't belong to her neither.
She stand there for a minute and try to remember the last time that she dress.
She wonder where these clothes that she got on come from.
Then that ever present pain bring her back to its attention
as a spasm pass thru her bottom and shake her down to her toes.

Help me, Jesus, she cry up to heaven.
Relieve me, Lord, from this pain that I'm in.
She stand up in front of the seat with her legs spread apart
and heish up her skirt, reaching down low to the hem.
Her stomach rumble and the cramps they pass
enuf for her to stop shaking and to try to sit down.
In one painful movement, she grab up the edge of her dress
so the material in the loose skirt won't fall down on the ground.
The wooden seat is smooth beneath her.
Just a wide plank, really, with a hole wore thin
from all of the bottoms that's done sit there before her.
She make sure she have something to wipe herself with.
She look in the basket that sit down on the floor.
It's some corn husks in there. That will just have to do.
Then she let loose her stomach and pass gas some more.
Belle cry while it seem like all her insides come loose.
Hard brown nuggets of sorrow leave her body in spasms.
She can hear them as they plop down in the green lime below.
Fat, white maggots crawl round in the hole underneath her.
They arch they bodies in protest in they dungeon below.
Her belly rumble and she pass gas in wet farts.
Long, slimy monsters that carry the odor of sin.
She rub the sides of her belly. And then Belle start to praying.
Then her bowels turn to mucous and come in long, bloody strings.

"Feel like all my fear and madness coming out the hole in my bottom.
It double me over, trying to find the way outside.
It hurt me so bad, I open my mouth up and wail
and bitterness roll out from the tears in my eyes.
The scream in my throat sound just like a song.
It match – throb for throb – the pain in my gut.
I can feel my belly being tore out from the inside.
Feel like my throat being rip out thru the hole in my butt.
I pray out loud calling on the name of the Lord.
'God, please. God, please. Take away this pain that I'm in.
My heart fill with loathing and my flesh is to ashes.
My breath stank. My body stank. And my stomach done fill
up with misery and pain. I'll do whatsoever You ask me.
Just let me stop hurting,' Mama say she cry out loud and pray.
"'You said in Your Word that You'd come if I call.
And I'm calling on You, Jesus. Have mercy, Lord,' Mama say.
"My head start to swim and I get real light-headed.
Feel like I'm getting stab in my stomach with the blade of a knife.
I'm so tired and so weak, I almost fall thru the hole in the toilet.
I reach out my hand to catch myself.
And what happen next change my life."

Mama say, "A hand reach out and grab mine. A hand bigger than yo' daddy's.
The hand fold itself round my fist way up past the wrist
and right away I am fill up with a sense of great calmness
and my body fill up with a incredible strength.
Light fill the dark toilet like God Hisself done reach down
from Heaven above and lift away the old roof.
I feel myself being set back down firm on the toilet.
And when my eyes adjust, in front of me, there a angel stood.

"The angel was dress in a long, flowing robe.
She was wearing a crown and fingering the end of her plait.
With the other hand, she was grasping ahold of my hand.
Then she bow down on her knee. Right in the toilet where I sit.

At first I can't hardly believe what I'm seeing.

I blink my eyes a few times to make sho' it ain't a trick of the sun.

Then the angel, still on one knee, look up at me and she say,

I am your humble servant, Belle. Sent to you by God.'

'Who you say you is? And why is you in my outhouse?'

I kinda stutter when I say it. My mouth can't hardly form into words.

'I am called Buffalo Calf Woman. I have been here forever.

I came with the Spider when She opened the grave.'

'Grave?' I ask. 'Like Jesus did with Lazarus?

Is you here to raise my son? Bring him back from the dead?'

The angel shake her head, no.

'Then you might as well go.

If you can't take me to Clyde, I ain't got no use for you then.'

"If I wasn't so outdone, I might just as well laugh.

A angel in a toilet talking about answering my prayers.

Then the angel cock her head and lean her ear up like she listening.

Like she waiting for God to tell her what to do next.

'Forgive,' the angel say. Just that one little word.

I feel a hatred so strong, I almost fall off of the seat.

'I don't know what that feel like,' I say and I sneer.

Feel like barb wire is squeezing my heart like a fist.

'I don't know what it look like not to see madness and hurt.

When I look in thru my eyes, I see blackness inside.'

'Forgive,' the angel she say again.

I look at her and say, 'Who?'

And then I say, 'How?'

"The angel say, 'That is good. All you have to do is be willing.

Ask God to help you. He will show you the way.

I was sent to make sure that you first forgive yourself.'

'Forgive me? Me?!! But, I ain't done nothing wrong,' I say.

Tears run down my face. 'No, you didn't,' say the angel.

'Life is a lesson we live. And God loves you still.'

'So God took my son just to teach me a lesson?

I ain't done nothing to deserve such a lesson as this.'
'Forgive.' The angel she say the word again.
The light in the toilet seem to get crystal clear.
I wipe the tears from my eyes so I can see her mo' better,
but when I look back up, the angel had done disappeared."

Belle breathe in a deep breath. The first with no pain since the fire.
The air in her nose done turn sweet as she ponder this thing.
God could just as soon have ask her to walk on water.
Turn water into wine. And then part the Red Sea.
"Forgive," she hear the angels sing somewhere up in glory.
Belle wonder if she have this thing still left in her heart.
She know she loved A.D. once. Back in the beginning.
Before Delta Rose come between them to tear them apart.

She wipe her behind on the corn husks and get up off the seat.
It's a lightness in her soul that don't have no bizness being there.
But when she breathe thru her nose, she find it's clog up with snot.
At the same time, it feel like she choking on pure heaven clean air.
Air like music that float all over her body
turning the sweat and the muss into something that's sweet.
She feel something like joy in her soul for the first time since the fire.
She don't know if this joy is a thing she want to keep.
What it feel like, Lord, not to be wrap up in sorrow?
What it feel like not to have nothing but blackness in your soul?
How you forgive a man that ain't done nothing but lied and cheated?
When you done give him yo' heart and you get back a dead son?
How you go bout forgiving yourself? And why would anyone want to?
That would be putting the pain of losing your chile out yo' head.
That would be acting like you didn't love him enuf or something.
But in her heart all she hear is, But your son is dead
and there is nothing you can do to change that fact now.
No matter how hard you try to run away from it.
This is a part of your life now. God has called your child home.
And there is nothing left for you to do but accept it.

I ain't never thought about what my mama feel when Clyde die.
And I still don't understand what it got to do with forgiveness.
And I never woulda thought no angel would come to no outhouse.
But today I seen her myself, so I got to believe it.
Mama say, "When I come back to myself, I'm standing at the graveyard.
All the coloreds Down Home buried in the same place.
It's in the back of Mt. Zion. I don't even know how I got there.
Just find myself standing beside my dead Mama grave.
I done walk all this way like the Hand of God Hisself
done took me and push me straight to this place.
Had just pick up my feet and move me where It want me to be.
I say to Mama tombstone, 'This been one crazy day.
A angel come to see me, Mama. Come right in to the outhouse.
The outhouse still there. Yeah, I guess you know that.
Same angel you told me about that one time.
Did you send her to me? Is y'all where Clyde is at?'
I think back to the day that I bury my Mama.
Remember standing at the grave watching them throw dirt in the ground.
Remember feeling the weight of the world on my shoulders.
I say, 'Mama, I didn't know what weight was. But I sho' do know now.
You always said I would if I just keep a'livin'.
Said one day I would know what life was really about.
I didn't understand what you meant. I don't know what I was thanking.
Lord, if I only knew then the thangs that I know now.'"

This another thing that she ain't said nothing about 'til today.
"This story done been pass down from each mama to her daughter.
You will tell the story of the Buffalo Calf Woman one day
to your own chile if she the one who done been chose."
"Who was the very first mama to see the angel?" I ask.
"She was a Indian woman who live a long time ago."
I snuggle up to her close and we settle back on the bed.
I feel shadows creeping up to Mama's windows and door.
"Mom Mattie tell me the Indian live somewhere she call the Great Plain.

That's land that reach from up north down the whole middle of the country.
It wasn't no states or nothing back when the Indians live there.
You get your long hair from that Indian woman, I reckon."
"The angel is a Indian? Is that what you saying?"
"The angel is a messenger that come to the women in our family.
She bring peace in a time of trouble to a woman in every age.
That's why she always come to a girl child in every generation."
"Tell me about the angel," I say again to my mama.
"You sho' you ready to hear this?"
"Well, I guess the angel thought I was
if she came to me out in back of the churchhouse today."
"Well, all right then," Mama say. The room filling with dark.

"First, let me say this. Cause I think it's important.
The story of a life always different each time that you tell it.
I don't know how much of what I'm fixing to tell you is true.
Truth seem like a story that is told to make you
see yourself a certain way. That's what I done figured out.
You become whoever it is that you be talking about.
Somebody else can see the same thing and tell the story different.
And I think that's what happen thru the years with the story of the Indian."
"What you mean, Mama?" I ask. I do not understand
why she is saying this to me instead of just starting to tell
me about the Indian woman and what she got to do with the angel.
"I don't know if the Indian woman even got the same name
thru all the years in the telling. Don't know if the angel do neither.
This just our family legend."
"Ok, Mama," I say and snuggle down into her pillow.

18
LONE WHITE MAN

The Indian woman sleeps,
and as she sleeps she dreams
she is in a dark space
A cave maybe
or a tipi

In the center of the room
is a large shining light
coming from a candle in a bowl
that is painted a bright
blue
The woman makes the color from berries
Her eyes are drawn
to the light in the candle
The light pulses and glows
When she looks more closely she sees
the light is coming from the four directions of the
world

Not from the candle at all
And then she sees roots bursting forth from out of the ground
Roots like from a tree
Like some knobby old arms
Like the ground they are in
can contain them no longer

From the west comes red light
From the east, the light's yellow
From the south comes black light
Martha walks over and straddles
the candle between her thighs
From the north, the light's white
It is that light that enters her
Shiny and bright
it wraps itself all inside her
and envelops her womb
Her body fills up with the light
but she does not feel warm
Her womb starts throbbing
like a woman in travail
Then an angel bursts forth
from up out of the ground

The angel is wearing a crown
that glows and shimmers and shines
The white light all around her
shines thru her red skin
Martha looks in her eyes
and sees the angel woman is sad
Martha wants somehow to comfort her
so she reaches out her hand
and the angel woman takes it
Martha's heart starts to sing
The angel woman smiles a bit

and her countenance changes
Martha, I will always be with you,
the angel woman she says
Then she does a strange thing
She turns and she walks away

How will I know you?
Martha asks. Her voice cracks
The angel speaks not a word
Then Martha notices her plaits
They reach down her back
and they are black as the night
She is wearing a cloak with the whole world sewn inside
Martha sees rivers and mountains
She even sees winged ones that fly
But all the land is a strange land
It makes her want to cry

Don't leave, Martha says,
the scream caught up in her throat
It is the scream that she screams
that first wakes Martha up
It is not the sound of the horse
that Robert Blue Hair rides on
It is the day that her brother
gives her to the white man

When she returns from the dream world, a thousand tiny spiders
are crawling thru the strands of her hair. They are whispering loud.
The spiders are saying her life is coming to an end as she knows it.
They say from her loins will spring forth all the colors of the rainbow.

Her mind is still reeling from the world of dreams all about her.
And the sound of Robert's horse is coming closer and closer.
So she does not pay attention to what the spiders are saying.
She brushes her hand across her head and the spiders go running.
Down her arm. Down her hand. They scurry under a boulder
that has sat by the tree since Creation's first smolder.
Martha will sleep with the ancestors before she finally knows
what the spiders' words mean that day. The colors of the rainbow
part anyhow. It doesn't take nearly that long
for the rest of what they say to come true. For everything to go wrong.
For none of her dreams to come true. That happens in a brief instant.
Martha hears it first in the sound of the horse's hoof beats.

She sits up where she sleeps under the cottonwood tree.
She looks out over the horizon and all she can see
is the dust Robert's horse has made, swirling clouds in the air.
Since starting the missionary school, Robert rides like the white man.
Telltale signs of him appearing long before he arrives.
The spiders run from Martha's shoulder and on down her left side.
Fleeing, Martha thinks, as tho something gave them a start.
And she longs to go with them. Her scared trembling heart
wants to follow them wherever it is they are going.
She watches as the spiders make a line and then go
into a hole in the rock. Safe in Great Mother's dark world.
Robert Blue Hair rides toward her from the direction of the sun.
He is her brother. And yet he is a brother no longer.
He lives now in the world of the white man and his god.
They were once very close, Martha and Robert, her brother.
Now he walks around with a book he says contains all of the knowledge
of the white man's god. The book's small with a cover

that is black and soft and is made out of cow leather.

Robert was one of the first children to go
to the Indian boarding school. Even before
attending was mandatory, he went to the Protestant School
that the missionaries had opened. They had 100 students.
When Robert went to the boarding school, he did not complain
or resist like so many of the other Indian boys did.
In fact, he and one of his classmates started a competition
to graduate at the top of the class. That brought him to the attention
of the white men who praised themselves for civilizing the Indians.
And they would present Robert as a good Indian example.
They even sent him and the smartest children to white universities.
He translated for the white government when they wrote all their treaties.
Robert said he could resist like the warriors and end up dead
or he could work for his people to protect them from the white man.

Robert and Martha used to talk about all kinds of things.
Especially the white man. He would explain their strange ways
and answer her endless questions. They would sit and talk about
the things Robert was learning. About his studies and such
when he started the white school. Robert was older but he
never seemed to grow tired of talking to Martha about things
that she was curious about. He was a good brother that way.
And that's what they were doing on that sparkling blue day
when Lone White Man came. The day he entered their world.
Martha was sitting with Robert, her mind pondering the things
he had just told her. That there are people who are black!
Whose skin is the same color as buffalo skin, or of dust.
Martha could not believe this thing. And yet Robert said it was so.
When he spoke the white man's language, his words sounded like smoke.
Robert spoke to Martha in English. He said it was important that she
learn to speak the white man's language. "I have seen their great feasts.
They have foods that I could have never even imagined!
Fruits and nuts that they bring from across the Great Waters.

And sweets that taste like sunshine." Martha could not believe what she heard.
She followed the smoke that was the sound of his words.
"A long time ago," Robert said like he knew,
"the white man painted his servant black. That makes it easier for you
to tell them apart. To keep them separate from the rest.
And now the black men have children born who are the same way
that they have been painted," Robert said. "All this is true, Martha, and yet,
they are a wonderful people. Their ways more like our ways."
She wrung water from her braids. She and Robert had been swimming.
Her head was filled with the smoke words, her mind dancing and spinning.
All of a sudden, Robert rose. Martha was so busy pondering the things
that Robert had told her, she did not even notice when
her brother started to walk along the path that led
from the eastern side of their house. Martha looked up and saw a two-legged
walking toward them from the direction of the river.
Robert Blue Hair walked over to this mysterious stranger.

He was covered in hair that was the color of clay.
Except for his forehead, eyes and nose, his entire face,
his chest, even his arms were covered with this strange growth.
Martha's hand went up to the nape of her throat.
Robert walked up to him. He lifted his hand
and said something in English to the lone white man.
Then she saw Robert extend his hand. And the white man grabbed his.
Then the lone white man fell to the ground as though dead.
Robert carried the two-legged inside and he laid him down.
Martha's father was shocked by this thing on the ground.
But her mother told him that she had had a strange dream
that this two-legged would come. "What does the dream mean?"
Martha's father asked her. That's when her mother said
she was told in the dream that this lone white man
would bind his future and theirs, like a knot never broken.
A shiver went up Martha's spine at the words her mother had spoken.
The lone white man slept for three days. When he woke, he asked for
some food. Mother gave him some venison they had shot

during the winter. And she gave him some water.
The two-legged looked at Martha's mother and asked her who she was.

He held his hand out to Martha when she brought him his food.
And she shook hands with him as she had seen Robert do.
He tried to talk to her then, but the sound filled her with dread.
Even after Lone White Man had been clothed and was fed,
he did not move from their house because it delighted Robert
to have a white man around with whom he could speak English.
He gave Robert books and he had lots of tobacco.
They'd sit under the cottonwood laughing and talking
till the moon rose high in the sky each night.
Eventually, they started to talk about Martha's life.
But he never told Martha. And now it is too late.
Just like the spiders whispered, her brother has sealed her fate.

Lone White Man lived with their People for many years.
He learned their People's language. And Martha learned more of his
from the conversations he and Robert would have long into the night.
Even after Robert left for school, Lone White Man and the shy
Indian woman would converse in both languages. Sometimes hers. Sometimes his.
He seemed happy with their family. Staying in their village with them.
After Robert had taught Lone White Man their language,
he started to study their People like they were an interesting specimen.
And she did not like the way he looked at her sometimes.
When he went to visit his people, he would bring back guns and knives.
Or axes made of metal. He used metal a lot.
He made a plow from the metal and tied it to the back of a horse.

When Robert agreed to have Lone White Man marry Martha,
the two-legged had made Robert Blue Hair believe that
he would never take her away from their People.
And Robert believed him. Robert has always been simple
when it comes to white people. She didn't know that at the time.
But Martha knew from the beginning that Lone White Man was lying

when he said he would honor her and her People's ways.
She could tell he was lying by the way his words made
the animals act. They would scream like the wind
every time he spoke to her. She told Robert about it
and Robert had laughed and said she was just being foolish.
He said she was full of old time Indian superstitions.
On the night that Lone White Man took her away,
she was sitting in the pasture. The same pasture where he had
first appeared to Robert and Martha. On the eastern side of the house.
He came up to her and told her that it was now time
for him to return to his family. Said he had gotten a letter that said
that his mother needed him. That his father was dead.
"Good-bye," Martha said. "This has nothing to do with me."
But Lone White Man said they were married, so he
expected her to go with him. To travel far to the South.
That is where Lone White Man said his family had a house.
He said, "I have been patient with you, but I can remain here no longer.
It is time I return to my people beside the Great Waters."
Martha said, "You are free to go anytime."
He said she had to go with him. They were standing outside of the house.
"But," she said, "what about your promise to Robert?"
"I have been patient," he said. "Just like I promised your brother.
Surely you knew that the time would finally come
that I'd take you with me." She said, "No, I did not.
I didn't know I would have to leave my family. I thought
we'd always live here with Father and Mother."
"I thought so too. And as long as my father lived
I had the option to stay. But now that my father is dead
I must return to help my mother. We have houses and land.
And she also needs help with managing all of the slaves."
"Your family owns men?" Martha asked him in disgust.
"It is the way of life in the place where I'm from."

Martha ran to her mother. "Mother! Mother!" she screamed.
"Please don't make me go. Please, Mother, help me!"

Her mother looked at Martha with tears running down her face.
"We must honor Robert's promise." That's all her mother said.
Martha forever remembered that night. Always remembered the moon,
how it hung full in the sky. Always remembered the tune
that the crickets had sung as she packed all her things.
And from that day forward, she became his captive.
Lone White Man became known as White Man Who Steals
the night he took Martha away from the place that she lived.
Forever after that night she would think of him in that way.
The White Man Who Steals. She never would speak his name.

They traveled many moons, through spring and then summer.
When they finally arrived, it was the beginning of winter.
Winter in this place near the Great Waters was nothing
like winter in the Great Plains where Martha was from.
After what seemed like forever, they finally got to the place
where White Man Who Steals and his family had their house.
They traveled by wagon. Martha traveled in back.
Though the trip took several months, Martha would never talk
to White Man Who Steals. She was filled with a rage
she had never felt before. He had loved Martha when
the journey from the Great Plains to South Carolina began.
But after months of her anger being directed at him,
he loved her less and less. And by the journey's end,
he wondered why he had ever loved this Indian.
He started to drink more and more during those long endless months.
After what seemed like an eternity, the wagon finally stopped
at the home of his family. His mother took one look
at Martha's face, and her whole body shook.
She took one step back and fainted dead away.
She could not believe her only son would disgrace her this way.
The Indian was an embarrassment. That's the way that she saw it.
But no one was more embarrassed than Martha,
and she would not step one foot in that house.
So she set up a cabin way out in the back

on a piece of property where their family kept slaves.
Just beyond their huts, near their family's graves.
Indians don't dwell among the dead normally.
But she felt better there than in the home of his family.
At night she would listen to the slaves talk about
their families, their problems, their dreams of freedom and such.

One night in her cabin, Martha heard a wolf cry.
Her howl filled the bitter blackness, stars sprinkled sparse in the sky.
They had been on James Island then for about six full moons
and he had not forced himself on her. Had not made her scream.
But on that night filled with darkness, in spite of moon and stars so bright,
he came to her with liquor on his breath. His pale skin glowed in the night.
He opened the door to Martha's cabin. She was mixing the herbs and roots
with which she helped heal the slaves' wounds. That's what she was doing
when he raped her the first time. Martha screamed and she screamed.
"You are my wife, you crazy savage. You will not deny me
the right to normal relations. It is your duty to share my bed."
His breath smelled of the liquor the white man drinks to make him brave.
His clothes were filthy, full of dirt and grime.
Her face was streaked with the tears that she cried.
The slaves in their cabins listened to her mad screams.
There was nothing they could do. They were more helpless than she
was. After he took her that first time, on that dark star filled night,
Martha became pregnant with White Man Who Steals' child.
Though she fought with all her might, she was soon overpowered.
He put his seed deep inside and nine months later
she gave birth to his child. A son with red hair just like him.
He came other times around the same time of the year.
And two more times she gave birth to male children with red hair.
They all looked just like him. Hair like flame and pale skin.
And as soon as they were born, his mother took all of her children.

These children barely knew her. And White Man Who Steals agreed.
So she never nursed them at her tit or bounced them up and down on her knee.

Kathya Alexander   **193**

A slave woman with a baby who had hair the same color
nursed them with her milk. Martha was never a mother
to the boys she gave birth to. Not a one. Not at all.
But, she wanted to be a mother. Not to them, but to the girl
whose spirit swam with her in the Great Waters on the day
after he raped her the first time. The girlchild's spirit came
to Martha floating on one of Great Mother's huge waves.
She saw the girl's dark hair floating behind her. She saw her dark face.
She looked like an Indian but not as Indian as she.
So Martha knew one day that this girlchild would be
a daughter to love her. Not like his three sons who were ashamed
to be seen with their Indian mother. And so she never tried
to demand their affection. It seemed the only way somehow
that she could show them she loved them. Even though it broke her heart.

When she swam with the girlchild on that first day,
the girl told Martha her name. Ringing Bell she had said.
She didn't speak with her mouth. They spoke spirit to spirit
as the water and the sand washed over her and her daughter.
She had come to the waters to wash the grime off herself
after White Man Who Steals had raped her. But after she met
her daughter's spirit, she thought of the incidents like
a penance she paid for something she wanted very much.
She knew her daughter was coming from very far, far away.
Martha could tell that when she saw her in the Great Waters that day.
His torture was the only way to bring her daughter home, you see.
The daughter birthed of her spirit that day in the great sea.
When she finally was born, her skin and hair dark as hers was,
his family all looked as tho they were in shock.
She is not like the others, Martha heard his mother say.
She looks like the Indian. And we cannot have that.
But the girlchild was her great joy. Now she knew why she was living.
She was the reason Great Mother put her here on this earth.
Martha taught her her People's ways and the Indian ways of knowing.
She felt a happiness she had not known since she was brought to this place.

The girlchild grew strong and beautiful. Though her skin became lighter,
her Indian blood shone through her face like the sun.
Martha took her one day into town with her for supplies.
It was a place that the Indian had rarely gone
for they often did not have the things that she needed.
Most often Martha hunted for roots and plants and whatnot
for the medicines she made away from the noise of the city.
And so she was uncomfortable and probably should not have gone
or taken her daughter with her. She could have asked the midwife,
but Martha had no idea that trip would one day change her daughter's life.
The girl met the man she would marry. Though they did not know that then.
She was still just a child after all. The child of whom Martha had dreamed.

Her daughter wore the clothes of the white man - a bonnet, a shawl
and a dark coat with buttons. Martha never wore things like those.
His mother would give her these clothes. Martha always had on the skins
that made up her dress. The child was only thirteen.
They walked together holding hands as they crossed the muddy street.
Her little fingers were clutching her mother's until a strong wind
made her braid fall from her bonnet when it was whipped from her head.
She ran after the hat. And just then some white men
with some slaves in chains just happened to be walking by.
One of the black men fell, and the daughter started to cry.
Her cry sounded like her name. It had from her very first sound.
It was the sound a bell makes when it is struck on the ground.
She ran into the street and grabbed the black man by the hand.
And from that time, their spirits joined.
Willie Boy.
And Ringing Bell.

19
PURE DEE AFRIKAN

The sky done got all dark and sparkly.
A chill wind done start to dance real slow.
The sun a gold ball in the sky disappearing
opposite my mama's open bedroom door.
The daffodils march straight and sure
in a line alongside the house to the back.
They waving like they is in prayer.
I lay my head on my mama's lap.

"The day he step on American soil, they say,
Willie Boy run into the woman he'd marry.
It was the Indian woman's daughter."
Mama ease back on the bed and spread her legs a little wider.
"He was a man who could still the souls of birds and other animals.
Say he could look in they eyes and soothe 'em with a touch.
He didn't love nobody on topside of this earth
except for his brother. And they say that he ate him."
"What!" I say. "He ate his brother?

What kind of person do something like that?"
The last of the sun shining past us thru the window.
The orange rays from the light making dust dance in the air.
"You lose everythang, you lucky you don't go crazy.
Add slavery to that, and I don't know what I'd be.
Being beat and treat like I'm some kind of animal."
Mama's eyes reflect the setting sun when she look down at me.
"Willie Boy wasn't born to be a violent man.
That come from being muzzled and beat with whips on his back.
Say he was a gentle boy when he was born in black Afrika.
It was that ride cross the water that make him finally snap."
"But to eat a human being. And your brother at that."
I don't believe a word of this is true.
And what's that got to do with the angel?"
"Be quiet," Mama say, "and I'm fixing to tell you."
I settle back against the head of the bed.
Mama eyes have something in them remind me of Chiller Theater.
Like a monster is somewhere off inside of her head.
I watch her face close while she tell me the story.

"Him and his brother get captured together.
They was out hunting or something for roots and whatnot.
Hear tell they daddy was a walking history book.
He something Willie Boy always call a griot.
His brother had been training to take over for his daddy
whenever it was that his daddy ever die.
And even tho it was forbidden, he passed on to Willie Boy
all he knowed. And that is why
Willie Boy ate him."
"But, Mama," I say,
"that just don't make no kinda sense."
"Listen, Mandy," Mama say to me.
"It's easy to judge when you ain't in it.

"Some white mens come and throw a net over them.
And made them march to where was anchored a great ship.
It was sitting on the biggest water the brothers had ever seen.
By then they was both dog tired. And then the brother took sick.
They herded them in with a whole lot of other Afrikan peoples.
Chained them to boards in the bowels of the ship.
Willie Boy never did get the sounds out of his head.
Heard them crying when he was wake. And specially when he was sleep.
'Member most of them Afrikans hadn't never seen white mens before.
They call them ghost people. And they shake down to they toes.
They think the white mens was some kind of spirit or 'nother.
Thought the ship was taking them down to a place in hell below.
The white mens separate all of the Afrikans
who talk the same language. Didn't want them to speak
to each other about what was happening to them.
Divide and conquer. To make them weak.
But, somehow, Willie Boy and his brother
ended up shackle to one another's legs.
So Willie Boy was allowed to stay with his brother.
And his brother kept putting his knowledge inside Willie Boy's head.

"He watch his brother get sicker and sicker.
Watch his spirit leave his body with every roll of the ship.
On the day his brother had teach him all that he know,
he ask Willie Boy to eat him. He say, 'Start with my lips.'
On his lips, his brother tell him,
is the story of they people. 'Don't you never forget
that we come from a people who stand proud and tall.'
Tell him he sorry to leave him. Then he die on that ship.
Say Willie Boy eat his brother's lips first
just like his brother had told him to do.
He bite off his lips in two big ole chunks.
Top lip first. Then the bottom one too.
When the full moon come up, Willie Boy start to holler
like he a werewolf or something. He wasn't human no more.

When the white men come to see what was the matter,
Willie Boy pray that they kill him. But all they did was throw
his brother's body in the ocean.
A part of Willie Boy drown that day too.
They led him off the ship, his hands shackled in front.
Willie Boy so crazy by now, he don't care what they do.

He march when they tell him and stop when they say,
walking to the noisy market where he was to be bought and sold.
He was hobbling along, not paying no attention,
when a horse was spook by a snake. Willie Boy grab ahold
of the horse's mane and pull it to him
just before he fell. A little olive skin gal
come and stood right next to him in the street.
She bent down to the ground and reached out her hand.
The horse tell Willie Boy he scared of this place.
Willie Boy tell the horse that here don't nobody care.
The little gal's mama reach out and grab her daughter.
She say some words to Willie Boy that he don't understand.
The horse tell Willie Boy the woman say thank you.
The girl look him in the eye and and grab ahold of his hand.
Her touch made Willie Boy feel like he human.
And he know, somehow, he gon' see her again.

"That little gal was yo' great granmama,"
Mama tell me now. She got her head in her hands.
"The angel come to the little girl too?"
Mama throw her leg on the side of the bed.
"Yes, she come to the little girl too.
But not for a while. She come to her when she grown."
"What the angel say to her, Mama?"
"She tell her to kill Willie Boy on the day she leave home."
"A angel tell somebody to kill somebody, Mama?
I thought angels come from God. And God wouldn't do that."
"That's the thing I'm trying to tell you, Mandy.

God can do whatsoever God lack."
"But what about what it say in the Bible?
The Ten Commandments say thou shalt not kill."
"God told Abraham to kill his own son, Mandy.
God can use you howsoever God will.
Hush now and let me tell you the story.
You hear enuf, you might not be so sho' of yourself.
What the angel do when she come to you, Mandy,
is to shake up your world. Turn you back on yourself."
"But, Mama," I say.
"Don't 'but Mama' me.
Do you want me to tell you this story or not?"
I settle myself back down on the bed.
My head is spinning and my face feel hot.

"When the white mens see what Willie Boy do to that horse,
they know he somebody who have got the touch.
That's what they call people who calm the souls of animals.
So he was bought by a rancher name of Colonel McClintock.
Old Marster McClintock have all kinds of animals.
Horses and cattle. He have hunting dogs too.
He start another business off of Willie Boy skill.
So Willie Boy don't toil the fields like the other slaves do.
That make some say he have a easy life.
But it wasn't like Willie Boy had no time on his hands.
He never did become friends with none of the other slaves
cause he talk to hisself. Or least that's what they said.
But Willie Boy wasn't never talking to hisself.
Didn't none of them others know what they was talking about.
Willie Boy was talking to the spirit of his brother
that live inside of his stomach and pooch his gut out.
Was a madness to Willie Boy. The other slaves called him crazy.
He run away all the time when the moon was full.
They capture him every time, crouching somewhere in the darkness.
One time he was covered with snakes, bellowing like a bull.

He was beat like a animal every time he was caught.
He bore scars on his back and all over his face.
Anything human he had in him after that trip cross the water
was beat out of him in this new world within the first few days.

After while strange things start to happen to the animals.
Cats give birth to dead litters. Or a two-headed cow.
Anything Willie Boy touch turn out to be abnormal.
And sometime birds would fall straight from out of the sky.
It took a while for Marster McClintock to put it together
that these things was connected to Willie Boy and his touch.
Some of the slaves had tried to tell him about it
but white folks don't never believe what we tell 'em. They call it superstitious.
The Indians speak of the Buffalo Calf Woman.
Say when She come, Evil will Evil destroy.
It was like that with Willie Boy and his white slave owner.
He was the Evil they created. And it become his pride and joy.
Being evil, I mean," my mama tell me.
"It's what Willie Boy become to keep hisself alive.
If it wasn't for the evil that was alive within him,
I thank he would have give up after his brother died.
And then you wouldn't have been here today.
You ever think how it work like that?
A crazy man and a wife that killed him
got your whole life hanging in the palm of they hands.

"Along with Willie Boy talking back and forth to the animals,
he also become a great hewer of wood.
He never did learn to write in the white man's language.
So he carve out whole stories of the life he once had.
Afrikan villages with little people cut in it.
His brother, too, from a single block of wood.
He even carve out the first meeting he ever have with the girlchild,
but it was years before he ever see Ringing Bell again.
He carve out the horse that change the course of his life.

He carve out the cape and the scarf and the hat
that the little girl wore his first day on new soil.
He even carve out the bell the little girl wore round her neck.
He remembered her face. He saw it in his dreams.
The braid that she wore that fell way down her back.
The curve of her nose. The tears in her eyes.
And he knew her when he saw her for the first time again.

"It was a place Willie Boy go to back off in a thicket of woods.
He lead the cows in that direction when the moon was full.
One day when he there, he come upon that same girlchild.
She was growed up now, but he knowed who she was.
She was wrap all around some wild-eyed white boy
who was acting like he was the girl's pride and joy.
Willie Boy could look and tell she thought she was in love.
And it hurt him in the place that had once held his heart.
Willie Boy creep more deep into the thicket of woods.
He don't want them to see him and so he stood
behind a old tree and he watch them so close that
the girlchild could tell that somebody was
with them out there. She start to fasten her buttons.
The boy grab her real rough. Willie Boy skin start to tingle.
She brush the grass from her hair. She feeling kinda shame.
She pull away from the boy and he call her a name.
He call her a savage like he hear his daddy say.
He hadn't never treat her like that before that day.
But the white boy was upset and he come and stand over her
and then he draw back his arm like he was fixing to hit her.
All this Willie Boy saw. And he wasn't never gon' let
nobody hurt somebody else that he love again.
So he creep up to the white boy and hit him over the head.
And the white boy fell to the ground like he was dead.
Ringing Bell cry out. She don't know what to do.
Willie Boy tell her, "I will always protect you."
"Protect me from what?" Ringing Bell she ask.

"I will protect you from everything," Willie Boy he said.
"You don't know what you've done. You don't know who this is.
His father is rich. And he never liked Will
to be with me anyway. Will Jenkins is his name.
And his father will kill us both when he finds out what you did.

"She knowed who Willie Boy was. Something about his eyes, she said,
when they finally got the time to talk about everything
that happen that day. She remember holding his hand.
But she was a Indian and he was a slave,
and they both knowed neither one of they lives was worth a plum nickel
to the white men who would find the body of Will
out in that thicket of trees way back off in
them woods where her and Willie Boy had left him.
And so they decide to just run away.
How they ever make it, the Lord only know.
She look just white enuf for her to be a white woman
and him her faithful slave so they never get caught.
They survive out in the woods in the Indian way
even tho White Man Who Steal put out a search for his daughter.
But he never hear nothing from Ringing Bell never again.
Nobody on James Island knowed her and Willie Boy had left together.
He done tried to escape so much that Willie Boy's master, I guess,
just figured the crazy slave had finally succeed at it.
Willie Boy built them a house in a whole 'nother state.
 And nobody never found them. Willie Boy kept her safe."

At first he was gentle with her. When he felt the madness coming,
he would always go away and stay somewhere off in the woods.
Ringing Bell didn't know he was crazy. How could she know that?
Willie Boy tell her how much he love her and she accept that as fact.
They built a life together, him taming animals and working wood.
And she, like her mother, sold medicines and herbs.
They ended up somewhere, I think, outside the city of Memphis.
Ringing Bell think this life is about as good as she can expect it.

She start to think different when, sometime in the next year,
Willie Boy slap her cross her face. He break the drum in her ear.
Willie Boy cry like a baby. He tell her over and over
how sorry he was. But he just couldn't control it.
It was like something in Willie Boy had just broke apart.
He didn't want to hurt her but he couldn't make hisself stop.
That madness he had tried to keep buried inside
become like a monster, like a thing alive.
His eyes would turn red when the moon would got full.
And Ringing Bell would try to hide, but Willie Boy would
always seem to find her. He tracked her like a dog.
Smelling the ground like the animal he had become.
And that's how Ringing Bell's life come to be.
Being beat all the time the same way that he
had been beat hisself. She bore scars on her back.
And sometime you could see finger marks on her neck.
When he didn't beat her, he'd rape her again and again.
In that way, Ringing Belle was living the life that her mama had lived.

"Did she ever see her Mama after they ran off that day?"
"Never did see her Mama, but she manage to send her a message
so that her Mama would know she was at least still alive.
If you can call it living, the life Ringing Bell had.
After a few years Ringing Bell become heavy with child.
That child was my mama. And her name was Mattie Bell.
You didn't never know her. She die before you was born."
"Did the angel come to her too?" My mama tell me again,
"The angel come once to every generation.
I thought she was gone 'til you seen her today.
You the one that she choose. Don't know why it was you.
But when she come, she gon' help you with something you got to go thru."

There are so many questions I still want to ask.
But Mama sit up and get up off the bed.
I don't know how much of what she said to believe

about the African man and the mix Indian girl.
But the angel came. And she look just like Mama said.
So if that part is true, why not all the rest?
These the kind of stories Mama tell me all the time
about people and spirits and animals all mixed up like
it ain't nothing peculiar. Like they all just the same.
And now the angel done chose me. But I still don't know what that mean.

20
IN MY FATHER'S HOUSE

"You say the mix girl ended up killing him, Mama?"
I ask my mama when she sit down again.
The sun done set outside her bedroom window
and the nite done come soft like a gentle rain.
Me and my Mama been talking all evening.
Talking like we ain't never talked before.
I been asking her questions about the angel.
She been answering my questions. But I wanna know more.
More about me and more about my family.
More about Daddy. And more about her.
But most of all, I want to know about the angel
and what she show herself to me for.

"Ain't you tired of talking?" Mama she say.
"We done talked and talked ever since we come home."
"No, I ain't tired," I say to my mama.
"Tell me about when the angel come
to the mix Indian girl who marry the Afrikan.

What she kill him for? What did he do?"
"He beat her and he beat all of her chir'en."
Mama say he beat her and do other bad things too.
"He was my mama's daddy, Mandy.
She say he mean as the day is long."
"But you never met him, did you, Mama?"
"Naw. He was dead fo' I was born.
But my mama talk to me about him.
Sometime when it was just her and me.
She always sad when she talk about him.
She say he the meanest man she done ever seen.
Not like my daddy. Papa was perfect.
Loved me and my mama in every way."
Mama look inside herself again
and move her lips like she is praying.
She always like this when she talk about her daddy.
He just die one year ago.
She scream when he die like she did today at church.
"My Daddy love me and my mama so."
Mama slide her hand across the bedspread.
Her knuckles swole up like little rocks.
I reach over and turn on the light on the nightstand.
The dark curl up in the corners like steam from a pot.
"But what about the mix girl and her killing the Afrikan?"
Mama sit with one leg cross the bed, one leg on the floor.
"He beat her and her chir'en one time too many, I guess.
Mama say her mama couldn't take it no mo'."

Mom Mattie was my Mama's mama.
She look just like a Indian too.
She have a long braid hang down her back.
Mama have her picture in the living room.
"What happen to the mix girl, Mama?
She ever get caught for what she did?"
"No, didn't nobody never catch her.

You know her name was Ringing Bell.
Call her that. She deserve that much.
Mom Mattie she name me after her."
She scratch her head with her fingernails
and dandruff fall out onto her clothes.
My mama name Belle just like the Indian.
But she don't spell her name the same.
"Ringing Bell is her name, but I call her Uncie.
I think that mean granmaw in the Indian language."
Mama say her granmama Uncie die
when Mama was just a little girl.
She die in a fire just like Clyde did
when the heater catch fire to the back of her skirt.
Mama say, "I saw her gown go up in flames.
And then Uncie she just take off running.
They probably could have saved her life,
but she was running so fast, couldn't nobody catch her.
I watch her burn." Mama shake her head
like she is trying to shake something aloose.
"I won't never forget that smell."
"What it smell like?"
"I can't tell you.
It's something you have to smell for yourself.
Lord knows, I hope you never do.
Fire and angels; that's our family history.
Uncie die in a fire. And my Clyde did too.
The full blood Indian pass down the story
of the angel that come to you today.
She tell her daughter all about it
same as I'm tellling you," she say.

I wonder why my family history
is fill with bad things like fire and stuff.
And I bet it's a lot of other bad things too.
Today I'm just starting to learn about some.

My brother Clyde. My great-granmama.
Half Indian. Half Afrikan. I never knew.
Mama grab her foot and rub the corn
where her toe done rubbed 'gainst her high heel shoes.
"The day Uncie kill him, she had cook his dinner.
The sun was setting and the moon was full.
He always go crazy during that time of the month.
I told you that's what slavery'd done.
So they was all expecting something to happen.
He come in the house snarling like a lion or a bear.
Mom Mattie say he didn't sound like nothing human."
"How old she was?" I ask her then.
"She must have been bout four or five.
Couldn'tna been no more than six.
Uncie had bore him four sons and a daughter.
And Mom Mattie was the baby out of the bunch.

"Willie Boy was a little bitty blue-black man.
Look like he been carve out of a block of wood.
He was the color of nite, his skin pulled tight
across his face like Uncle Jesse skin do.
Mama say he'd come in they room at nite
and climb into they beds with them.
He do thangs to his chir'en no daddy should do.
And that's why my Mama hated him.
Even tho she wasn't old enuf to remember,
I guess some thangs you can't forget.
Mama say he would rub all up against 'em.
That's when my Mama started getting sick."
"She watch her Mama kill her Daddy?
I think that would have made me sick too."
"My mama say that killing her daddy
was the best thing that Ringing Bell ever do.

"He sit down at the dinner table.
And he ask Uncle Clement to give him a drink.
But first Clement took a bite off of his chicken.
And Willie Boy hit him in the face.
Hit him so hard, his eye fell out.
Right on the table, my mama say.
My mama start to scream like a banshee or something.
And Willie Boy hit her in the face.
He pick Clement eye up with his greasy hand,
still full of chicken grease and crumbs,
and push it right back in the socket.
Then he finish dinner like nothing ever happen.

"When Willie Boy was thru eating, he laid down on the bed.
And pretty soon, he was snoring loud.
Uncie wash the dishes then sent the chir'en to the porch.
Then she put a pillow over Willie Boy head.
Mama say she was looking thru the window
so she see everything her mama do.
She say Willie Boy was flailing his arms
and making these clucking sounds like a chicken do.
Uncie sit on his face 'til he stop jekking.
When he still, she get the chir'en's coats and hats.
She tell 'em they is going on a adventure.
And she say they ain't never coming back."
"What happen to him after she kill him, Mama?"
"My mama say she didn't never know."
"Didn't nobody never find his body?"
My Mama say, "Not as I knows."

"Mama say the angel told her mama to get that pillow.
Then the angel come to lead them thru
the dark nite while they was all traveling.
She tell Ringing Bell where to go and what to do.
Uncie say she see her clear as day.

Look like a Indian woman with plaits down her back.
Mama say she have a crown on her head."
"Just like the angel I seen look like!
What the angel say to her, Mama?"
"She always have a message when she come," Mama say.
She have a strange message when she come to me.
All about God's thoughts and about His ways.
I do not know what this message mean.
When she come to Mama, she say, 'Forgive.'
That seem easier to understand.
Mama say, "You will understand it when you need
to understand. That's how the angel work.
She give you a message for when you need it the most."
Today I needed it cause of my Daddy.
Cause the church had made it like he never was.

But Mama say, "Yo' Daddy was a bigger man
than to get upset about a piece of cloth.
Respect come from the life he live
and can't nobody take that away from him."
I think I would have acted different
if Mama had told me about it before
I got in the church. But my head was hurting
and that make me act crazy sometime I know.
Maybe now the angel will help my headaches
like the fire angel did that time
when she flapped her wings to relieve the pain.
Maybe this is what growing up is all about.

Mama continue with the story about the angel.
"Mom Mattie say she was always a little ahead of them.
She lead them thru the darkness 'til they come
to a shack somewhere back off in the woods.
They wouldn't have never found it if hadn'tna been for the angel.
She lead 'em to it straight and sho'.

It was a light in the window and a light on the porch.

Inside, there was a fire in the fireplace too.

The angel say, 'In My Father's house, there are many mansions.

This one He prepare just for you.'

Mom Mattie say her voice sound just like a rainbow."

"And then what did the angel do?"

"She just up and disappear right before they very eyes."

"God made them a house?" I ask my mama.

"That's what Mom Mattie say," my mama reply.

"And that's when yo' mama see the angel?"

"She saw her the first time on that day.

But Mom Mattie see her another time too."

"When that was?"

But Mama do not say.

"Mandy, I'm tired and I am thru

talking about all this for right now."

"But, Mama," I say. But it don't make no difference.

I can tell she is thru talking to me.

I can hear Sissy in the kitchen washing the dishes.

Mama get up off the bed. I can hear both her knees crack.

She place both of her hands down at the small of her back

and bend over a little to stretch her muscles back out.

Then she bend over and kiss me smack dab in the mouth.

"I'm gon' go in the kitchen and get me something to eat.

You want anything? "

"I want something to drink.

But don't go yet, Mama," I look at my mama and say.

"Tell me more about this Afrikan who ate

his brother."

"I'm thru talking. This enuf for one nite."

"But, Mama, it's important to hear the story about my life."

"You done lived all this time and you ain't never knowed

what happened before today. You can wait a while longer."

"But I can't wait, Mama. Things is changing all the time."

"That's what's wrong with colored folks. Y'all done all lost yo' minds.
I need some time to myself now. Chile, you just don't know.
It ain't the kinda world where a colored chile can just do
whatsoever she want. It's this Civvie Rights nonsense.
Y'all all act like it's gon' change how white folks feel about us.
But just remember that laws don't change the heart of a man.
Don't none of it make no sense. Everybody want to take a stand.
Well, freedom ain't no defense against them dogs and water hoses
them white mens turning on folks. Y'all need to learn about patience."

I know Mama still thinking bout that march in Selma today.
How them people got beat 'til blood run down they face.
I know she worried about me too. About why the angel done come.
Somehow, I know that she hoped that I wouldn't be one.
She never thought it'd be me who would have to go thru it.
But seem like the angel always come to the oldest or the youngest.
And if the angel done came, something bad coming too.
Mama look out the window like she looking for answers to
all the problems that face her. The sky black tinged with red.
Remind me of the eyes of the Afrikan. Like a man who gone mad.
Mama turn her face up like she looking God straight in the eye.
Like the face of God is in the stars in the sky.
Then Mama start to pray like she forget that I'm here.
Like this a conversation she having that only her and God can hear.
"What you demand, God, is a whole lot to ask.
And yet You is a God who sees future and past.
Who sees thangs I can't see. The world in the hollow of your hand.
I cannot do nothing but what you lead me to, Lord.
And where you leading my chile, well God only You know
why you having things turn out the way that they going.
But I am only thine handmaid. Put here to do Your Will.
You ain't never left me. And you ain't gon' leave me still."

Then Mama act like a peace done settle into her soul.
Can't say she look happy. But she look peaceful with knowing.

Knowing that God is guiding her. Knowing that He answers her prayers.
I wish I could say that I knew all the answers that
God was telling my Mama. But I know I'll soon understand
what God wants from me too. Cause He chose me and that's
not even something that I never thought about God would do.
If He see something in me, maybe soon I'll see it too.

Me and Mama don't never talk about the angel again.
She done explain to me all she going to explain.
She say I'm gon' just have to wait to see what God will do
and what the angel coming is gon' have to do
with my life. She say, "You get ready for
a change that's gon' come. Cause it's coming for sure."
Then she get up off the bed and she go into the kitchen.
I can hear her in there. She is talking to Sissy
about Quinton taking her back to school.
They is going to leave later on this evening.
I was gon' ride with them when he take Sissy to college
but now Mama say since I done got my period
I need to stay home. She get a hot water bottle
and tell me to press it down right onto my stomach.
Blood and angels is mixed all up in my head.
And I keep wondering about the words that the angel said.
But I guess I am just going to have to be patient and see
exactly what all of this means that the angel said to me.

III
BLACK IS BEAUTIFUL

21
ONE SUMMER MORNING

When Belle wake up that morning she go out to the truck patch,
the garden she plant at the edge of the back yard.
In her hand she is carrying the silver metal foot tub.
She break the fingers of okra from off the six foot tall stalks,
not even paying no attention to the spiny splinters on the plants
that stick into her fingers like little pieces of glass.
Quinton he stop putting his bags in the car
and he follow her to the back yard when he hear her out there.
She can hear Quinton walk in the garden thru the tomatoes,
careful so he don't step on the cabbage and peas.
She hand him the tub and they work together in silence.
Somehow they both know that they gon' have to agree
that neither one ain't gon' give up what they think about the other.
He gon' do what he gon' do and she is gon' have to just pray.
There ain't nothing else Belle can do but ask the Good Lord to keep her
child safe from the trouble he gon' get hisself in.

Belle and Quint had been arguing about the white woman
that Quint had brought to the house. Brought her three or four times.
Belle hadn't never been there and had not knowed about it.
But she come home early yesterday and seen the woman in the yard.
Standing there big as you please. Holding hands with Quinton.
When Belle saw that she thought she would have a heart attack.
She got out the car she'd been riding in with the white woman
that Belle work for three days a week cleaning her house.

"I'll see you Friday, Belle," Miz Donahue had said to her,
never taking her eyes off the white woman who had not dropped Quint's hand.
Belle rush over to Quinton and snatch his hand out of the white woman's.
Miz Donahue smile and drive on out of the yard
looking back again in her rear-view mirror.
Belle could not hardly breathe. She standing there in shock.
"Quinton," Belle said, "I need you in the house."
And she had walk in the door, leaving them both in the yard.
There ain't nothing more dangerous to her than a white woman,
nothing more able or likely to cause injury or harm.
Everything about a white woman is fraught full of risk and of danger,
and yet here Quinton is holding one by the hand in her yard.
Seem like it was always a white woman that was the cause of her trouble.
What is it about colored men needing to put they lives in danger?
Hadn't enuf of them died over white women to know better?
But they still run after white women like they got the can't-help-its.
That's what she had said to A.D. It hadn't made one bit of difference.
He swore he didn't love her but he wouldn't let her alone.
She didn't know about the white woman when her and A.D. got together.
If she had she wouldn'tna never gave him her heart like she done.

The sun shining thru the vegetables like a ladder from heaven.
Quinton standing over there looking like he is covered in sin.
She start to singing a hymn. Quinton start to sing with her.
It is the only harmony that this morning gon' bring.
Belle start the hymn way down low in her throat.

It is one of the songs that they sing in church
when the deacons start the worship service with a song of praise.
God put a song in her heart each and every day
that He give her. That is how He make His presence known.
The song in her mouth come out like a moan.

> *Soon I will be done*
> *With the troubles of the world*
> *The troubles of the world*
> *Troubles of the world*
> *Soon I will be done*
> *With the troubles of the world*
> *Going home to live with God*

"Where did you get this white woman from?"
Belle ask Quinton yesterday when he come into the house.
"And why y'all holding hands out in the open like you crazy?
Don't you know that's what them white men kill Emmett Till about?"
Emmett Till is the name that have become a colored mama's warning.
What they done to that boy was a sin and a shame.
He wasn't nothing but a child. They say he whistle at a white woman.
Everybody know that was a lie. Just the reason they gave
as a excuse to kill and then rip him to pieces.
They gutted him like a deer. Actually, even worse than that.
Them same white men would have had more respect for a animal,
would not have tore his hide apart like they did to that child.
Even if Emmett was from up North in Chicago,
he would still have knew not to say nothing to a white woman.
Not in Money, Mississippi, most especially.
You learn that at your mama's knee when you is born colored.

Them white men had came and dragged him out of the bed.
When he was found he'd been drowned and had got his throat cut.
His mama, Mamie Till, ran his picture in Jet Magazine
cause she said she wanted folks to see what they done to her son.

And even tho that had been nearly 10 years ago,
Emmett Till's name was a prayer from every colored mama since.
His death had did just what them white men want it to do.
His death become a warning for every colored man to leave
white women alone. So you can imagine how Belle felt
when she ride up in her own yard and seen a child that she birth
holding hands with a white woman. When Quinton come in the house
Belle hit Quinton up side his head before she even thought.

"I say who that white woman is that you bring to my house?"
"Her name is Elaine."
"And why she standing out in my front yard?"
"She work for SNCC. We work in the same office.
She done work for SNCC for two years here in Little Rock.
She rode the bus during Freedom Summer.
That woman done put her life on the line
more times than I can count. Even Stokely Carmichael
vouched for her, praised her as a Civil Rights organizer."
"I don't know nothing about nobody name Stokey Carmichaels.
But I know about white women. And how dangerous they is.
And you know it too. Don't act like you don't.
Keeping company with a white woman gon' end up with somebody dead."

"Elaine was one of the original Freedom Riders.
She started working with SNCC back in 1961
when there were just 13 people in the group that refused
to separate themselves on their way to New Orleans.
She even went to an all Negro college,"
Quinton tell Belle, his voice filled up with pride.
"If it wasn't for white women just like Elaine
the Civil Rights Movement would almost surely have died.
You need to thank that woman for all she did," Quinton say,
"for your rights and mine." Belle is shaking her head.
Thank a white woman for standing out in her front yard.
She don't know how she can get her child to understand

that holding hands with a colored man almost as dangerous for the woman,
for all of them. They house could have been burn down.
All of them could be kill. And Quinton too stupid to even see that.
He mad about her raising her hand to him. But she would do it again.
She wish she had hit A.D. upside the head
the first time she hear rumors about him and that woman, Delta Rose.
She didn't believe that A.D. would do nothing like that.
But now she believe what her lying eyes is trying to show her.

Delta Rose the only daughter of a red-neck white lawyer.
Belle Mama use to work at they house when she well.
The white gal and Belle ain't exactly the same age.
But the girl like to play with her when Mom Mattie go to they house to sell
them the eggs and the butter that she sell around town.
Mom Mattie add to they living any way that she can.
She do cleaning when she able. Wash and iron white folk clothes.
And Belle always go with her. For as long as she can
remember back in her life, she done work 'long side her Mama.
Cause Mom Mattie was weak. Sick a lot of the time.
Belle had seen A.D. over to the white people house working.
But what she was seeing slip right thru her eyes.

Delta Rose was round bout 11 when A.D. first meet her.
She was 16 and A.D. 12 the first time they have sex.
She had hair look like fire. A.D. hadn't never seen nothing like it.
He start to have them dreams about her that make little boys sheets get wet.
That was back when her daddy and A.D. daddy, Levi,
have a run in over a tract of land they both claim that they own.
It's land that join together somewhere down near The Bottoms.
The dispute had been settle friendly. So the families had done
business with each other from time to time.
Over the years, A.D. start to do little tasks round they house.
Levi Anderson talk that man out his land with a smile.
And Delta Rose take a liking to A.D. from the start.

She was just slick enuf to make they friendship look cute.
Like a attraction to the family cat. Or for a stray dog
that come to the back door looking for hushpuppies.
The first time they lay together wasn't no reason but cause
Delta Rose want to have sex. It start out innocent as that.
She was curious. And A.D. was hard as a rock.
They both promise not to tell. They both know what they do is dangerous.
That make it even mo' better. A game they play every few months
or so. Careful-like so as not to cause no attention.
They was children. That ain't no excuse. But it's the truth just the same.
If they had left it at a children's game, no one would have got hurt.
It's the game they play when they grown that's the sin and the shame.

If such a relation become general knowledge,
the colored man in question most likely be kill.
I guess that's why it was hard for Belle to believe
the danger A.D. put hissself and her in.
Carrying on with a rich white woman.
All the Negroes Down Home gossiped about what was up.
Belle might have heard some rumors about her husband,
but she don't put no stock in mess such as that.
But, if you don't believe your lying eyes,
life sho' do seem to have a way
to show you the things that you don't want to see.
Like the Lord did to Paul on his way to town one day.
Sometime the Lord will see you on the back of a jackass
and blind you with a great light. And then knock you down
on the side of a dusty road somewhere.
He'll blind you and then drop the scales from your eyes.
And Belle was blinded by her love for A.D.
She think about it now and wonder how she could have been so stupid.
And I guess because God take care of fools and babies,
He didn't never let them white folks come after her husband.
Even when her love had died, she kept her family together.
After she learned the truth, she shouldn'tna never tried to stay.

It was all because she thought he would have got off too easy.
What she think she gon' prove hanging on to him that way?
"Why I don't love me more than I hate him?
What was wrong with me that I accept something like that?"
Even after they first dance, Belle learn that A.D. go to her.
Wasn't a time when she had A.D. all to herself.

Quint say, "You act like me and that woman was out in the yard kissing.
All she did was take hold of my hand.
She just gave me a ride home from the office in Little Rock."
Belle look at her chile like he done went stone cold mad.
That's got to be it, she think. He done plum lost his mind.
"Quinton, you done lived in the South long enuf for you to know better.
Don't act like you don't. Ain't no chile of mine
done lived under my roof they whole life and don't know that
even looking at a white woman is enuf to get you kill.
Let alone in the public holding a white woman by the hand.
If a white man had drove up, all she had to say is you raped her."
Quinton was near bout the same crazy as his daddy.
"That is ridiculous, Mama," Quinton say with a sneer.
"How I'm gon' rape a woman who is totally dressed?
And why would I do it out in the public like that?
Ain't nothing you saying making one bit of sense."
"You think what them white men done to Emmett Till make sense?
When do sense have anything to do with white folks killing coloreds?
Don't act like the world done change just cause you want it to.
You got to understand that, Quinton, or you is headed for trouble.
Ain't nothing gon' change. This world gon' go on the way
that it's been going since the time that this country first started.
You thank white folks gon' give up the life that they live?"
"They ain't going to have no choice. That's what you don't see, Mama.
Things are changing. And we cannot stop and give up now."
Even tho his Mama want him to, he will not quit working with SNCC.
It took them too long to get the Little Rock office going.
And Quint had moved back home just in time to make a impact hisself.

Belle say, "Quinton, this is just the way that thangs is.
Don't you go out there and get yourself killed."
Quinton say, "But, Mama, things have got to change."
Belle say, "You is my child. Change do not mean a thang
if you is dead. Cause that's all that's gon' happen.
These white folks gon' kill you just as sho' as you born."
"But Dr. King say if there ain't things that you willing to die for,
then you are not really a man."
"That man is a fool,"
Belle say, her voice filled with fear and with trembling.
"He gon' get killed too. You just mark my words.
But, I ain't worried about how Rev. King live his life.
I didn't give birth to him. I give birth to you."
"I can't sit back and do nothing while I watch all my friends
out there marching and fighting each and every day.
It is up to Negroes to bring change to this country.
White folks like Elaine putting their lives on the line every day.
You have lived all your life with signs that say colored only.
We cannot go into places that say only whites.
We are living in a segregated society that is based on skin color.
And I don't care what you say, you know that ain't right."

Quinton walk over to Belle and grab the handle of the foot tub
and he take all the vegetables into the house.
"Where is you going?" Belle she ask Quinton.
"I know you ain't going to that white woman's house."
He had put the clothes he had packed into the trunk of his car.
He said, "I can't live here anymore. I will still help you out
with taking you everywhere that you have to go.
But all this arguing we doing is wearing me out."
"Wearing *you* out? I done heard everything now,"
Belle say as she put the vegetables into the sink.
He probably would have moved into the apartment with Elaine,
but she was staying in a place with some other members of SNCC.

"I'm going to stay with Lil Wren, Mama," Quinton said.

He kiss her on her mouth. She know just who Wren is.

Belle see her all the time when she come play at they church.

Lil Wren play the piano and wear high price clothes.

"You fixing to move in that house with that old woman?" Belle say.

"Don't that woman have near bout a whole house full chir'en?"

"What does it matter how many children that Lil Wren have?"

Quinton say to Belle. He putting the rest of his clothes in

the car. He got a Pontiac that look like a tank.

"You can't move in that woman's house. Y'all ain't even married."

"There you go with all your old fashioned notions again.

It doesn't matter to Wren whether or not we are married."

"Well it matter to me if you is living in sin.

You jump out of the skillet and into the pot.

Now you want to shack up and live with a woman out of wedlock.

That matter to me. And it matter to God."

"Just pray for me, Mama," Quinton he say to her.

He kiss her again then he put his tailored suits in the car.

Belle watch him as he pull out of the driveway,

a prayer on her lips as she offer her son up to God.

22
SCHOOL DAZE

After her daddy died, time had start to go funny.
Some things Mandy remember and it is some things she don't.
It make her feel like she is losing control over her mind.
And Quint and her mama arguing is not helping things none.
Her head always hurting and she always feeling sick.
And now Quinton done left without even saying a thing
to Mandy about leaving. Didn't even tell her goodbye.
Seem like everything keep changing in her life all the time.

After he got out the hospital, Mandy thought A.D. was all right.
Nobody but Belle knew that A.D. had been told
over 10 years ago that he'd only live another decade.
Mandy still had trouble believing her daddy was gone.
A.D. was sho' that the Lord would give him longer than that.
And so he had lived like his life wasn't never going to end.
Belle didn't think she would never forgive him for that
cause now here she was having to clean up all his messes.
He died owing everybody. Belle couldn't stand to be in debt.

She believed in living on only what she had in her pocketbook.
A.D. had always live his life like whatsoever he want
regardless of how it affect her life and the children.

Life without her daddy is still too sad for Mandy to remember.
But only, it seem like, for her most of the time.
All the rest of the family going on just like always.
Tears keep welling up in her eyes and she always feel like crying.
Sissy getting married to a man she met in Pine Bluff at the college.
Lucky score a winning touchdown on the football field last nite.
Vernell and Grady done file for divorce again.
They still the same. Always fussing and fighting.
Cleo done got put in jail again for drunk driving.
That happen not long after A.D. had died.
Belle ain't even noticed Mandy. And Mandy ain't telling nobody
that time done went all funny and she can't remember exactly
when things in her life have actually happened.
Like Cleo. He in jail. But exactly when he went, she don't know.
And Mandy know her and her mama done had that conversation.
But she just can't remember. It's the same way at school.
She don't know why but she is always in trouble.
Miz McQuincy be talking bad about her just cause the boys like to hang out
with Mandy as much as they do with each other.
After she sat on the bleachers with the boys, the teacher called her a whore
in front of the whole class. The woman just mean and hateful.
Mandy just sit at her desk with her head held up high.
And that just make Miz McQuincy start screaming at her.
But Mandy don't care. She just stay mad all the time.
Belle hadn't took no notice to what is happening to Mandy
cause she too busy trying to pay off all A.D.'s debt.
She know that Mandy is missing her daddy,
but Belle been too busy putting they life back on track.
It is Jesse who helping Belle pay off all the bills.
If it wasn't for Jesse, she don't know what she would do.
And she done almost paid off everything A.D. owe.

It make Belle feel bitter every month when the bills come due.

"Come try this skirt on for me so I can see how it fit you,"
Belle say to Mandy calling her into the living room.
They been watching the television together that evening.
Watching little colored children try to desegregate schools.
It remind Belle of when she was a little girl in the country,
when education for coloreds was not accepted as fact.
Back then getting a education was a privilege only for white folks.
Not like today when the law say that everybody has got
to send they children to school. Mandy don't know what a blessing
it is for her to get to go to any kind of a school.
That's why they move from Down Home. So every one of they children
could get the chance at a education. Not have to stop going to school
to work the fields and the crops. Belle put pins in the dress
to hold the material together. She is making Mandy another wraparound skirt.
This one is flowered on one side and black on the other.
Mandy love two-sided dresses. They a whole lot of work,
but Belle do not mind, Mandy like them so much.
But today she keep looking at Mandy all upside her head.
Mandy so wrapped up in herself she do not even notice
that one of the children on the television done got pushed down and fell.

Belle tell Mandy the story again about when she was a girl
way back when she was growing up down in the country
when only the white children get to ride on the bus. Colored children have to walk.
And the white children would pass by and chunk mud rocks at them.
She say the school that she go to is bout 10 miles each way.
But Mandy done notice how the school keep getting further and further with each telling.
Belle done told Mandy this story for all of her life.
Mostly when Mandy don't want to get up in the morning.
Belle say, "We traipsed down long roads where dust rose up when we walked
or they was muddy in the springtime because of the rain.
In the winter, them roads would be hard as a rock.
And we walked 'em barefoot for most of the year.

In the winter we would cut us out some cardboard foot shapes
and put them down in the bottom of our shoes to make soles.
It didn't do much for warmth, but I woulda did anything.
Walked that much and further just for the chance to go to school.
Chir'en today is ungrateful. That's just what y'all is."
Seem like every story Belle tell seem to come back to this.
"You got buses that will take you to yo' very own schools
but you rather go to school with chir'en who don't even want you near them."

They watching the pictures on the television of colored children on a bus.
And these white women trying to turn it over. And they screaming and they fussing.
Mandy ain't never seen white women who look so mad and so mean.
These is white mamas. With children she coulda played with
when Belle took Mandy with her to they house to clean.
All them children want to do is go to school just like Belle wanted.
Why white people hate them so much? That's what Mandy want to know.
Her mama say this gon' happen. But Mandy hadn't believed it
so she had filled out the form and decided to go
to the white school in Jacksonville. But Belle do not know it.
She think Mandy going to the colored school where she done always went.
Now after seeing all these children on TV getting turned over in buses,
Mandy starting to have second thoughts. She don't know what to think.

All summer long her head done been hurting.
Cause when Belle find out she gon' give her a whipping.
Cause when they give them the Freedom of Choice cards to sign,
Mandy write Belle's name where it say "Parents." If A.D. was still alive,
Mandy is sure that he woulda gave her permission to go.
Cause A.D. for integration. But her mama say no.
But now President Johnson done got the Civil Rights bill signed.
That means that Mandy can go to school wherever she decides.
So Mandy and Jewel had decide they was gon' do something new.
So when them cards come in the mail, her and Jewel had decided to
sign they mamas names on them Freedom of Choice cards
that say now they going to school in Jacksonville, Arkansas.

That's the nearest white school to where they live out in the County.
And all a Negro child need now is permission from they parents.
Belle say she ain't never heard of nothing so stupid.
And what Mandy seeing on television now is making her wonder.
Seeing this happen change the child. Now she know like her mama always say
that she somebody who can be kill. Like the little colored girls on TV,
with her same fat plaits and her ashy knees.
She know she gon' have to tell her Mama soon what she did.
Mandy ain't told her mama about always getting in trouble
or about the bad word that Miz McQuincy had call her.
She want to get away from the colored school. Want to have a new start
somewhere don't nobody know her daddy. Where ain't no chains round her heart.

Mandy had not said a word about school all that summer.
And now Belle and Quinton arguing about some silly white woman.
Belle feel like she cannot trust her children at all.
She know Mandy lying to her. All this taking a toll
on Belle as much as it has been on Mandy.
Belle know this got to do with Mandy losing her daddy.
She believe that Mandy would have talked to A.D.
"But she done stood in my face and flat out lied to me,"
Belle say to Miz Francis. Miz Francis know too
that Jewel done sign Francis name on them Freedom of Choice cards too.
They had found out one day when Francis went to the mailboxes to get
her and Belle's mail from the boxes that all stood together like a fence
along with 10 other families that lived on the highway.
Mandy usually brought in their mail, but she had missed it that day.

Francis open her letter from the school first. She just laugh when she read
that Jewel had signed up for the white school over in Jacksonville.
"Why that lying little haint," Miz Francis had said.
"Open this," she told Belle handing her all her mail.
"What is it?" Belle say, taking the stack of envelopes.
"Open that one," Francis say. Belle tear the letter open
and read it out loud. It say Mandy got permission to go

to the white school in Jacksonville just like Jewel's say too.
"You know if one of them done it, the other one doing the same.
I can't believe them lying hussies would actually sign both our names
to a school document. And ain't said nothing about it."
Belle say, "That's cause they know that they is in for a whipping.
I'm gon' beat Mandy until my arm won't lift up no more."
"Uh uh," Francis say then. "Let's hold out a little longer.
I knowed something was strange about how Jewel been acting.
She been jumpy all summer cause she got a guilty conscious."
But Belle can't hold on to her anger cause her daughter is so pitiful.
Moping round like don't nobody care nothing about her.
And Belle love her last child like she love her own breath.
And she can't have Mandy give up just cause her daddy is dead.

Belle call Mandy name and she come back with a jerk.
She tell her to come over where she at so she can try on the skirt
that she sewing for her. Mandy walk slow cross the floor
with tears shining in her eyes. "What is you crying for?"
her Mama ask her. But she can't say a word.
Belle say, "You see now what I tell you?" Mandy see little colored kids in the dirt
with they new school clothes all messed up from the mud on the ground.
Mandy know she got to tell Belle. But she can't tell her now.
She gon' have to wait 'til all them images is gone.
When she ain't feeling so sad. She feel another headache coming on.
"You like your new dress, Mandy?" Belle look at her and she say.
"Yes, Mama," Mandy answer, to the throb of her headache.
Belle take the pins out the dress. One of them stick Mandy's skin
and she burst into tears. But she still don't tell her mama about the trouble she's in.
Belle hold her child in her arms and she just let her cry.
And that make Mandy finally believe that everything is gon' be all right.

23
DEMONSTRATE

When school started this year, nothing bad at all happened.
The white kids got along good with the few of us Negroes.
It wasn't nothing like I watched on the television with Mama
when white women was trying to turn the school buses over.
It is only about 20 Negroes in the school.
Carol Jane and Red had forged they mama's name too
on the Freedom of Choice cards to go to Jacksonville.
And I was glad I made the decision to try out the white school.

Miz Montgomery was mad. But since I was gon' be there,
Carol Jane and Red didn't get in too much trouble.
Cause Miz Montgomery still like me. She bout the only one in Uz
that ain't saying I'm some kind of bad influence on they daughters.
That's cause all the mamas think I was the main ringleader
for getting everybody to go to the white school.
I will admit it was my bright idea,
but everybody was real happy to go along with it.
Miz Montgomery just say, "If Mandy went and jumped

in the Arkansas River, would you two jump in too?"
But she just laughed to herself. That's how Miz Montgomery is.
She don't never see me as a bad girl like Miz McQuincy 'nem do.

Jewel told me her mama said my mama told Miz Francis
that she wasn't mad because she was happy I was going to get
a chance to do something new. Of course, she didn't say that to me.
I think she was just tired when she had to go up to the school
when Miz McQuincy finally call and tell her about something I did.
I was real surprised because my mama don't really like white people.
She always scared they going to do something bad
to coloreds. But she didn't hardly fuss at me or nothing
when she find out what me and Jewel 'nem did.
She put my name on her checkbook because Mama said
that's what the white women she work for do for they kids
so they could buy things like lunches and other stuff that they need.
Mama say, "You gon' be just as good as all of them white chir'en,
no matter that we ain't got as much money as them white people got.
I ain't gon' have you going there looking like you less than them."
She even buy me new clothes from where the white people shop.

So when we integrate the white school there wasn't no trouble at all.
Don't none of the white kids mess with us when we walk down the hall
or when we sit in our classes. And I am just as smart there
as I was at the colored school. The white kids don't even stare
at us strange or nothing. The only difference I can see
is that I don't run everything like I used to at the
colored school. Like, I don't get the lead in the play
like I did at the colored school each and every year.
Cause this year they doing Romeo and Juliet.
At the colored school, we never did do no plays like that.
All the plays that we did was wrote by somebody colored.
Last year we did the play, Amen Corner, by James Baldwin.

My English teacher name is Miz Wilson. She is perky and blonde.
She say I recite Shakespeare better than any child she ever taught.

> *My only love sprung from my only hate!*
> *Too early seen unknown, and known too late!*
> *Prodigious birth of love it is to me,*
> *That I must love a loathed enemy.*

Miz Wilson encourage me to audition. She work with me after school.
I thought sure I would get the part. And Miz Wilson is sure too.
She is from somewhere up North. So she don't act like all the rest
of the teachers who done lived in Arkansas all they life.
And even tho in the audition I tore Juliet up,
wasn't none of them white folks gon' have none of they sons
save no colored Juliet out on no balcony. No way.
So me and Jewel decide that all us coloreds gon' create
our own arts department. Miz Wilson said it wasn't fair
cause I was the best Juliet she ever saw at Jacksonville.
"Amanda," she say. (I decide when I go to the white school
that I want to be called Amanda and not Mandy no more.)
"You will need a sponsor. And you must have a teacher
who agrees to do that before you can go get permission
from Mr. Whitlock. But I cannot see a reason
he wouldn't give you the okay to put on your own play this season."

I want to do Shakespeare too. I really like Shakespeare a lot.
But I know I can't talk none of the other kids into that.
Miz Wilson say she will help us put on whatever we want to do.
So us kids decide we gon' do a all colored talent show.
Everybody gon' be in it. Since it ain't but 20 colored kids
that go to the white school we gon' need all of them
to put on a good show. Since Miz Wilson say that we
got to get permission from the principal, Jewel and me
go to the secretary's office and set up the appointment.
But when we ask he say no. We was so disappointed.

He say they don't have money budgeted for two separate events
and their play is a tradition. We say, "But all they got are white kids.
That's not fair," I say. But Mr. Whitlock just say,
there is nothing he can do. Jewel say, "We'll see about that."

I get so mad at Mr. Whitlock who act like he don't have a clue.
Like he don't understand how the white teachers treat us as inferior.
The ways that they show they expect less out of us.
Not that I care. To me it is all for the better.
That's why I came to the white school anyway.
Cause I was tired of the colored teachers who care about me too much.
Who always expect excellence. No matter what the situation.
No electricity. No food. No running water.
At the white school the teachers always feel sorry for us
when we don't turn in our homework or something.
At the colored school, the teachers would always say,
'You can always come here and eat if you're hungry.'
Although I didn't really know no colored people who was hungry.
Not with the food that grow wherever you put your feet.
Everybody raise something. Fruit, vegetables, or animals.
It might not be what you want, but everybody got something to eat.

That's the thing I like the most about being at the white school.
Cause don't not one person at that school know my mama.
So if I want to cut school or not turn in my assignments,
the teachers don't never try to get in touch with my mama about it.
Especially since my mama had turn off our phone.
Somebody had call and they had charged it collect.
Mama thought it was Quinton but he had denied it.
So now we ain't got no phone. She say that will stop that.
Now we have to get our phone calls over to Cud'n Thetta's.
And she is on Jewel's party line with her nosy old self.
So she always be listening in to our conversations.
Cud'n Thetta the person in Uz who criticize me the most.

When I tell Mama about Mr. Whitlock, she say, "That's what you get.
You the one who decide to go to school with white chir'en.
What did you expect? To be welcome with open arms?"
"I thought at least they'd be fair," is my answer to Mama.
"You think white folks is fair? When you done ever seen that?"
But I don't care whether white folks have been fair before or not.
We students at the same school now. And I think that should mean
that we would all be treated the same. And if we not, then we
gon' do something about it. That is one thing I know.
I don't say nothing to Mama about it cause I know she won't approve.
So I talk to Jewel, and me and her decide to call a meeting
with all the colored kids at school and put on a demonstration.
We decide we gon' do like the Children's Crusade
that they had in Birmingham when all them children went to jail
to end segregation. We don't think we will go to jail for this.
Segregation is already over. So it shouldn't be that deep.
When the kids in Birmingham did a protest, they just got up from their desks
and walked out of their classrooms. So we decide to do that.
We gon' make signs and everything, and then march around the school
and won't none of us go back in until Mr. Whitlock agree to
let us have our talent show. Everybody done already decided
what they gon' do in the show to show off all of our talent.

When them kids in Birmingham decide they gon' do their walk-out,
they got the DJs on the radio to get together and announce
a secret code that tell the kids what's happening at what time.
So since Quinton is a DJ, I ask him to tell Sweet Willie Wine,
the DJ that have the early morning radio show,
to announce what we doing and ask all the kids to come
to help us with the march. Quinton do just like I ask.
So on the day of the walk out, over 200 colored kids show up
and march around the school. Some of our white friends walk out too.
We hold up signs that say, "Negro children deserve art too!"
At first Mr. Whitlock said that he gon' kick all of us out
until them white kids get up with us and they all walk out.

Cause even the girl who got the part of Juliet in the play
know I did a better job than she did on audition day.
So Mr. Whitlock can't do nothing but agree to let us do
our own talent show. And it was a big deal too.

Some kids recite poetry by James Weldon Johnson and Dunbar
to showcase there are colored poems that's as good as Shakespeare's are.
Me and Jewel and Red act like we the Supremes
and Miz Francis even lend each one of us one of her wigs.
Mama make our dresses out of something from her white lady
so we have long formals and everything. And we all look so pretty.
Maurice Smith was James Brown with a cape and everything.
We end up with a bigger audience than the white play even did.
After that Mr. Whitlock said we can do our own thing every year.
And it became the biggest program they ever have at Jacksonville.

> *Stop! In the name of love*
> *Before you break my heart*

Mr. Whitlock say me and Jewel is always the main people
who want to start a revolution. And he do not want that.
But we was always putting our heads together and figuring out what to do.
And we would get together with Betsy Mae and Red
to remind the white folks they can't treat us any old kind of way.
Carol Jane wouldn't hardly do nothing cause she is a scaredy cat.
But after the demonstration work so good for the talent show,
we got together and start to think about what we could do next.
We always wanting to do what we see on television.
Marches and sit-ins and stuff such as that.
But Mr. Whitlock would finally give in to anything that we asked him.
He took all of the fun out of having a protest.
Cause tho we small in number, we make it up with being loud.
Betsy Mae is the leader of the loud colored bunch.
She came to the white school a whole year earlier.
So she knew the ropes and was good at conning Mr. Whitlock.

Kathya Alexander   **237**

I start messing round with Clinton Moore cause he on the football team.
I know I'm not in love with Clinton or nothing.
But I'm in the 9th grade and Clinton is a junior.
That is the only reason that I start to kicking it with Clinton.
Plus Clinton got a car and he is going to the prom.
That mean I get to go to the junior prom too.
I start cutting school with Clinton. We'd go up to Pinnacle Mountain
and so far my mama ain't learned nothing about it.
Plus I get to wear Clinton's team ring and his football sweater.
That make me look groovy and make all the other girls jealous.
That's what the white girls do. Especially the cheerleaders.
They wear their boyfriends' stuff. But they act like they better
than everybody else. Cheerleaders always like that.
The cheerleaders at the colored school acted like they better too.
My mama white lady's two twin daughters
was cheerleaders before they graduate from the white school.
And my mama get hand-me-downs from her white lady's children.
So I got two uniforms just like the white cheerleaders wear.
I let Carol Jane wear one and I always wear the other
on Fridays when it is time for our Pep Rally day.
I don't get to see Clinton that much after school
since he stay in Jacksonville and not with the coloreds in Uz.
And my Mama say I am too young to receive company yet
so don't even think about going nowhere with no boy.

Whenever my mama let me, I go to the ballfield after school
and play ball with Betsy Mae. All the kids in Uz meet there too.
On Fridays Nikki Davis be out there in the ball field.
Her tennis shoes always clean and her clothes always new.
It is something about Nikki that always make me uncomfortable.
I don't really know her that good so I don't know what it is.
For one thing she always be staring at me.
I wish she wouldn't do that. It always make me feel
like she want something from me. I don't know why I feel that.

But she is real good friends with Carol Jane and Red
since her mama pay them to come and clean up her house.
Nikki she don't like Jewel cause she use to date her boyfriend.
So we don't never really hang out together
when she be in Uz. That is ok with me.
I never would have thought things would turn out like they did.
The way things would change between Nikki and me.

24
PARTY OF TWO

Miz Francis come over to the house and walk straight to the kitchen
where Mama is at. They giggling before she even get good in the door.
They whispering like it's something they don't want me to hear.
Miz Francis almost skipping when she walk cross the floor.
My head done been hurting ever since I woke up.
I been waiting for Mama to finish cooking breakfast
so I can eat to see if that will help my headache.
But now I want to use this chance to get away from my mama.
"Can I go to Miz Francis house, Mama?" I go in and ask her.
"You come back home in a hour," my Mama answer me back.
"They ain't got no school," Miz Francis say. "Let her stay for a while."
"All right," Mama say, "Act like you got some sense."
This week is spring break. And at the white school they give you
the whole week off. The colored school is two days,
Friday and Monday to make up a long weekend.
Miz Francis and Mama start whispering even before the door close.
I walk thru my front yard and on out beside the highway.
I decide not to cut thru Miz Lucille's front yard.

Just as soon as I get to the highway where I can see them,
Red and Carol Jane and Nikki come out of Carol Jane 'nem's house.

I guess Nikki Davis must get a whole week off too.
She go to a colored school, but it's in North Little Rock.
Her mama live over on Baker's Acres.
I think Miz Payday and Nikki think they better than everybody else.
Citified my mama call them. Living over in they brick house.
They pretty much keep to theyself. And with Nikki not living there during the week,
most the time when she in Uz, I don't even know that she here.
Miz Payday always be arranging some kind of demonstrations against
the white folks downtown that own all of the businesses
that discriminate against coloreds. They having another one soon.
Next month they doing protests against Woolworths and Sterlings.
Mama say Miz Payday need to leave the children alone
and leave this Civil Rights mess in the hands of the grownups.
Miz Payday work with Quinton and the students from SNCC.
I think that's another reason that my mama don't like her.
Another person who got Quinton doing something she don't agree with.

Nikki lift her hand up and wave. Carol Jane she look up.
She see me and show her white teeth when she smile.
Carol Jane is the color of the midnite sky.
And her hair is long. A little longer than mine.
"Can you come over to my house later on?"
Nikki she ask me. "We having a party."
"I don't know. I don't think so," I say to Nikki.
"I don't think that my mama is going to let me."
Carol Jane say, "Mama say I can't come unless you come."
That ain't unusual. Since Miz Montgomery really like me
she always want me to be around wherever Carol Jane and Red at.
"Can't you at least ask? Why you acting so funny?"
"I ain't acting funny. It's just that I'm hungry.
I got to go eat cause I got a headache."
Nikki walk over to me and put her hand on my shoulder.

"Are you sure you all right?" Nikki she say.

"Yeah, I'm all right," I say to Nikki.

I move away from her hand. Feel like my skin there is burning.

"We got food at my house. You can eat over there if you want to.
But come over either way around six for the party."

"I'll go ask my mama if I can go to the party."

But something telling me not to go. It just don't feel like I oughta.

"Well, we got to go to the store. You want to walk up there with us?"

"Naw, y'all gone ahead."

"You sho' you all right?" Nikki ask me.

"I keep telling you I'm fine. Why you keep asking me that?"

My voice go up a notch and it get kind of shrilly.

"I was just asking. You ain't got to get mad."

"Yeah, Mandy," Carol Jane say. "Why you acting so silly?"

"If you don't come, then we can't come," Red she say.

Red is real high yellow. She don't look nothing like her sister.

"Sammy Lee 'nem coming. Wait, you'll see.

This party gon' be the best! The least you can do is ask her."

"Ok, ok. I'll ask her. I already told you that.

Y'all ought to come by Jewel's when you come back from the store.

Did you invite Jewel?" Carol Jane drop her head.

I feel like something is up. I feel it down to my core.

All of sudden Nikki ask me, "Mandy, how come you don't like me?"

"Who said I didn't like you?"

"I can tell how you act.

And don't try to deny it. You know I'm telling the truth.

I ain't done nothing to you. So I don't understand."

"I feel like you lying to me. You ain't telling me the truth.

And I know Carol Jane in on it. I can see just like you.

If you want me to like you – and I don't understand that -

but if that's really what you want, you need to tell me the truth."

"Ok. That's a deal. I'm throwing this party for you.

I really want to get to know you. And I couldn't think of no other way

to get you over to my house. Maybe we can be friends."
"That still don't make no sense to me," I say.
"What's this about, Carol Jane?" I look at my friend with a glare.
Carol Jane ain't never been able to lie. She too much like her mama.
Miz Montgomery too nice. And Carol Jane just like that.
If she can't tell you the truth, she rather just to avoid you.
"Yeah, that's the truth. Or least that's what she told me."
But it's something bout the way she say it. She don't look all the way up.
And she give me that goofy smile that she do.
Grinning up on one side. Make her show her dog tooth.
"Y'all still lying to me. If I didn't need to eat,
I would think more about it and try to figure it out."
By now we done walked all the way up the highway
and we standing in the driveway where Jewel 'nem house is at.

"I wish you would let me help you," Nikki say at the driveway.
"Help me do what?" I ask her.
"You look like you hurting real bad."
"So, what? You don't even know nothing about me."
"You dealing with something inside you. Any fool can see that.
I know you hurting from losing your daddy.
I know about that kinda hurting. I lost a daddy myself."
My eyes fill up with tears. Ain't nobody never ask me direct-like
if I had some feelings about Daddy that I want to share.
And ain't nobody wanted to hear bout no hurt.
'Cept to say not to have it. So, I just ain't talked to nobody.
I done kept it inside myself for so long that I'm aching.
And I been getting headaches, I think, from getting back to normal
too quick. Seem like that's all I done heard.
'A.D. would want them kids to get back to normal.'
Mama she kept me out of school for a week.
She let everybody else decide when to go back on they own.

Lucky went back to school the very next day.
Sometimes I wish I could just kick things like Lucky.

Daddy died on a Sunday. And he was right back out on
the football field by the end of school on that Monday.
 I want to run and tackle somebody. Make somebody else feel the hurt.
But that is not something a girl get to do.
Mama don't let me decide nothing. She decide for me herself.
While all the boys in Uz do pretty much what they want to.
But if you a girl, you get called out your name.
Like the day when Miz McQuincy say that I'm belligerent.
That's the main thing about Uz that I do not like.
Why it is that girls get treated so different.
Get put out the church if you pregnant. But if you the boy,
his life do not change. That don't seem fair to me.
But when I say this to Mama, she say what make me think
life got anything to do with fair. That is her answer for everything.
Nikki reach over and wipe a tear from out of my eye.
I didn't even know that I was standing out there crying.
"Thank you, Nikki," I say. She don't seem so strange to me now.
I bet she don't never get to talk to nobody about her daddy neither.

I kick the gravel up when I walk down Jewel long driveway.
I see her standing in the window. She looking like she watching to see
what is going on. I turn back and say to Carol Jane and Nikki,
"I ain't coming if Jewel can't come to the party with me."
Jewel been standing at the door watching the whole carrying on.
She say, "Who that with Carol Jane and Red?" as I walk in the kitchen.
"That's just Nikki. She is having a party.
They was asking me did I want to walk up to Protho Junction."
"She having a party? What kinda party she having?
Is it gon' be some boys there?"
"Yeah, seem like she done invite everybody."
I reach in the cabinet so I can get me a plate.
"Jewel," I ask between bites of tomatoes
sprinkled with pepper and salt. She look at me and say, "Yes?"
"How come we ain't never really talked about my Daddy?"
"I didn't know you wanted to. I thought you was trying to forget."

"Why would I want to forget about my Daddy?"
"Well, that's what I did when I moved in with Mama and Daddy.
I had to forget all about I had another whole family.
That I had sisters I loved. And a brother who loved me best.
That was the baby. Remember that time when you met him?"
I remember a baby with snot hanging from off his nose and his face.
Seem like he had ringworm. And he had a head full of tetter.
"Mama said forget about them. And that's just what I did."
"No you didn't, Jewel," I say. "Sometime we even go visit."
"Yeah, every once in a while, Mama will take me to go see them."
She say, "We can talk about Big Daddy just as much as you need.
"You want me to fix your plate for you?" Jewel a real Southern woman.
Ain't nothing a good meal can't fix in her mind.

Mama say I can go to the party when I go home and I ask her.
Miz Francis still there. And they both look relieved.
I don't know why but they both get a smile on they face.
They want me to go to this party. Maybe even more than me.
Jewel do my hair up in a ball at the top.
She say she do it like that so that when we slow dance
and the boys start to sweating all over you while you dancing,
you can dance all you want and your hair won't turn back.
She pull her hair up too. I put a headband on mine
that just outline the ball. That way when I dance
and my hair start to sweat, the headband will keep it in place.
That way it won't fall all down into my face.
Jewel put on a dickey that have maroon and pink stripes.
Then she pull a v-neck cashmere sweater over her head.
She ask me to make sure that her hair still in place.
I take some hair out her ball and I pull a few strands
in the back on her shoulders. It make her look like she got
hair like white women got. I can't let nothing hang down
if I know I'm gon' be sweating. But it's okay for Jewel
cause Miz Francis done got Jewel's hair relaxed.
Mama won't let me. I ain't gon' even think about it.

How she try to keep me a baby. And it seem like she would
start to change some things now that I done become a woman.
But she ain't changing her mind just cause some blood between my legs.
I still ain't told Jewel that I started my period.
I don't know why. I tell Jewel everything.
But I don't want to tell her about the blood, for some reason.
And she ain't noticed yet. Even tho Jewel start hers
over two years ago. She always have cramps.
If I done been cramping, I ain't noticed it yet.
But, then, all I been thinking about is the pain in my head.
"You ready?" Jewel say, and we walk down her steps.

Me and Jewel walk together over to Bakers Acres.
We walk there down the highway so our feet will stay cute.
If we cut thru the yard, they gon' be all covered with grass.
And I ain't about to get grass stains on my new maroon shoes.
We can hear the music soon as we come out of Jewel's house.
I can hear Gladys Knight singing her record about the grapevine.
If I hadda only knowed when I walked out of that house,
what I know now. How the name would be mine
that was being sung all over the grapevine.
But, wait, I'm getting ahead of myself.
From now on, whenever I hear Gladys Knight and the Pips,
I will remember a angel. And about God and His ways
even tho it's been years since I saw the angel.
Seem like all that stuff Mama told me don't have nothing to do
with me being chose to do anything.
But all I had to do was wait to see what God was gon' do.

> *Just about, just about, just about, just about*
> *To lose my mind*
> *Oh, yes I am*

25
TIMBREL AND DANCE

Me and Jewel walk up into Nikki front yard.
Sammy Lee and Marcellus is hanging out on the steps.
Jewel act like she gon' walk right by Sammy Lee.
But he pull on her arm, and they go round the house.
I go on in the living room. The door is wide open.
I see Carol Jane and Nikki standing by the punch bowl.
They both turn to look at me when I walk in.
Nikki she smile. Carol Jane she come over
to where I'm standing. She just glad not to be home.
Glad that Miz Montgomery let her go somewhere.
"Where Red at?" I ask her.
"She somewhere outside.
All the girls that's got boyfriends is somewhere out there."
"Dance with me, Mandy," Nikki say all of a sudden.
The room is lit dim and she got a lava lamp on.
"I don't feel like dancing right now, Nikki," I tell her.
"Maybe I'll dance with you later on."

It ain't nothing unusual about girls dancing together.
In Uz we do it together all of the time.
Cause our mamas usually don't let us be around boys.
So we just dance with each other. Actually, most of the time.
Nikki walk over and grab Clarence. With his green-eyed self.
Got eyes that look like they belong on a cat.
Clarence put down his cup on the table by the punchbowl.
Then he follow Nikki to the center of the room and they dance.
James Brown is singing about it being a man's world.
Clarence acting like he James Brown. He keep shaking his head
like he got processed hair that's falling all over his face.
Clarence acting a fool, with his crazy self.

Just then one of my favorite songs comes on.
I love Little Stevie Wonder. And this is my song!
It's another slow dance. So everybody keeps dancing.
I move into the corner to give everybody more room.
Any other time, I would be dancing too.
But everybody else is already all paired up.
So I'm just standing on the edges all by myself.
The lava lamp make the room spin round slow motion-like.
The words of the song slipping and sliding in my head
and then travel down a dark tunnel to the bottom of my heart.
I stand and sway in time to the music.
I close my eyes and move my body back and forth.

> *With a child's heart*
> *We'll face the worries of the day*

All of a sudden, I feel somebody's arms round my waist.
I open my eyes. Everybody looking at me.
I'm standing in the middle of the living room crying.
I didn't even know it. And Nikki the one got her arms around me.
Nikki guide me around to the back of the house.
Then she wrap both of her arms around me again.

I lay my head on her shoulder like that's where it belong.
My heart feel like it's breaking into little droplets like rain.

"Why you crying, Mandy?" Nikki ask me and hand me some tissue.
She sit down on the steps that lead onto the patio.
I ain't never seen no patio except in magazines and on television.
I think Miz Payday and Ricky Lee must be rolling in dough.
The thing I like most about Nikki is that she don't never ask,
'You *still* missing your daddy?' like everybody else do.
That's why I don't never talk to nobody about him no more.
It's like there's a deadline to sadness and I done passed it for sure.
I don't care that Daddy done been dead for two years.
My heart *still* hurt for him each and every day.
 And Nikki seem to be the only one who understand.
That make me like her now. Cause she make me feel safe.

"I didn't even know I was crying," I say. And it's the truth.
But as soon as I say it, the tears they start up again.
Seem like I been doing this forever since my daddy died.
Start to cry about things. And don't even know that I am.
But this time I know. "I just miss my Daddy.
I miss my Daddy so much sometimes that it hurts.
I still can't believe I ain't gon' never touch him again.
Can't believe I won't never sit again on his lap.
That's all it is. I just miss my Daddy.
Miss the man who made me the thing that I am."
"I'm just glad that you got the chance to know your daddy.
Glad he was somebody who was worth being sad
about. What's the thing you miss most about not having your daddy?"
"It's so many things, Nikki, I can't even list them.
I miss the way his car sounded on the gravel when he got home from work.
And I also miss the smell our house had.
A sweet mixture of his sweat and Royal Crown in the steam
that the bathroom had on Sunday mornings after he finished getting dressed."
"Why don't you spend the nite with me, Mandy?

Mama is going out and we'll have the house all to ourselves."
"I don't think my Mama gon' let me."
"I'll tell my Mama to go ask her herself."
Just then Jewel walk up on us from around the side corner.
She look at us both funny. Then she reach out her hand.
She say, "We can leave any time you want to, Mandy.
This party ain't nothing… Oh, hi, Nikki," she say.
"It ain't that I'm saying that your party ain't nothing.
I just want to take care of Mandy."
"Where Sammy Lee?" Nikki say.
"Don't know and don't care." Seem like Jewel spit that at Nikki.
Nikki just laugh in her throat. "Come on, Mandy," Jewel say again.
"Good night, Nikki," I say. "I will see you tomorrow.
And thank you for everything. You really helped me today."
We start to walking cross Cud'n Thetta's back yard.
We get to Jewel house first. She stop and look back.
"Mandy, you sure you all right?"
"Yeah. Don't worry. I'm skrait."
When I get to my house, I walk around to the front.

Most times, I usually just go in the back door
when I take the shortcut thru Cud'n Thetta's side yard.
But this particular nite, I decide not to do that.
Instead I walk around our house so I can go in our front door.
The first thing I notice when I reach the side of the house
is Deke Jones's car parked around on the other side.
Now this is a side of the house that don't nobody never park on.
This the side of the house people park at when they trying to hide.
Cause it is partially hid by the corn stalks and the peas
that Daddy had growing on two and a half of our acres.
I have seen Deke Jones a lot since the funeral.
I don't think nothing about it. He was a friend of my daddy's.
The front porch light is on. Maybe that's why they can't see me.
But I can see them real clear thru the windows cut in the door.
You know them doors that's got the three rectangles in them?

Well, on our front door, we got us some of those.
I lean into the glass just to open the door,
and I see Deke Jones and Mama sitting on the small couch
that sets directly across from the front door.
Mama's feet on the coffee table. And he got his hands up her dress!

I push the door open and Mama cover up her legs
real fast with a blanket she got throwed cross the couch.
Deke Jones so much into what he is doing,
he don't even hear the door. His head don't turn around.
Mama say, "Hey, Mandy. You sho' is home early."
Deke Jones get the message and get his hands from between her legs.
"I wasn't expecting you 'til sometime after 10 o'clock."
She steadily closing her thighs and pulling down her dress.
"Mama, can I stay all nite with Nikki?
It ain't no school tomorrow." Mama she look relieved.
She say, "Yeah, I thank that will be all right.
Make sho' you get some pajamas and a change of clothes that is clean."
My head is pounding as I walk down the hallway.
I can't hardly see as I gather up my clothes.
My head is throbbing to the beat of angel wings.
And it feel like ain't no air still left in my room.
When I get back in the living room and I can see the couch,
Deke Jones is on one side and Mama sitting way over on the other.
They whispering and giggling like two silly teenagers
who mama done walked in on them doing some heavy petting.
"Nite, Mandy," Deke Jones say. "You have fun at the party."
I don't even say nothing. I just walk on out the house.
I can hear Mama yelling something out at me.
But I just keep walking. I don't even turn around.

My mind is racing while I walk back over to Nikki's.
I'm so mad at my mama that I can't hardly see.
If she had walked in on me doing what I just saw her doing,
she probably wouldn't never get thru whipping me.

No wonder she is ready for me to get over missing Daddy.
She ready to get on with her life so she want me to get on with mine.
And if that wasn't bad enuf by itself,
she sitting there with some man who got a wife!
A married man! Good God up in heaven.
Miz First Lady sitting there getting felt up like a slutty teenager.
Well, I guess she definitely ain't no first lady no more.
The way that she acting is just like a whore.
I'm so tired of everybody being so hypocritical.
I think back on Easter Sunday when she get so mad at me.
Her not wanting me to embarrass her in the public!
But I guess it's all right if the things you do is things can't be seen.

Nikki standing over in a corner by the kitchen door.
She laughing and talking to Carol Jane and Red.
Red is the first person who notice I'm back.
"Hey, Mandy," she say. "What you got in that bag?"
"I got clothes for tomorrow. I'm gon' spend the nite with Nikki.
If you sure it's all right with your Mama, that is."
"Yeah. Let's take your things back into my bedroom.
Come on. Follow me. I got two twin beds.
And Trisha and Lil Ricky is at my grandmother's
so we will have the whole house all to ourselves
until Mama get back. No telling when that will be.
Since her and Ricky Lee separated, I can't never tell."
I put down my clothes and go back in the living room.
And then I pull Nikki out onto the dance floor.
People start to leave the party around 11:30.
By midnite, everybody done pretty much gone home.

Carol Jane and Red had to leave at ten.
I told you they mama don't hardly let them out of the house.
When the last person leave, me and Nikki start to clean up.
Miz Payday left with a man about a hour ago.
Me and Nikki go to the kitchen and start washing dishes.

Miz Payday had told her the party better not go
on much past eleven. And she said she would check.
She asked Miz Irma next door to check just to make sure.
Said she was gon' look to make sure the lights was all out.
And if they wasn't she was gon' give us trouble for sure.
"This my mama's first date," Nikki say all embarrassed.
"Since Ricky Lee moved out, she acting just like a whore."
"I know just what you mean," I say to Nikki.
"No you don't," Nikki say. "Maw Belle don't act that way."
"You would be surprised. She ain't the saint that you think.
Since my daddy died, seem like everything done changed.
Don't your mama do all them protests and demonstrations?
Do she ever let you go to any of them with her?"
"Yeah, she always make me take a part in the protests."
"Think I could go with y'all sometime? When is the next one?"
"Maw Belle gon' let you take a part in a protest?
I didn't think she was down for all the demonstrations and stuff."
"She don't care bout my daddy. So I don't care about her neither.
Just let me know when y'all going to do the next one."
"Ok," Nikki say. "Let's go outside on the patio."
We thru with the dishes. She grab a blanket off the bed.
We go out in the back and lay it down on the beach chairs.
Then Nikki act like she falling and end up in my arms.
Then the air stop moving. And I know she gon' kiss me.
When she do, she slip the tip of her tongue in my mouth.
I ain't saying that I ain't never kissed no boys or nothing.
But I ain't never been French kissed like that except once.

"Nikki, you a bulldagger?" I ask all of a sudden.
I hadn't planned to ask that. The words are Mama's not mine.
"That's a nasty word. And I know I ain't nasty."
Nikki look at me like she got a bad taste in her mouth.
"But if you mean do I like girls as well as boys,
then I guess the answer to that question would be yes.
I have made love to girls. And I've let some boys kiss me."

"Don't you think that's strange? Having sex with a girl?"

"Mandy, Mandy, Mandy…" Nikki sing out my name.

She sing it to the tune of that Stevie Wonder song.

"I think God put me in your life just to show you

that you can't let people tell you what's right and what's wrong.

You ever hear the story about Peter and the blanket of food

that God handed him down from heaven one day?"

I know this story well. My daddy even let me preach the sermon.

"God told Peter, how dare you call what I make

something nasty?" Nikki say to me. And then I tell her,

"But God wasn't talking about no unnatural acts."

"What makes a thing unnatural?"

"Against the laws in the Bible."

"Well, if that's the case, how come all us still eat pork?

The Old Testament say don't eat nothing with a split hoof.

I know some Muslims who think that is the sign of the beast."

"Mama say all the Black Muslims going straight to hell."

"I ain't saying nothing against your Mama but you need to think for yourself."

Then Nikki get up and start to fold up the blanket.

The mosquitos getting worse so we about to go in.

I feel like it's something in this conversation I am not getting.

Something that start with Deke Jones and his hands between Mama's legs.

"So you saying it ain't no difference between right and wrong?"

"I'm saying 'wrong' is denying what the Good Lord have to offer.

His ways are not our ways nor are His thoughts our thoughts.

I'm standing here offering you a sympathetic shoulder

for you to cry on. But you would rather cry in a room

full of people who don't care nothing about you.

And you judging me as something less than yourself?

I ain't the one everybody at that party think is crazy."

My head start to swell. And my heart almost stop.

These the same words that the angel say to me.

"Mandy you all right?"

"I saw a angel one time, Nikki.

My Mama say she seen the same angel too.

She say it come to the special women in our family.

And the angel said the exact words that you just said to me."

"What you mean you saw a angel?" Nikki ask me.

"I saw her behind the church on Easter Sunday.

She say, 'His ways ain't our ways and we don't think like He think."

"I love you, Mandy," Nikki say all of a sudden.

"I wanted to say that to you all nite long."

"A girl can't love another girl, Nikki."

"God's ways ain't our ways and His thoughts ain't our thoughts."

And then she kiss me. And I do not pull away.

I remember the other thing that the angel say when I saw her.

So even tho me and Nikki kissing, I still remember to pray.

26
BLACK POWER

I am watching Stokely Carmichael on the television
and shelling purple hull peas. We been shelling all week.
I am sitting on the floor with a bowl between my legs.
My thumb is sore and my fingers purple and green.
Every year about this time our three acres of land
is full of crowder peas, black-eyed peas, peas of every kind.
And so now all I can do every day after school
is shell peas and more peas. My fingers hurt all the time.

Outside in the yard, the chrysanthemums drooping and raggedy.
I had ask my mama if we could plant some this year
since they was Daddy's favorites. She didn't want to, but she said yes.
But now the smell make my head hurt and fill my heart up with fear.
The willows who weep try to reach into our windows.
They scratch their slithery fingers up against the old screens.
Seems like I been feeling fear a whole lot here lately.
And the words of the angel just will not leave my head.
His ways ain't our ways and His thoughts ain't our thoughts.

To me that seem to mean that things not gon' go the way
I think they should go. Cause God don't think like I do.
I can't talk to nobody about this except Nikki
when she home on the weekends now that school is done started.
We were together all summer. And now she staying in Uz more
than she used to since Miz Payday and Ricky Lee separated.
Miz Payday always going to some kind of meeting or another
so me and Nikki babysit. My mama don't like it.
But up until now she ain't stopped me from being with her.
But now everything about me and Mama done change.
She so mad at me now, all we do is argue and fuss.

I listen close to the speech that Stokely Carmichael is making.
He is part of James Meredith's March Against Fear.
James Meredith was the first colored man to integrate
the law school at the University of Mississippi.
He had planned to do the march pretty much by hisself
from Memphis, Tennessee to Jackson, Mississippi
to show that signing the Civil Rights Bill
and the Voting Rights Act ain't made one bit of difference
in the lives of most colored people all over the South.
He had ask only a few colored men to come and march with him
cause he didn't want all the press that come with King and white people.
But on the second day of his walk, a white man had shot him.
Thank God he didn't die. Mama say it just go to show you
how tired white folks is of all these marches and stuff.
"He just lucky that white man just shoot him with buckshot,"
Mama say. "Cause it sho' coulda been a whole lot worse."

After he got shot, Negroes come from everywhere.
The Southern Christian Leadership Conference led by Rev. King
and the Student Non-Violent Coordinating Committee,
the young people's arm of the Civil Rights Movement,
which was led by Stokely Carmichael at that time,
come to carry on the march in James Meredith's name.

And they ended up with almost 15,000 Negroes
who marched off and on during those 220 miles.
When the marchers arrived in Greenwood, Mississippi
and tried to set up camp at Stone Street Negro Elementary
the police came and arrested Stokely Carmichael
and charged him with trespassing on public property.

The police held him for hours before he can rejoin the march
at the local park where the marchers have set up camp
and was beginning to do a night-time rally.
15,000 Negroes! I will never forget the sight.
White folks went crazy seeing all of these Negroes
all together at one time, marching and singing freedom songs.
And since this is the first all Negro demonstration,
even the white folks who like us is tired of all these Negroes.
Rev. King and Stokely Carmichael been arguing the whole week
cause Stokely Carmichael call us Black for the first time on television
and Rev. King was calling us Negroes like everybody always do.
But even Rev. King was saying Black by the time the march was over.

"That man is crazy," my Mama she say.
"I thought King was crazy but I done seen everything now.
I ain't black. Just look at our skin.
All of us is the same color of chocolate brown."
"Black don't have nothing to do with color,"
my brother Quinton turn and say to my mama.
"Is white folks the same color as the white paint on the walls?
No. But don't nobody say nothing because white is always better.
That's what Stokely is saying," Quinton he explain.
"Stop letting them make you think that black is less.
The white supremacy machine will keep running over you
as long as they can get you to think like that."

Quinton come home in the evening so he can help with pea picking.
Even Lucky have to help after his football practice.

I agree with everything that Quinton is saying
but Mama already mad at me so I do not say nothing.
But I don't know, is what I'm thinking to myself.
Cause whenever you get in a argument with one of your friends,
the thing that will hurt somebody's feelings the worse
is if you say to them, "You ole black thang."
Playing the dozens is a game that is based on that.
"Yo' mama so black…" it always start out.
But Stokely Carmichael is saying that Black is beautiful.
This is something that excite me just to think about.
Cause now Stokely Carmichael is saying that our blackness can't hurt us.
That my nappy hair and full lips is a good thing, not bad.
After going to the white school for over a year
that is a thought that I like to have in my head.
Cause when you see the white girls keep getting chose for prom queen
and everything else, it start to get to you.
So I hold Stokely Carmichael's words in a corner of my heart,
but I just keep shelling these peas like Mama tell me to do.

They showing Stokely Carmichael back from the police station.
He mad as all get out, and he just jump up on
the speaker's platform and almost run over Rev. King!
He just take to the stage and grab the microphone
out of Rev. King's hand and start yelling Black Power.
Rev. King look like he tired. Like he is about to cry.
Like he know he done lost control over the demonstration
cause the whole march is in the hands of the young people now.

Stokely explain to all the people watching on the television
that Black Power ain't got nothing to do with no violence.
He say we have tried to get white people to do the right thing
thru Civil Rights legislation and thru forced integration
and Black people is still getting killed by the Klan.
James Meredith had tried to not even draw a crowd
and even then he got shot by a white man.

So now Stokely Carmichael say Black folks have got to organize
and take control of our own communities for our own self
since it is clear that white folks don't want us to be a part
of their communities and political institutions.
He say we need to build a machine of our own.
And he say that we need to demonstrate against the police
and to defend ourselves from their brutality and aggression.
He say it is them who is violent but they want us to think
we wrong when we defend ourself against their oppression.
Since our demonstration at school last year turn out a success,
I been thinking about all the other things that we can do.
Now after listening to Stokely Carmichael the thing I decide
is to start a Negro student club at the high school.
And I decide I'm gon' call it the Black Student Association.
Nobody else in Uz done start to call theyself Black.
But now Mama done found out about me and Nikki,
so I don't know how that is going to affect all my plans.

By now everybody done started to talk
about me and Nikki. This relationship we have.
For the longest time, me and Mama pretend
like ain't nothing no different. Like there ain't no whispering.
No elephant in the room. But I guess Mama done tripped
over it one time too many. Now I know that she know
cause she hit me this morning in the face with my diary
where I done wrote down all of my secret thoughts.
She got some kinda nerve. That is what I keep thinking.
If this ain't the pot calling the kettle black, I don't know what it is.
She can have a secret relationship with a married man,
but get mad at me about Nikki. I thought a sin was a sin.

After the party that nite, me and Nikki go crazy.
All that we want to do is be in each other's arms.
We could only see each other during the school year on the weekends
since she stay with her grandmaw the whole week long.

We spent the whole summer together. And I did not have one headache.
Nikki buy me stuff and Miz Payday do too.
Mama ain't crazy about it, but she didn't say nothing about it.
And she let me stay over Nikki's as much as I want to.
Mainly cause I think so she can be with Deke Jones.
She act like she just being nice but I know that's what it is.
Her and Deke Jones is still sneaking around,
so she don't care what I do long as she is with him.
All summer long Nikki had been home with her mama.
Now that school start, I been staying all night every weekend.
Miz Payday know all about me and Nikki too now.
But all she say to us is to be more discreet.

The first time it happen, the first time we got caught,
was when I sent Nikki a homemade sweetheart's card.
Miz Payday opened it. It had curlicues on it
and twisted red ribbons turned to satin music notes.
I had spent hours working on that card.
The sweetheart's card was meant to be a song.
I poured all my love onto the poster board.
But I guess it musta sung out too loud.
I guess it sung out too strong.
However it happen, it was the card Nikki mama
got her hands on. But I can't say nothing bad
about Miz Payday cause she was cool when it happen.
She just sat us both down and told us for the first time,
"Y'all need to be more discreet. Mandy, suppose your Mama
had gotten this card instead of me."
But me and Nikki don't know how to be nothing different.
Don't know how to be nothing except what we being.
Two girls with hearts that is as big as heaven.
With a love that drown us and take away our breath.
When school start, I had start to keep a diary.
It was something I saw Gidget do on television.
So much done happened since the nite of the party.

The nite that I dance to that Little Stevie Wonder song.
The nite that I open my heart up to Nikki.
The nite that I know what it feel like to be in love.
What it feel like to be happy. Seem like I had forgot.
Sometime I feel like a part of me died alongside my daddy.
Nikki's love for me make me come alive again.
Now you tell me what about that is so wrong.
Nikki say I am everything she ever wanted.
All that she live for. It's as simple as that.
She make me feel just like my Daddy use to.
Like I can't do nothing wrong. I love feeling like that.
Feeling so accepted. For just what I am.
And nothing I do gon' affect our love at all.
Nobody ever love me like that. Nobody but Nikki.
Except for my Daddy. And my Daddy been dead for such a long
time. Me and Mama been fussing so much,
sometime I feel like she don't love me at all.
She too busy making out all the time with Deke Jones.
Letting him feel her up all up and down her legs.
But she mad at me. She is such a big hypocrite.
She say me and Nikki is sinning and we gon' go straight to hell.
I wonder do she think God like what she is doing
having my Daddy's friend rubbing her all over her legs.

Mama was greasing my scalp that nite when there was a knock on the door.
I jump up so fast, I knock the grease and brush on the floor.
I answer the door with my hair all over my head.
I know that it's Nikki. I just know that it is.
Cause her and Miz Payday had their court date that day.
Nikki testified too, and I want to hear what she say.
Cause Miz Payday done swore that Ricky Lee ain't gon' have
a dime for his new woman. And no place to live.
Turn out Nikki stepdaddy had been running around
with a bartending woman on the other side of town.
Miz Payday had found out about it when she found a receipt

for a watch he had bought her. And she have a fit.

"Gal, sit down and quit running like you is crazy,"
Mama say while I got my hand still on the knob.
"You ain't leaving this house. I want you to know that Mandy.
Don't let it cross yo' mind. Don't even thank about it."
I can see Nikki thru the window in the door.
I'm going. I don't care what my Mama say.
She ain't never liked Nikki much. Always said she is funny.
And if I hang around with her, people will look at me that way.
Nikki is smiling. She is beckoning me out.
Miz Payday got the motor still running in the car.
I look back at Mama who is waiting to see
if I am going to flat-out disobey her.
I grab my headscarf and quick as a flash,
I am out the door and onto the ground.
I can hear Mama screaming my name out behind me.
I pretend I don't hear. I start talking loud
so Miz Payday won't hear my mama calling me neither.
Me and Nikki both exchange a quick, secret glance.
Mama not dressed. She is in her nightgown.
So she won't come after me. Or at least I thought that.

Nikki and Miz Payday is laughing and giggling.
They been shopping all day with the first check that they get
from Ricky Lee Davis and his other woman.
They feeling like victory. And they want me to share in it.
Miz Payday say, "I got something for you."
"Something for me?" I ask her real shy.
Nikki say, "Yeah, just wait 'til you see it."
I look at the stars that is throwed cross the sky
like a quilt or something. Something that's been sewed there.
The night is real dark and real clear and real crisp.
The wind is whispering like the other gossips in Uz.
Danger, it is saying to me. Danger. Beware.

We had been in Nikki's house for about ten minutes
when my Mama throw open they back side door wide.
And she just bust on in. She fuss out Miz Payday.
Call her no kind of a mama. To take somebody's chile
when they Mama done told 'em that they cannot go.
Miz Payday she just keep rolling her neck while she saying,
"How was I suppose to know what in the hell that you said?"
Mama grab me by the arm and pull me out the house with her.
Miz Payday keep trying to say something to Mama.
My mama keep walking and smacking me on my butt.
She done pulled a switch off a tree from somewhere
while she was walking. When we get to our house,
she start screaming and beating me. Saying how crazy I am.
"Don't you never leave this house when I tell you you can't.
Is you crazy, Mandy? Is that what you is?"
I don't say a word. It ain't nothing to say.
I just keep putting my hands on my butt and my back
trying to stave off the lightning that live in the switch.
Every time she hit me, it feel like a electrical shock.
"You ain't to leave this house no more after school,"
Mama say when she get tired of beating on me.
"Now you go to bed and learn to act like you oughta.
You better learn how to act like you have got some sense."
"You don't care about nothing but Deke Jones," I say to my mama.

"What you say to me? I know you crazy now."
"Quit beating on me." I have not shed one tear.
She raise her hand up in surprise and in shock.
"Mama," I say. "Don't you hit me no more."
I am looking her dead in the eye.
I think that is why she stop anyway.
Cause I guess it ain't no fun if I ain't crying and screaming.
This is the first time I ever look her in her face
and stand toe to toe. I don't know what come over me.

But I know that something inside me done changed.
I look at her like I dare her to hit me again.
"Girl, if you don't get out of my face, I might go to jail,"
Mama say. But she don't hit me no more.
I turn on my heel and walk into my bedroom.
Something done happen inside me. I don't know what it is.
But I know that everything between me and Mama done changed.

All the next day, I just laid in my bed
putting castor oil on all of my whelps.
Carol Jane and Red come by the house.
They scratch on the screen just as quiet as a mouse.
They give me the present from Nikki. But I don't let them in.
I talk to them out of my window. Carol Jane is real sad.
She say Nikki tell her to tell me that she
love me and that she is thinking about me.
Her mama won't let her come over to my house.
She say the way my mama act make Miz Payday want to knock her out.
After the way my mama acted, I want to hurt her myself.
But I don't say this out loud. I keep that thought to myself.
I open the package that Carol Jane give to me.
It is a little heart and chain that's made out of real gold.
I ain't never had nothing made out of real gold before.
I can feel the tears sliding out my eyes down my nose.
Everybody in Uz got a opinion about me and Nikki.
Got a opinion about what me and her is all about.
I just wish everybody would just mind they own business.
Wish they would focus on they own life and keep our names out their mouths.
But me and Nikki is the new gossip in Uz.
Me and her ain't been too careful about the love that we share.
I been telling myself that we acting like any two good friends.
But I know that ain't true. I just been fooling myself.

At the end of his speech, Stokely keep screaming Black Power!
And all the people in the crowd scream the words back at him.

Mama tell Quinton to get up and turn the television off
and she tell all of us to bring the peas in the kitchen
so she can blanche them to get them ready for the deep freezer.
The walls is almost dripping from all of the steam.
I get up and pour all my peas in the huge iron cooker,
and listen to Quint and Mama argue while I get ready for bed.
She really mad at me now but she taking it out on Quinton.
But Quinton don't care. He say he gon' do what is right.
That mean he gon' keep working in the Civil Rights Movement
and he gon' see who he want to. Don't care if she white.
Mama keep saying she is scared for her children.
She say me and Quinton act like we some kinda fools.
Quinton ask her what I done that make her think I am foolish.
She just say she should have never let me go to the white school.
She don't say nothing about what I said about Deke Jones.
She ain't said nothing about Nikki neither but it's just a matter of time
that she try to turn everybody who love me against me.
But when Quinton find out he just tell me that I
need to be more careful about the things that I'm doing.
He say what me and Nikki do is nobody's business.
And he tell me I can see her when I come to his house.
But it's gon' be a long time before Mama gon' let me
out of this house that she done turn into my prison.
School and back home is all that she let me do.
But I'm gon' find a way to keep seeing Nikki.
And I'm gon' do it even if it mean that I have to skip school.

I like what Stokely was saying about being in control
of your own life. Not letting the people in authority
determine your destiny. I'm gon' do what he said
both at the white school and when it come to me and Nikki.
I don't care what Mama say. What she think is old fashion.
And what the people in Uz think is old fashion too.
I decide I'm gon' start to wear my hair in a Afro.
What difference do it make? Cause people gon' do

whatever they want to when it comes to making judgments.
No matter what I do, they gon' decide that I'm bad.
Miz McQuincy do it at the colored school and I wasn't even doing nothing.
So I'm gon' take control of my life just like Stokely Carmichael said.

The next year we talk about starting the Black Student organization.
Everybody want to do it but we can't agree on the name.
We sitting in the lunch room at the colored student table.
We all sit at the same table except for Tommy McDade.
He sit with the football team. It is mostly white boys.
But since Tommy live on the air base, that is the people that he
be around more than he be around us anyway.
But he couldn't go to the white school before last year
so he always went to the same school as all the colored kids.
I been knowing Tommy since we was all in the first grade.
He was in the A Group in Miz Jennings classroom like I was.
It was me and him and Cookie Johnson and Calvin James.
We the smartest kids. And Miz Jennings would always
have us help out the other kids with all of their lessons.
So I ain't got nothing against Tommy sitting with the white kids.
We gon' decide and then tell him. He'll go along with the program.

Some people don't want the club to be called Black nothing.
But most of them had watched Stokely Carmichael when he
did his Black Power speech that nite on the television.
Everybody in Uz was watching the same thing on TV.
So I finally decide we gon' go with that name
cause we had been arguing the whole lunch and it was almost time
for the lunch bell to ring. So all 20 of us voted
and all of us voted for the Black name except five.

At the white school, they don't let the Black people really do nothing.
It still ain't no Black kids in the plays. And it sho' ain't no cheerleaders.
So we decide the Black Student Association gon' put on our own prom.
The white kids welcome to come. That would make for more people

since it is still so few of us Black kids at the white school.
We all decide that we gon' wear some daishikis.
Our theme for the prom is Black Is Beautiful.
But we know we got to get a couple of the white teachers
to agree to be chaperones. Some of the white teachers treat us
like we ain't no different than the white students sometimes.
And the white teachers who act like they don't really like us
just stay out of our way. And so that is just fine.
When we go and tell Mr. Whitlock we want a prom for the Black kids
he say no like he always do when we ask the first time.
And when I explain to him like Stokely always talking about
how he has no moral compass, he look at me like I done lost my mind.
Since now Clinton a senior, I get to go to the white prom
that the school have every year. Mama already made the dress.
She don't know Clinton my boyfriend. Thought he had just asked me again.
This was before she found out about Nikki so she had said yes.

But when I tell my mama about us having a Black prom,
she say she ain't buying me two dresses. She say that is just crazy.
But since I am going to the white prom and the Black prom too,
I can't wear the same thing to both. I need to get a daishiki
to wear to the Black prom. We all gon' dress like we African.
Mama could make me a daishiki but she don't think that I need
to go around dressing like some Africans no way.
She said she might change her mind about the white prom the way that I been
acting here lately. She tell me don't forget
that I am still on punishment 'til she say that I'm not.
But she done already told me that I could go to the white prom,
but she ain't gon' spend one dime on me after that. Not a one!
She didn't take me off punishment until the middle of summer.
I thought I was gon' die stuck in that hot house all the time.
We still tipping around each other like strangers.
And when school start this year, she don't know that I'm
skipping school so I can go to see Nikki.
She gon' kill me if she ever find out.

But right now I got to worry about the dress for the Black prom.
Worry about one thing at a time is the way that I thought.
I am so disappointed that I decide to just pray
since this whole Black prom idea is one that I thought up.
I call Sissy in Illinois and ask her to talk to Mama for me
since I know that she know how to soften Mama up.
And since the angel told me that God's ways ain't my ways,
I still believe that a miracle is always ready to happen.
As soon as I think that, I hear thunder outside.
And I believe that mean God is telling me He is listening.

27
A GIFT FROM A KING

The air today is real hot and humid
from the storm that come thru yesterday.
It is only April but it feel like summer.
Inside the house feel like 100 degrees
from the water that's boiling in the iron cooker.
The sun bake everything on the back porch.
The tin tub that's hanging on the outside wall
shine orange from the rays of the evening sun.

"Don't bring them nasty clothes in here,"
Mama say to Quinton when he get home from work.
He got a new job on a garbage truck.
"You leave them clothes out on that porch."
Quinton get undressed outside the kitchen door.
First his shoes and then his shirt.
Everything he got on stink to high heaven
and his hair and face covered up with dirt.
Since Quint got this new job he been staying with us.

He ride to work on the truck every day
with Mr. Willie Lee Williams and Mr. Mose Sampson.
Cause both of them work on the garbage truck too.

I drag the tin tub off of the wall.
Mama got the water heating up on the stove.
We use to bathe like this every day
before they bring running water to Uz.
But even tho we got a real bathroom now
and don't have to use the tin tub no more,
Mama won't let Quint come in the house
'til he done cleaned hisself up some.
I hate this job that Quinton got!
He ain't been working there but a week
but he come home stinking like a toilet
and it's done made more work for me.

Mama lift the big cooker from off the stove
and hand it to Quint thru the back door.
Sweat is running down all our face.
That make me just hate his job even more.
Because now this is my daily job
to get Quinton's tub and water ready.
Mama put the water on at four o'clock
so when he get home, everything be ready
for him to clean hisself up with.
Quint pour the hot water in the tub.
Then he go round to the faucet out back
and fill the heavy cooker up
with cold water. He do this two more times.
He pour the cold water in the tub
until it's cool enuf for him to get in it.
Then I leave so he can take off the rest of his clothes.
He strip down to his underpants
right outside in the back yard.

Then he hold the hose over his head
and shake it back and forth while the water run
thru his hair. Finally he get in the tub.
He set hisself down with a sigh.
I can hear him but I'm sho' not looking.
I wouldn't like to have to bathe outside.

Quint working on the truck to get money for college.
He going to Philander Smith.
A lot of Black people go there who from Little Rock.
He got a music scholarship.
But he still need money for books and stuff.
He even going to stay in the dormitory.
He could stay at home my mama tell him.
Staying at the school is a waste of money.
But Quint say that he want to have
what he call a real college experience.
Quinton say stuff like this all the time.
He my second brother that's done been to college.
Jake just got two semesters to go
before he graduate with his Bachelor's and Masters too
from the college in Conway. Him and Vernell go together.
They in a special program they have at that school.

Since Mama think Quint is wasting money,
she say he gon' have to earn it for hisself.
That's why Quint working as a garbage man.
"One monkey don't stop no show," he say under his breath
when Mama tell him to get a job.
He ask Uncle Jesse to talk to Governor Faubus
about getting a job at the Capitol where Daddy use to work.
Now Uncle Jesse the one who empty trash for the Governor.
Governor Faubus tell Uncle Jesse being a garbage man
is the quickest way for Quint to make some money.
The garbage workers in Little Rock is on strike

just like them garbage men over to Memphis
who marching with Rev. Martin Luther King.
They marching to get better conditions.
I can see why mo' better now that Quint on a truck
cause what they have to do is just plain old nasty.

Quint don't really want to cross the line.
He say Governor Faubus just think he slick
cause our church is helping SNCC in the strike.
The new pastor let them use it to organize stuff.
Quint say Gov. Faubus must have found out.
Uncle Jesse say, "He ain't said nothing about it to me tho."
I hear him and Mama talking after I went to bed.
I hear them thru my bedroom door.
Quinton do not want to ask him for no help.
He call Governor Faubus a segregationist.
But Mama tell him what his politics is
should not make Quinton one bit of difference
if it help him to get where he need to go.
This another thing him and Mama argue about.
Quint say his friends at SNCC would never forgive him
if they ever actually found out.

Mama tell Quint, "You need that job.
That's a good job. It pay good money."
Quint say, "All money ain't good money. You know that Mama."
Mama say, "All money good money when you ain't got it.
That's what we left Down Home for Quinton.
So you chir'en could have a chance to go to college.
I don't know why them men on strike any way.
Colored folks need to be thankful that they got a job."
"You done seen the way I come in here looking.
Maggots falling from out my hair.
Nobody should have to work in conditions like that.
That's why they hire Black folks to do it. It just ain't fair."

Mama say, "I ain't never seen a time
when fair had nothing to do with life."
If life was fair, my mama say she reckon,
them people wouldn'tna killed Jesus Christ.
"Old man Faubus just offered me that job
to see if I was going to take it.
He know about me working with SNCC
and he gon' use this job to try to stop me."

"Mandy," Quint call. "I'm ready for my hair."
I take the foot tub out to the porch.
I pour the water over Quinton's head.
The water that is in the tub
is cloudy now. So I can't see thru it.
I pour some water over his head and face.
Quint put some shampoo on his palms
and rub his hands all thru his head.
"Ewww!" I scream, and I drop the foot tub.
Two maggots fall out from out his head.
This is why I hate this job Quint got.
He come home with maggots all over him every day.
They don't even give them a place to shower
once the work they do on the truck is done.
So they have to drive home smelling like rotten meat
and with nasty things crawling all over them.

Quint pick the maggots from out the water
and squeeze them both between his fingers.
He rinse his hands in the dirty water.
Then he put his hands in his hair and scratch like a demon.
Quint he got that real good hair.
Wavy, straight, and kinda curly
like music wrapped around his head.
His hair always been his crowning glory.
A week ago, not for a million dollars,

would Quint have ever put his hands on a maggot.
I guess you can get used to anything.
He pick 'em up now like they ain't nothing.

I go fill up the foottub again.
When I come back, his hair filled up with suds.
I pour the water over Quinton's head.
The surface of the water is black with scum.
But don't nothing fall out his hair this time.
I'm glad cause I don't think I could take it.
"Go get me the towel," Quint say to me.
I run and get it off the kitchen table
and then I go back in the house
so Quint can get from out the tub.
He wrap the towel around his body
while I go in the bathroom and fill that tub up.

I put some Joy in Quinton's water
so he can have a bubble bath.
He gon' take another bath when he get in the house.
He go thru this same thing every day.
And he gon' take a shower again
before he go to bed tonite.
Then when he get up, he gon' start his day
with another shower. Seem like cleaning hisself
done become his life when he at home.
That's all he do. Bathe and shower over and over.
He say he can't get the smell from out his nose
so he use a lot of Old Spice cologne.

Quint get out of his second bath
just in time to watch the news.
Walter Cronkite reporting on the television.
All of us is sitting in the living room
watching the news clips of Rev. King's speech.

The one he made in church last nite.
Uncle Jesse walk in thru the front door.
He always come home just in time
for the 6 o'clock news. Quint settle in on the couch
and everybody crowd round the TV.
They showing a picture of Mason Temple in Memphis
and standing behind the podium is Rev. Martin Luther King.

Quinton been saying he like Stokely Carmichael better
than Rev. King. The young people feel like
Stokely Carmichael is the voice of the new generation.
But he still want to show Rev. King the respect
that he deserve too for this march he having.
Quinton say he would have went to Memphis too.
But he working on the strike here in Little Rock
even tho he working on the garbage truck too.
Quint say he feel like such a hypocrite.
Mama say, "You want to go to school or not?
Now yo' daddy dead, you got to pay yo'self.
You ain't got the same choices them other chir'en got."
Lil Wren been basically taking care of Quinton
until she learn about that white girl.
I thought she would have throwed him out,
but she didn't. All she ask is that Quinton tell
the white girl to quit calling her house.
But I guess Quinton thought that was too much to ask.
So he just go and enroll in college.
He say, with a degree, he can take care of hisself.

Then Walter Cronkite get a strange look on his face.
He put his finger up side his head.
He say, "Dr. Martin Luther King, the apostle of nonviolence
in the Civil Rights Movement has been shot to death
in Memphis, Tennessee."
"What?!!!" we all scream.

"Naw, Lord," Mama moan. Walter Cronkite talking but I can't hear.
Quint get up and turn the television up.
"Shush! Shush!" Mama say, her hand to her ear.
"Police have issued an all points bulletin
for a well-dressed white man running from the scene.
Dr. King was standing out on the balcony
of a second-floor hotel room
tonight when, according to a companion,
the shot was fired from across the street.
In the friend's words," Walter Cronkite say,
"the bullet exploded in his face."
Mama scream like something haunted.
A groan that fill her mouth and throat.
Tears running down everybody face.
Quint opening and closing up his mouth.

"Police, who had been keeping a close watch
over the Nobel Peace Prize winner because
of Memphis' turbulent racial situation
were on the scene almost at once.
They rushed the 39-year-old Negro leader
to a hospital where he died of a bullet wound
in the neck. Mayor Henry Loeb
reinstated the dusk to dawn curfew
he had imposed on the city last week when a march
led by Dr. King erupted in violence.
Gov. Buford Ellington has called out
over 4,000 National Guardsmen."

I go put my head in Mama's lap,
but she don't even know I'm there.
The green leather couch springs sag with a moan
and the wet done gone from out the air.
Walter Cronkite is on the television
showing a picture of the president on a balcony somewhere.

Miz Irma open the door and walk in our house.
She sit across from the TV, crying and staring.
"In a nationwide television address,
President Johnson expressed the nation's shock.
Dr. King had returned to Memphis on yesterday
determined to prove that he could lead a peaceful mass march
in support of the sanitation workers
most of whom are Negroes. Dr. King had this to say last night
about the situation in Memphis."
Then they show some more news clips from his speech last nite.

> *I may not get there with you.*
> *But I want you to know tonight, that we, as a people, will get to the*
> *promised land!*

"He seen his death," my Mama say.
"He sho' saw it," Miz Irma agree.
Everybody got tears running out they eyes.
I feel some tears on my face too.
I look over to where Quinton is sitting.
He clutching his fist and shaking his leg.
He trying to keep his tears from falling.
I go and hug him around the neck.
I realize this is the first time
that I done touched him since he got his job.
I wonder do them people in Memphis
feel that way when they garbage men come
home from work. Wonder if they family
stay away from them like I have done with Quinton.
That must be a really lonely life.
I'm glad Rev. King work for them people.

Then Quinton bury his head in the crook of my neck.
He cry like his heart is about to break.
He always try to be such a man.

But this killing done strip his mask away.
I wonder do he know that I ain't touched him.
He use to play football with me all the time.
Even tho he don't stay out the bathtub now
long enuf for nobody to pay him no mind.
Quint wipe his eyes and walk over to Uncle Jesse.
He say he ain't going back to work no more.
He say he sorry. Uncle Jesse say,
"You was just doing what you thought
you had to do. Don't worry yourself."
"But, Rev. King," Quint say. Then his voice crack.
Mama look at Quint but she don't say nothing.
He look at her and say, "I ain't going back."

And then he walk out to the back porch.
I can hear him take the tub from off the nail
where it is hanging against the wall.
Then Quinton start to bang it and bang it
upside the house like he trying to kill it.
Like the tin tub has done something wrong.
Like it's to blame for Rev. King
when it was Mama who made him take that job.
I get up and start for the back porch.
I don't know what I think that I'm gon' do.
But Mama catch me by the hand.
She tell me to leave Quint alone. And so I do.
Another one of our neighbors open our front door.
"Y'all watching the news?" Miz Gertharine ask.
Then she sit down on the couch with Mama
and put her head in both her hands.
"It's a crying shame," Miz Gertharine say.
"We knowed it was just a matter of time
before some cracker kill Rev. King."
Her nose is running from the tears she crying.
She wipe the snot on her dress sleeve.

Mama come and hand her a handkerchief.
"Umph, umph, umph," Mama keep on saying.
More neighbors come in and sit on our couch.
Seem like everybody want to be together
to watch this horror that's come to our people.
"All Rev. King was trying to do
was help them po' sanitation workers.
Why somebody kill him for something like that?"
We watch the television all evening long.
Riots is breaking out everywhere.
Quinton say that he ain't going to college.
Mama say, "Oh, yes you is.
You think not having a education
is gon' show some honor to Rev. King?"
Quinton just walk back out of the living room.

I follow Quint into his bedroom.
Quint take some money from out his pocket
and he hand all of it to me.
"You can have this, Mandy. I don't even want it."
"But, Quint," I say. "This your paycheck.
After all you went thru to get that money,
you deserve it. Keep it for yourself."
"I don't want no blood money, Mandy.
Buy the stuff you need for your Black prom
since Mama said she was not going to buy
two dresses that do not even serve the Lord.
I just don't want this money," Quinton reply,
I say, "I guess I don't want the money neither
since it is blood money like you said."
Quint say. "Take it, Mandy, but always remember
that Dr. King was a gift to this world.
He is the first person to ever lead a protest
to try to make this world a little cleaner."
I take Quint's money from out his hand

and put it all in my back pocket.
"But how you gon' get money for school?
Mama gon' be mad if you drop out."
He say, "This is a secret between me and you.
Don't you tell Mama nothing about it."

We stay up all night listening to the television.
When I finally get ready for bed,
my eyes is swole up from all the crying.
That night I dream of The Three Kings
who come and bring they gifts to Jesus.
My pillow's damp and my room is hot.
In my dreams, Rev. King still living.
And I see him walking over a mountain to God.

28
THE PROTEST

After Rev. King die, Mandy decide that the Black prom
was not enuf of a demonstration. And so she decide
that the Black kids need to stay out of school for the funeral
after Mr. Whitlock tell all the Black kids they would not be allowed
to stay at home to watch the funeral on television.
The day that Rev. King had got killed was on a Thursday.
President Johnson had declared a national day of mourning
for the entire country on that following Sunday.
But the big funeral, the one everybody gon' be watching,
was gon' be held that Tuesday at Ebenezer Baptist Church
where Rev. King and his daddy had both been the pastor.
All the Black kids decide they gon' stay home to watch.

It was riots going on all over the country.
Black folks was tearing up the cities and white folks was scared
even tho not one white neighborhood had got one lick of damage.
Black folks was tearing up they own neighborhoods.
Dr. King always said that riots was the language

of the unheard to get freedom and justice.
A way to tell the American government
that they had failed to live up to their promises.
But some Black organizations had decide to do some sit-ins
in Little Rock so people could channel the anger and rage
into something more positive than just burning and rioting.
Miz Payday organization was the Little Rock Roundtable
and they had decide to do a sit-in at Sterling's.
Cause Black people still couldn't sit at the lunch counters there
even tho President Johnson had signed the Civil Rights Bill four years ago.
White folks in Arkansas act like they don't care what he said.

The stay-home protest at school had not even made a whimper.
All the Black kids stayed home just like Mandy had planned.
But the principal just give all of them an excused absence.
So, Mandy felt like they needed to do something else
and since Miz Payday was gon' do the sit in at Sterling's,
Mandy decide all the Black kids should participate too.
So, she ask all the kids to meet her downtown at the store,
but everybody was scared. Mandy was scared too
cause she know that her mama ain't gon' let her be no part of
no kind of protest against no white folks downtown.
So her and Nikki had cook up a plan for Mandy
to meet her and Miz Payday that Saturday in Little Rock.

It just so happen that the church had plan a revival
that same week after Rev. Martin Luther King got kill.
Mandy knew that her Mama was gon' cook on the last Saturday.
Even tho they had a new pastor, Belle still act like she is
the First Lady at the church cause the new pastor's wife
she kinda act like she slow. All they children slow too.
So all the usual duties that a First Lady have,
Belle she had decide to just continue to do.
And one of them duties include cooking dinner for the preacher
who speak at the revival. His name is Rev. Darden.

He had been a good friend of A.D. before he died.
And this the first time he been back since the new pastor take over.

Quinton came home that week so he could help out his mama
to get ready for the preacher. So he is back home again.
He gon' be staying at home for the rest of the week.
Rev. Darden had always liked Quinton. And that man sho' could preach.
When the Spirit hit him, he jump up and down.
And he was lite on his feet when he touch back down to the ground.
Maybe if Belle had gone to church instead of staying home cooking
things woulda turn out different instead of the way that they did.

Belle and Mandy was still having they problems
about Nikki. But since Mandy had been skipping school
and meeting up with Nikki at least one day every week
Mandy was happy with everything and Nikki was too.
That was the thing Mandy like most about going to the white school.
The teachers didn't never contact her mama about nothing.
That's why she could skip school at least one day a week
and Belle had not found out nary a thing about it.

Since she had been keeping things quiet and not making no trouble,
Belle thought that Mandy had finally got some sense.
Belle even start letting Mandy keep company with boys.
She had decide that maybe she had been too strict
about boys and Mandy, and maybe that was the reason
that Mandy had started all this craziness with a girl.
And since Mandy seem to be acting a whole lot better here lately,
Belle think everything about Mandy had went back to normal.
And because Mandy so smart, she turn in all of her homework
and make all A's and B's on her tests and everything
so Belle just think Mandy doing all the things that she ought to.
And Mandy make sho' she show Belle all the good grades she getting,
Cause it ain't nothing that Belle would have never even thought,
that Mandy was lying to her the way that she was.

With Mandy going around thinking she halfway grown
and that she ain't a little girl no more.

Mandy know that in order for her to take part in the protest
that Miz Payday organization is having downtown on that Saturday,
she got to figure out a lie that Belle will believe
so she won't know that she meeting up with Nikki and her mama.
When they skip school that week and put they heads together,
Nikki and Mandy thought about it and they had decide
that Mandy was gon' have to stay all night in Little Rock that Friday.
And since the revival was going on, she thought she could get away with the lie.
So Mandy go to Belle and she ask her mama
if it's all right for her to go and spend the nite
over in Little Rock with Sammie Lee and Miz Priscilla
after she go to revival that Friday nite.
Mandy know Belle always go along when it come to going to church.
She look at Mandy side-eyed but she had said yes
when Mandy ask if she could spend the weekend with Sammie Lee too
and come home Sunday after church. Belle even helped Mandy to
pick out the clothes she want her to wear on that Sunday.
Said she could ride home with her and Quinton after service was over.
So Mandy had clean the house and then she cut the grass
and hung out the clothes before her Mama even ask.
She had been the sweetest child in every single way.
Belle know something is up. Don't care what Mandy say.
But Belle give her enuf rope for her to hang herself.
And that is why after the way things happen, Belle so mad at herself.
Cause she know Mandy have got something up her sleeve.
But she don't know it's gon' turn out as bad as it did.

The real reaon Belle said yes was cause she was busy with the dinner
that she have to cook for the preacher for Saturday nite.
So didn't nobody go to church that Friday but Mandy and Quinton.
Her mama stay at home. She still had to fry
the chicken for the preacher who carrying on the Revival.

Quinton was gon' be a part of Miz Payday demonstration too.
But he didn't know nothing about what Mandy and Nikki
had schemed up in lying about what they was gon' do.
Quint had picked up the preacher on they way to the church
while Mandy was still in the car sitting in the back seat.
And then, instead of taking her to church, Quint drop her off at Sammie Lee's.
But he don't go in the house. See, that is the thing.
Quinton didn't talk to Sammie mama like Belle woulda done.
Or any other woman in fact. He too deep in conversation
with Rev. Darden about how Jesus woulda acted during this
whole nonviolent Civil Rights situation.
So Quinton didn't even know that Sammie's mama wasn't home.
She was spending the weekend with her sister down in Gould
and wouldn't be back 'til Sunday evening. Sammie and Mandy had worked it out
that Mandy would stay all nite on Friday. Priscilla didn't even know nothing about it.

SNCC was gon' help out Miz Payday and her organization
even tho SNCC had already been part of a demonstration
the day before. But SNCC had still showed up
cause the young people was so mad about Rev. King being shot.
When Belle had heard that Quinton was going to take part
in the sit-in at Sterling's, she call Payday a red-headed tart
who sleep with other women husbands. She been mad ever since
that nite she pull Mandy out her house. Belle say she only care bout herself.
As far as Belle concern, Payday can't do nothing right.
She would have lost her natural mind if she knew what Mandy had cooked up
to go on that protest with Payday. Belle say that protest don't mean a thang.
Say Payday don't care about no Civil Rights. She just trying to get herself seen
on television like that woman, Daisy Bates, was always doing.
Daisy Bates own the colored newspaper. Payday don't do nothing important.
And Daisy known to use her some children. So Payday is using her some too.
That's why Payday had ask Nikki to get some children from her school
to take part in her sit-in. Daisy had one the day before.
And she didn't leave it for no child to ask, so Daisy'd had a whole lot more
people than Payday did with her. Daisy had 500 people when she went inside

and sat down at Woolworth's lunch counter. Payday had SNCC and about 35
people with her at Sterling's. And cause of Daisy the day before,
them white folks was ready this time for all of them uppity Negroes.

Nikki just tell her mama that Saturday they was picking somebody up
who gon' be part of the protest. Payday didn't even know who it was.
She don't know she picking up Mandy when she go to that house
or that Mandy even in Little Rock. First thing Payday ask
is, "Mandy, do Maw Belle know where you at?"
And Mandy lie to her and say, "Yes, M'am. My mama know that
I'm going with you today."
"She ain't said nothing to me.
I thought we was just picking up a friend of Nikki's,"
Payday say. Whatever Mandy told her, she wasn't doing nothing but lying.
But Mandy know they ain't got no phone. So Miz Payday can't call her Mama.
So Payday take Mandy down to Sterling's. True, it's against her better judgment.
And, of course, you know Mandy the one who end up getting in the most trouble.

Instead of joining in with Daisy like somebody who got some sense,
Payday call her march a second wave of defense.
Her and her 35 marchers go up to Sterling's big as you please.
They stand at the front door and then they get down on they knees.
I ain't never seen Payday at church. God probably don't even know who Payday is.
But her and them Negroes get to praying. Then, honey, they march right on in
to the front door of Sterling's. And that white sheriff standing there waiting.
Payday in front with SNCC's founder, a white man name of Bill Hansen.
Hansen known to like colored women. He married to a colored woman right now.
Belle say, "I know Payday sleeping with that man. Ain't no sense in lying about
that." Belle say, "Enuf lies been told already."
Belle messing with a married man herself. But still she being judgmental.
This is why she losing her daughter. Belle say that they ain't
having no intimate relations. She still want to be known as a saint.
Big sins and little sins. Christians good about that.
Judging people on qualities they don't even possess.
So Payday and Bill Hansen walk into the front door

and head straight to the lunch counter. And with them is four
children, which include both Mandy and Nikki.
Then the rest of the group come in and kneel. And Quinton come in with them.
He surprised to see Mandy but he had got there late
so he didn't have time to do nothing but go on with the protest.
The sheriff, Cull Campbell, knock Bill and Payday to the floor.
And his deputies start to pushing the children back out of the door.
Nikki see the white man hit her mama, and she start to screaming and hollering.
Mandy see Nikki start for the sheriff and she raise her hand up to stop her.
That's when she accidentally hit a white woman. And, of course, it was the sheriff's wife.
She say, "Nigger what you hit me for?" Then she push that child aside
like she ain't nothing but a feather. Lift her way up in the air.
And Mandy come down on the counter showing all her fare-thee-well.
Quinton try to get to her but he can't. He trip on Bill on the floor.
Everything happen so quick. It was the biggest mess, Lord.

Mandy jump up trying to get to Quinton. She acting on nothing but nervous energy.
And then she push out both her hands at anybody who in arm's length
and happen to smack the white woman again in the face while she flailing.
Course the white woman act like she killing her. She yelling and screaming,
"Arrest that nigger!" the white woman say. "That pickaninny dare to touch me.
You take that gal right to jail or my husband will see
that you lose your job." Her face and neck done turn red.
And then one of the deputies turn around and smack Mandy upside her head.
Slap her with his open palm. Seem like you could hear it round the block.
Mandy just standing there crying. The child was actually in shock.
Just then, Quinton come and pick Mandy up. Her legs is shaking like jelly.
And they all manage to get to Payday's car where she done parked in the alley.
What Mandy see when she look back at where Cull Campbell is running
is a angel standing in the doorway with her wings spread wide across it.
She got a look on her face that make it light up like a candle
is glowing from inside her. She turn and she smile at Mandy.
Payday already in the car. And she got the motor running.
The white folks that's in the doorway is standing there wondering
why they can't run after them. They all in the door screaming.

But they can't see the angel in the doorway, and they can't see her wings.
Quinton put Mandy down then. He look scared as Mandy ever seen.
He jump under the steering wheel and they all pull off speeding.

When they walk into the door, Belle she just started to screaming
and beating them with a belt. Both Mandy and Quinton.
Quinton grab the belt with one hand. He not mad at her or nothing,
but he is a grown man and he ain't taking no whipping.
Belle sit down on the couch like all the air been suck out of her.
Then she hold out both her arms and gather her children around her.
They cry together for a while. Belle ask them a few questions
but mostly they just pray together and thank God for all His blessings.
Cause they all know it could have turn out even more worse than it did.
"Y'all alive," Belle say. "That's all that mean anything."

So now it's done come to this. Belle got to send her child away.
Mandy in her bedroom packing. She is going to stay
with Sissy in Illinois. Belle and Mandy both been crying.
Mandy putting her clothes in the suitcase and she is going around mumbling
underneath her breath. Belle don't even want to know what she saying
cause she come too close to losing her. Belle cannot even imagine
what Mandy could have been thinking. What had went thru her mind.
And how much of a failure she is when a child of hers can decide
to put all of them in harm's way. Put them in danger like she did.
She had thought it would be Quinton, but it had been Mandy instead.
When Belle asked Mandy about it, all Mandy had said
was, "I wanted to make a difference. What's so bad about that?
That sheriff shouldn't have hit me. All we was trying to do
was make things better for Black people. That is something that you
should want for me too, Mama."
"Of course I want that.
What I didn't never want for you is the very thing that done happen."

Belle had already heard rumbling about what them white folks is saying
about finding that nigger gal who dare to hit a white woman.

Right now it ain't no more than rumbling. Belle is sure about that
cause ain't nobody said who Mandy is. Or at least not as yet.
That's why Belle got to send her away. She failed Mandy, pure and simple.
If her mama couldn't keep her out of danger, then maybe her sister could do it
better than she can. When Sissy said that Mandy could stay
in Illinois with her, Belle fall down on her knees and she thank
the Good Lord Above. Of course, Mandy do not want to go
cause she do not want to leave Nikki. Belle think that is just more
reason for her to be grateful. To get her away from Nikki too.
Sometimes God answer your prayers in a different way than you
would have solve them yourself. But Belle know God do not care
about how she want her life to go. She do not even dare
to question how God lead her life. She just do what it is that God want
her to do. Whether it make sense to her way of thinking or not.

Cause things could have went way different. And it is just that thought
that make Belle feel the worse. Cause she know she had been caught
up with Deke Jones and her concern to find her own happiness.
What if she had been focused on her child instead of being so focused on herself?
She say seem like she would have known that after all the years she had thought
she could put her faith in A.D. And look how that had all turned out.
When I went to Uz afterwards to check in on Belle and on Mandy,
I was just wanting to lend Belle a hand. So I tried to make myself handy
and do things that would help them. Little things round the house
like the washing and canning. Anything to help out.
Belle's eyes was filled with sorrow, and she say to me, "Ree,
all I want is to keep my child safe. And, yes, I wanted to be
happy myself. I guess that was selfish of me."
"That ain't selfish at all." I hand her a glass of ice tea.
"My joy done always faded quick. Don't I never deserve no joy too?"
I looked at my sister and said, "Belle, of course you do."
"What it's gon' take before I learn that nobody but God know about
contentment of spirit? How to find joy in your heart.
Ephesians 6 and 10 say, 'Be strong in the Lord and He
will give you power to stand against the devil and all his schemes.'

How long it's gon' take me to learn that the devil always ready and willing
to test my faith in God? And the quickest way is thru my chir'en?"

She cried then like I ain't seen her cry since the day she lost Clyde.
She didn't carry on like this even when she lost the child
that died before Mandy was born. Her name was Gloria Daisy.
"I can't lose another child, Ree. I thank that might finally drive me crazy."
"I know. I know," I said. "That is just why I come.
I'm hoping to help make things a little easier now Mandy is leaving home."
I hold her hand in mine and we sit together at the table
until she straighten her back and say, "Well, I know God is able."
We both get up then. She take her tea to the kitchen.
And I go to Mandy's bedroom to help her pack all her things.

29
A LONG WAY FROM HOME

sometimes I feel like a motherless child
sometimes I feel like a motherless child
sometimes I feel like a motherless child
a long way from home
a long way from home

When Belle wake up this morning her heart is heavy laden.
It thump in her chest like God is beating on a drum
so hard she can feel the bones at the back of her rib cage
fluttering back and forth in rhythm to the old gospel song.
She finding it hard to smile about anything this morning.
It ain't nothing funny about the way that things done turn out.
But she still know that God is gon' take care of her baby.
She just got to believe that and don't allow doubt in her heart.
She look at the paper peeling off the walls in the kitchen.
Deke Jones coming tomorrow. He said that he could
peel off the wallpaper and re-do the whole kitchen for her.
Still and all, she don't know where she'd be without him.

He gon' paint it yellow. Belle love a yellow kitchen.
She use to have one Down Home before they move here to Uz.
But A.D. daddy didn't put in sheetrock when he build the house,
so Belle had to wallpaper to hide the ugly beaver board walls
that would not hold paint. Soaked it up like paper.
Well, it was just pressed paper. Cheap and make do.
That's how everything was when they first move to Uz.
Everything done too fast. A.D. being careless like he do.

The television in the living room got on a program about
Martin Luther King. They interviewing a whole lot of people
who work alongside Rev. King in the Civil Rights Movement.
Everybody been wondering who gon' keep the whole Civil Rights Movement going.
Belle listening to the TV and cooking while Mandy is packing.
They both is sniffling back snot and they wiping away tears.
What she watching on TV about Martin Luther King
is a way for her to show her sadness and Mandy not know that it is
her leaving that her mama is really crying about.
Rev. King ain't even been dead for one whole month.
Gertharine done come over to watch the show with them too.
She sipping coffee at the table and watching the TV in the living room.

One woman they interview name is Xernona Clayton.
She one of the last people that see him before he go to Memphis.
Belle she think Coretta keep that woman too close.
She done found out the hard way you can't always trust women.
Xernona say she loved Martin, but she was really best friends with Coretta.
"I used to travel with her whenever she toured.
You know she was trained as a classical singer
and I always went with Coretta whenever I could.
She fell in love with music in the one room schoolhouse
where she lived down in the country in Alabama.
Her teacher had taught her music appreciation
and had given Coretta her love of classical music."
She say Coretta had put her singing career on the back shelf

when she married Martin and they had the children.
She thought she would start singing again one day.
"But, like many women, she never could do it.
Even tho that was her major at the Music Conservatory
where she got her degree in Boston. She went on a scholarship.
But she gave up her career to support Martin and the Movement.
People don't really understand what a saint that woman is."

Belle pour in the clabber milk and mix the contents with her fingers,
pulling the sticky dough mixture from the side of the bowl
and folding it over and over until it is just the right texture.
She wipe a tear from her eye that is sliding down her nose.
That make her laugh to herself. Sorrow such a useless emotion.
She ain't got no time for sadness. She got these biscuits to make.
Gertharine call to the kitchen, "When you say that Sissy is coming?"
Belle say, "She be here directly. And Sissy ain't never late."

Sissy had married a man that she met at the college.
Ray Silas fell in love with her when he heard her sing on the stage.
He from Crossett, Arkansas, and been raised to help family
so when Sissy want to help Mandy he did not hesitate.
Belle done spent all the last week with getting Mandy ready.
Sewing and washing, making her all the new clothes
that she will take when she go to live with her sister.
Cause Sissy coming today and she gon' take Mandy home
to live with her in Illinois. That child can't stay in Arkansas.
Sneaking off to that protest. And then hitting a white woman.
If it wasn't for the angel, she would already be dead.
Fools and babies Belle laugh, tears dropping into the biscuits.

Xernona Clayton say, "The day before Martin went to Memphis,
Coretta had a dinner party over to their house.
Whenever he was home she made him eat with the children.
And that day she invited us too. All told, it was about
a dozen of us who had come to the party.

Ralph Abernathy was there. King Sr. and his mama.
We hadn't spent time together like that for the longest.
I can still remember the sound of him laughing.
Cause he hadn't laughed a lot, seem like, for quite a while.
Things in the Movement had started going bad
after he went up North and started the protests in Chicago,
plus coming out against the Vietnam war and
the infighting that was happening between him and SNCC.
They were being led then by Stokely Carmichael
and he and a lot of the youngsters were falling prey to the hate
that the white people had been slinging at them the whole time.
It all had put Martin in a depressed state of mind.
Nonviolence was his mission. On that, he would not compromise.
So Coretta had decided that having the little dinner
might make Martin start to feel a little better.

"And it had made him feel better. We laughed all that night.
He was joking and seemed like his heart was a little bit lighter
than I had seen him for the longest time.
Ralph was acting foolish. Martin was smiling.
He came over to where I was sitting at the piano.
He told me, 'Xernona, I bet you didn't know I could sing.'
'Why no, Martin,' I said. 'I didn't know that.'
He laughed and he said, 'Well, Xernona, I can!
Give me a B flat,' Martin said to me.
When he opened his mouth and he started to sing,
the room filled with the sound of his rich baritone
and after that everybody in the whole room started singing.

> *i'm gonna sing if the spirit say sing*
> *i'm gonna sing if the spirit say sing*
> *if the spirit say sing, i'm gonna sing o lord*
> *i'm gonna sing if the spirit say sing"*

Belle mind went back to all the times she had heard A.D. sing.

That man would sing you a song at the drop of a hat.
He had sung for her the very first time that he met her.
Had sung out her name with his head stuck down a well.
She shoulda ran away from him then. Shoulda seen what he was.
More show than anything. But she have to admit she like that.
Just like she is sho' Coretta liked being Mrs. Martin Luther King.
And, like Belle, she gon' have to figure out who she is now without him.
Everybody had heard rumors about Rev. King sleeping with other women.
That is something Belle know that a preacher known to do.
So she didn't never think that man was no god or nothing,
not like the other colored folks did. Just like they knew
how he treated his wife. Just cause they saw them on television.
We live in a foolish world. Where foolish thoughts reign supreme.
Belle had put a stop to all that singing for her A.D. had been doing.
After she find out about Delta Rose, he never sung to her again.

Mandy come from the bedroom and walk into the kitchen.
She speak to Miz Gertharine, and then she say to Belle,
"Mama can I talk to you please?" She sound real respectful.
Belle wipe her hands on the dish towel and come on in the back
where I had been helping Mandy sort the clothes she was taking.
Quinton had came over yesterday and brought her a new pair of shoes.
He said it was the expensive kind like Lil Wren like to wear.
He'd said to Mandy, "Sorry I didn't take better care of you."
Belle had always thought it'd be Quinton that would get into trouble.
What with how casual he was with the white women that he
was always hanging round. But it turn out to be Mandy.
Still a white woman tho. It always seem that she
could not disconnect her fate from the hands of a white woman.
A.D. messing around with that white woman Down Home.
She know she can't question what the good Lord got in store for her life,
but why its always got to be a white woman dear Lord?
And then she laugh to herself. Because of course she know the answer.
It is the same thing that the Good Lord had answer when Job
had questioned God about the way his life had turn out.

God had said to him that it is the thing we fear most
that is gon' come upon us. And Belle done seen that happen.
In this life you got to learn to fear nothing but God.
She done had to learn that lesson again over and over.
She pray she done learned it for the last time now.

"Mama," Mandy say, "can't I please stay at home?
I promise I won't lie to you never again."
Belle say, "I ain't sending you to Sissy as a punishment, Mandy.
I'm trying to keep you alive. The fact you still don't understand
that make me know even mo' that you can't stay here in Uz.
You don't understand the danger of being a colored chile in the South.
You still don't believe you can be like them four little girls
who died when them white folks came and blowed they church up.
People will come looking for you. You done hit a white woman.
That's the most dangerous thing that a colored could ever do.
And not only will they come and drag you out of the house,
they could come to our church and blow you up in it too.
I can't take that chance. And I don't understand.
All your life you done said you can't wait to leave Uz.
Now you got the chance. And you staying with Sissy.
She ain't no punishment neither. This is someone you love
and who love you."
"I love Sissy too, Mama.
And I know she love me. She my favorite sister."
"Well, what is it then? Is it all about that girl?"
"Don't bring Nikki into it."
"She done upset yo' whole world.
And you still trying to protect her. Her and her mama too.
I don't want to talk about it no mo'. You still got packing to do."

Belle go to the kitchen and open the stove. The heat come out to kiss her.
She take the pan out the oven and turn over the ham
that she got cooking on low in the big cast iron skillet.
She move her hair out her face with the back of her hand

and she offer a prayer up to her Good Lord And Savior.
"Lord, please protect my chile. Keep her safe in Your hand."
She take the platter and spoon up the smothered potatoes.
Then she call Mandy and me from out of the back and
she invite Gertharine to have breakfast with us if she want to.
Gertharine have the sense to go on to her house.
"Well, Mandy," she say, "if I don't see you fo' you leave,
you tell Sissy hello and you take care of yo'self."

The three of us all eat our breakfast in total silence.
We watch the television from the dining room so we can all see it where we sit.
Xernona Clayton saying Martin Sr. start up the next verse of singing.
"He had a powerful voice that was a deep rich bass.
He came and stood by the piano, his hand on Martin's shoulder.
I kept playing the music, keeping the tempo upbeat and fast."
Belle start to tapping her feet to the tune of the music.
Mandy's eyes filled with tears. She looking down in her glass.

> *i'm gonna do what the spirit say do*
> *i'm gonna do what the spirit say do*
> *if the spirit say do, i'm gonna do o lord*
> *i'm gonna do what the spirit say do"*

Xernona say, "Coretta came from the back where she was checking on the children.
She laid her head on Martin's shoulder and she put her arm thru
his elbow where he had his hand resting on the piano.
Then she started the next verse in her beautiful soprano.

> *i'm gonna love if the spirit say love*
> *i'm gonna love if the spirit say love*
> *if the spirit say love, i'm gonna love o lord*
> *i'm gonna love if the spirit say love"*

Belle know the attraction of a shoulder to lean on.
She even wish A.D. was here now for her to rest on a little.

But then Mandy wouldn'tna been acting like this if A.D. was alive.
It took everything coming together like them domino pieces
that knock each other down. Things have got to line up
in a certain particular way in order for life
to turn out the way that it do. That is why Belle
go where the Lord lead her. She don't try to fight
His direction. His guidance. Just like with all of His chosen,
each one got a life that they preordained to live.
And every whirlwind in life lead where God want them to go
mix with just enuf of that thing that God call free will
to fool you into believing that you got some control.
To fool you into thinking if you do what He say
He will follow a set of rules that is the ones that you need
to give you a sense of satisfaction and relief to your days.

Xernona say, "We were all gathered around, justa laughing and singing.
Ralph Abernathy was the next one to open his mouth.
Ralph couldn't sing worth a damn and we put our hands over our ears,
but Ralph didn't care. He just sang even louder.

> *i'm gonna march if the spirit say march*
> *i'm gonna march if the spirit say march*
> *if the spirit say march, i'm gonna march o lord*
> *i'm gonna march if the spirit say march*

"We all knew he was thinking about Martin's trip in the morning.
I was taking him to the airport for the march he had in Memphis
for the garbage worker's strike. They'd started it all by themselves.
He said the least he could do was march with them for safer conditions.
Everybody was tired and the Movement members were splintered.
But Martin had said that he had to go
and support those men striking off in Tennessee.
Because those garbage men were all Negroes,
the City wouldn't listen to their grievances and conditions.
Another Black man had been killed by the trash crusher last week.

They'd called and asked Martin to come. And, of course, Martin
agreed to take part in the men's fight against injustice.

"There were hundreds carrying signs that said I Am A Man.
Andy Young was going with him. And they would meet up with Jesse.
We didn't have any idea what was waiting for him
out on that balcony of the Lorraine Hotel in Memphis.
But it wouldn't have made Martin one bit of difference if he did.
He was always going to go wherever it was the Lord led him.
He always said only God could determine the time of his death."
Then she paused and said, "I think often about the last verse I heard him sing."

> i'm gonna live if the spirit say live
> i'm gonna live if the spirit say live
> if the spirit say live, i'm gonna live o lord
> i'm gonna live if the spirit say live

Belle turn the television off and we all get up from the table.
I clean the kitchen while she make sho' Mandy doing all that need to be done.
She go into Mandy's room. Of course, the trunk sitting there half empty.
"What is you been doing, Mandy? You ain't near about done."
"I been packing since yesterday. All my stuff will not fit.
I just took some clothes out so I could make room for my shoes."
"You ain't got to take everythang with you, Mandy."
"But," she say, "I ain't coming home no more."
Then Mandy stand and face her mama from across the bedroom.
"I do understand, Mama. Watching that lady on TV
make me look at things different. I'm sorry it take me so long.
And I'm sorry I worried you and put my life in danger last week.
I just wanted to do something to help the Movement along.
I guess I wanted to be like Rev. King. I wanted you to be proud.
I wanted to be there the day you sat at that lunch counter at Sterlings.
I didn't think about what all that could happen to me.
And I realize now that I was just being selfish.
And I just hope you will forgive me for the way I been acting.

I been mad about Daddy for so long I ain't gave no thought to
how you feeling yourself. But I could tell from that story
how Miz Coretta was hurting. I want you to be happy too."
Me and Belle both got our mouths hanging open.
Don't tell me that God don't perform miracles every day.
Belle kiss Mandy and say, "Thank you for saying that, Mandy.
You sound like you growing up now, I am happy to say.
Now you gone and get done. Sissy gon' be here in a minute.
She call Thetta and say that she is on her way."
Just then we all hear a car drive up in the front yard.
"That sound like them now." Tears streaming down all of our faces.

Belle go to the door. "Get that trunk closed up there Mandy!"
she holler from the front. Mandy throw in her shoes
and she close up the trunk. She drag it to the front door.
And Sissy husband, Ray Silas, take the trunk to the car.
Then he close the back up. Sissy talking to Belle.
When Mandy come out, she go and give her a hug.
"Don't worry, Mandy. Everything's going to be all right.
Just wait and see," Sissy say. "We are going to have so much fun."
"I know Sissy," Mandy answer. And she hug Sissy back.
"Y'all come on inside," Belle say. "It's still plenty food left."
Ray Silas can't even talk for all the food stuffed in his mouth.
Belle give them the food she done wrapped up for the trip
so they can be careful about the places that they have to stop.
She make sho' everything in the car that need to be there.
She pray, "God take care of my chile. Keep her Yours. Keep her safe."
And she start to sing under her breath as she watch the car drive away.

> *Jesus paid it all*
> *All to him I owe*
> *Sin has left a crimson stain*
> *Oh but He's washed*
> *Me Whiter*
> *Than Snow*

The End

ACKNOWLEDGEMENTS

I have to start by acknowledging my advisors at Goddard College - Beatrix Gates, Reiko Russo, and Aimee Liu. This book would have never been completed without you. Thank you for encouraging me, challenging me, praising me, and criticizing me. Each of you helped make this story what it is today.

Thanks to Aunt Lute who believed when nobody else did. To Frida, who read the manuscript first; to Joan who worked tirelessly thru thick and thin, the ups and downs and ins and outs; to Emma who restored my joy; to Shay, clean up woman extraordinaire; and to everybody on that first phone call who loved the very things that every other publisher had rejected. I can never thank you enuf for the beauty you brought to this journey. May you always exist for women writers like me.

To Paula C, who so generously gave her time to read the manuscript and sing its praises when I needed it most.

To both the Paulas and Snigdha who listen to me whine and who always give me such great advice during our cocktail hour.

To Patrice, Dave, and Ben for the back cover photo and for dragging me into the 21st century. Thank you!

To Georgia McDade and the African American Writers Alliance who listened to Mandy stories for so many years while I was figuring it out.

To C @ *Just Finish The Damn Thing Productions*

To Aathina, the unicorn who calmed my fears.

To Aunt Mama, who always believed.

To Olubayo, who sat on the porch and listened to me read chapter after chapter, always with a twinkle in her eye, and for letting me know which parts she didn't understand - even when I didn't want to hear it. And for her unwavering faith that this novel would get published one day.

Thanks always to my suns, Eric and Karioki. You are my most splendid creation.

And THANK YOU GOD for making sure that I'd just keep a'livin' to see this day.

KATHYA ALEXANDER is a writer, playwright, storyteller, and teaching artist. She was a Writer-in-Residence at the prestigious Hedgebrook Women Writer's Retreat and won the Fringe First Award for Black to My Roots: African American Tales from the Head and the Heart at the Edinburgh Festival Fringe for Outstanding New Production and Innovation in Theater in Edinburgh Scotland. She has also won awards from 4Culture, Seattle's Office of Arts and Culture, Artist Trust, Jack Straw, Seattle Theater Group, Freehold Theater, and Seattle Parks and Recreation. She was a freelance writer for the now defunct award winning Colors NW Magazine and The Initiative, and is a regular contributor to the South Seattle Emerald. She has been published in The Pitkin Review, Arkana Literary Magazine, Pontoon Poetry/Black Lawrence Press, and Native Skin Magazine. She has also been published in anthologies by the African American Writers Alliance (AAWA) and in Raising Lily Ledbetter: Women Poets Occupy the Workplace by Lost Horse Press. Her playwriting credits include *The Negro Passion Play* ; *Black D*ck Matters* ; *Hands Up! Don't Shoot!* ; *Think Before You Do*; *With Hope And With Morning* ; *David & Jonathan: A Modern Day Retelling of the Biblical Story* ; *Homegoing* ; *A Revolution of Hope* ; *emotionalblackmale* ; *HumaNature* ; *Dream'n* ; *Native Sons and Daughters* ; *A Taste of Prison* ; *Three Strikes on Trial*; *Nappy Roots* : *A Fairy Tale* ; and B*lack to My Roots.*

Kathya's acting credits include *House of Dinah* , *And Jesus Moonwalks The Mississippi*, *The Negro Passion Play* , *Zooman and the Sign* , *The Amen Corner*, and *Before It Hits Home* . She is a founding member, producer, and Resident Playwright of Brownbox Theatre: Reimagined Black Theater in Seattle, WA. She has been a professional storyteller for 20+ years, and told stories monthly as part of Aunt Mama's Story Table at Starbucks in Seattle for 15 years until it was closed due to COVID. Her experience as a teaching artist includes residencies for Seattle Public Schools, and she was part of the Freehold Theater residency at the Washington Correctional Center for Women. She has also taught for Powerful Schools and the Seattle Youth Violence Prevention Initiative in addition to several community based programs for adults and children. Her most recent experience was working with BIPOC youth on a play about gun violence funded by Seattle Parks and Recreation. She is a proud member of the Creative Advantage Arts Partners Roster, the African American Writers Alliance, and the Seattle Storytellers Guild. This is her debut novel, published by Aunt Lute Books.

Our Mission: Founded in 1982, Aunt Lute Books is an intersectional, feminist press dedicated to publishing literature by those who have been traditionally underrepresented in or excluded by the literary canon. Core to Aunt Lute's mission is the belief that the written word is critical to understanding and relating to each other as human beings. Through the centering of voices, perspectives, and stories that have not been traditionally welcomed by mainstream publishing, we strengthen ties across cultures and experiences, promoting a broader range of expression, and, we hope, working toward a more inclusive and just future.

Land Acknowledgement: We, Aunt Lute Books, acknowledge that we do our work of uplifting marginalized voices and striving toward justice via the written word on the unceded ancestral homeland of the Ramaytush Ohlone who are the original inhabitants of the San Francisco Peninsula. As the indigenous stewards of this land and in accordance with their traditions, the Ramaytush Ohlone have never ceded, lost, nor forgotten their responsibilities as the caretakers of this place, as well as for all peoples who reside in their traditional territory. As Guests, we recognize that we benefit from living and working on their traditional homeland. We wish to pay our respects by acknowledging the Ancestors, Elders and Relatives of the Ramaytush Community and by affirming their sovereign rights as First Peoples.

You may buy books from our website.
www.auntlute.com
aunt lute books
P.O. Box 410687
San Francisco, CA 94141
books@auntlute.com

This book would not have been possible without the kind contributions of the Aunt Lute Founding Friends:

Anonymous Donor	Diana Harris
Anonymous Donor	Phoebe Robins Hunter
Rusty Barceló	Diane Mosbacher, M.D., Ph.D.
Marian Bremer	Sara Paretsky
Marta Drury	William Preston, Jr.
Diane Goldstein	Elise Rymer Turner